IS IT IN HIS KISS?

"You look gorgeous."

She burned with pleasure. "Thank you. I'm ready," she said after several quiet seconds.

"Do you want to get something to eat while we wait for Willow?" He climbed the stairs, each step bringing his mouth closer and closer to hers.

She yielded to the attraction that lived in her and said, "No, I really want you."

His hands captured her around the waist, as a current of wanting connected them. Tilting her head back, she closed her eyes, afraid at what she might see if she looked at Van. She wanted to see the desire that had flowed like hot lava yesterday, but was afraid the brown depths would be clouded with suspicion and distrust.

His mouth approached slowly and their lips met. Kissing Van crushed emotional shackles, and she heard herself groan. Spirals of ecstasy curled through her when his arms completely encircled her. Fox groaned long and low again.

As if a fairy had granted her wish, she opened her eyes and what lay on her heart was mirrored in his gaze.

COMMITMENTS

CARMEN GREEN

ARABESQUE
BET.
BOOKS

BET Publications, LLC
www.bet.com
www.arabesquebooks.com

ARABESQUE BOOKS are published by

BET Publications, LLC
c/o BET BOOKS
One BET Plaza
1900 W Place NE
Washington, D.C. 20018-1211

All Kensington Titles, Imprints, and Distributed Lines are available at special quantity discounts for bulk purchases for sales promotions, premiums, fund-raising, and educational or institutional use. Special book excerpts or customized printings can also be created to fit specific needs. For details, write or phone the office of the Kensington special sales manager: Kensington Publishing Corp., 850 Third Avenue, New York, NY 10022, attn: Special Sales Department, Phone: 1-800-221-2647.

First Printing: September 1998
10 9 8 7 6 5 4

Printed in the United States of America

ACKNOWLEDGMENT

Thank you to Doctors Ted and Michelle Wilson for all your technical advice and for being so wonderful whenever the family got the notion to visit.

Many thanks to Rita Herron and Stephanie Hauck for the critiques and helpful suggestions.

Booksellers Emma Rogers, Nia Damali, and Jane Harp, you may think you're just doing your jobs, but you're giving us writers a hand up. Thank you for your efforts. They are noticed.

Without writer friends pushing from behind, sometimes I don't know if I would have made it. Thank you Jacquie T., And thank you Monty, Jeremy, Danielle, Tina, and Stacy for pulling from the front.

Faith—knowing what you cannot see is there.

CHAPTER ONE

Fox Giovanni hurried along the Manhattan sidewalk letting her coltish stride carry her toward Twenty-third and Eighth Avenue and the luncheon to celebrate her new promotion.

Her tongue glanced along her lips, the urge for a cigarette nagging again. She resisted succumbing. Resisted filling her lungs full of the strong bitter flavoring. Smoking in public wasn't an accepted practice of the newly appointed vice president of securities and investments for Fields, Inc.

Tucked into Café Ormond around the corner was her boss, and self-appointed champion of clean lungs of America who'd insisted she attend this congratulatory celebration for a job well done.

And though Fox had summarily vetoed an in-office party, a working lunch was acceptable.

In the back of her mind, Fox knew she deserved the praise and the promotion for turning around an unprofitable division. She had indeed worked her fingers raw for it, but she couldn't be careless and take a moment of this success for granted. A moment spent basking in one's accomplishments, and the competition would slither by.

Her steps lengthened.

A private, *working* lunch with her boss wouldn't be a total waste. She could at least reiterate her new ideas.

She hurried down three stairs into Café Ormond, her favorite Italian eatery. As usual, the lighting in the deco-lored room softened the raucous red and white tablecloths against glossy oak furniture.

Tall, dark-haired Antonio approached, his face breaking into a welcoming smile. "Check your coat, Ms. Giovanni?"

"Yes, thanks."

Shrugging the black Ann Taylor from her shoulders, she rubbed gloved hands together, then extracted her numb fingers from the furry cashmere caverns. She entrusted the expensive indulgence, the only one she'd allowed herself this year, to Antonio. "Where is he?"

"In the back room. Right this way. Andrew!" A young boy snapped to attention at his uncle's sharp call and accepted Fox's coat carefully over his plump arms. His face looked a prepubescent ten, though he seemed short for that age.

Fox's gaze caught and held to the boy's, who looked at her with the eyes of an angel. Her step faltered. She couldn't recall being his age or relate to the innocence shimmering in his eyes.

He touched her arm. "How do you do, Madame?"

"Fine, thank you." At a loss for more to say to the young man, she moved on down the aisle as he hurried to check her coat.

As it had been given to this past month, her heart raced, and warmth spread through her. Too young for a hot flash, she wished the heat away as she willed her heartrate to slow down. She caught up with Antonio, who'd already stepped around the spindled divider and through a dark door.

"Congratulations," the room full of people shouted, then massacred a round of "For she's a jolly good fellow."

Fox's smile dropped into place as she registered the scene. If it were possible to surprise her she would have been surprised, but it wasn't and she wasn't.

In the center of the melee of her peers stood her boss, Mr. Albert Chesterfield, a grin wide as his belly on his cherub face. The jowls of his chins shook as he approached.

"Gotcha, Ms. Giovanni."

Eleven years ago, he'd hired her to work in the mailroom and insisted on using the formality of her last name. At the time, Fox couldn't understand the need for such pomp with a clerk. He told her then she would do great things for Fields. She needed to earn people's respect now.

Today proved she'd earned it. "Impossible, sir. But nice try." Fox greeted her boss with a firm handshake. "Thank you. You shouldn't have."

"Please be seated," he said to the staff. "I'd like to introduce you to the woman who will take Fields and put it on the international map." People applauded as Mr. Chesterfield eased her aside.

To the group he said, "Why don't you place your drink orders while I speak to my new vice president?" His fatherly gaze reached deep inside her.

"I know you hate surprises. That's why you'll make a hell of a vice president."

Fox let some of the irritation that bubbled inside her show. "The sentiment isn't lost on me, sir. But we could have had a sandwich at the office."

"That wasn't good enough." He angled closer. "You can have your birthday stricken from your personnel records and I have to abide by that. You can even continue to make your perfunctory appearances at office parties and holiday functions." His stomach strained the buttons on his shirt when he stuck his chest out. "I respect your choices. But I wanted to say congratulations, my way."

Annoyed at the burning sensation behind her eyes, Fox

tried to extract her hand. No one had ever cared enough to throw her a party.

An overwhelming sense of loss filled her. How did a promotion party become the first party of her life? Easy. When you had no family, birthdays and anniversaries didn't have much meaning.

Explaining herself to Mr. Chesterfield would only spark questions, so she reached for her cloak of control and drew it around her. Here she was comfortable.

"Who's minding the store, sir?"

Chesterfield smiled, clapping her once on the back, then removing his hand. This was the most her boss had touched her in eleven years.

"Never mind about business for one afternoon."

He turned to the group of business economists she'd been tasked to lead only a week ago. Among them were both men and women who respected, hated, and feared her.

Fox's program for success was simple. Sign on, or sign exit papers. Her confidence at being top in her game was hard earned. Business economists were in great demand with the unsteady overseas economy, and the companies she dealt with wanted to be sure their investments were safe.

Her forecasts for financial and economic trends had been dead on and profitable for five years, and by Chesterfield allowing her the opportunity to prove herself, Fields had earned a place on *Fortune's* Top 100 list. This was the pinnacle of her career and she took a private moment to bask in the joy of it all.

Glancing to her left, Fox noticed two of the female project managers chatting quietly, and for a split second, she wanted to join them. She brushed the increasingly common feelings aside and faced a truth. Out of all the people in the room, she couldn't count one as a true friend.

Not one to share office gossip or gripes. No girlfriend

among the five women to commiserate with a failed relationship or morning-after insecurities.

Distance was something she understood all too well.

Being abandoned at two and placed in the New York City foster care system hadn't helped to bolster close relationships. Now, a handshake to seal a deal was all the intimacy she needed.

Fox put some distance between herself and her boss, and wiped her hands against navy wool slacks to dry the clamminess, wishing she were behind her desk taking a call from the French office. Business would close overseas in an hour.

Her heart tripped and began to race. Through the smile she'd perfected years ago to put others at ease, Fox breathed deeply. Perspiration gathered atop her lip, and annoying beads of moisture slicked her back. She felt as if she were a contender in a marathon. Surely if her heartbeat didn't slow and this hot flash pass, she'd melt.

Or faint. She struggled to hear Chesterfield's words of encouragement, only she couldn't. His mouth moved, but the sound didn't reach her ears.

Her heart galloped. *Bumpbumpbumpbump*. Then, mercifully, slowed. Her ears cleared and sound flooded in.

Chesterfield, who'd stopped talking, gave her a curious look.

Fox's step was sure as she approached the table and took the seat of honor at the head.

"Thank you for coming. I'm glad you all could find time to take off from work, leaving phones unmanned and screen savers monitoring the office."

A good-natured groan rumbled around the room as a slice of pain zipped through her chest. Fox arched, her back hitting the slatted oak chair. She tried to steady her hand, as she reached for her ice water. After a few sips, she began to breathe deeply again.

Perhaps filet mignon had been a bad choice for dinner

last night. Concerned gazes stared back at her and a smile or two dimmed.

When in doubt, the appearance of control was as good as the real thing, and she straightened in her chair so the lines of her Donna Karan milk-white blouse hung arrow straight.

"Seriously, I appreciate the sentiment behind this gesture and I know that as we enter the twenty-first century, we'll reap rewards together. Thank you."

At her nod, waitresses distributed menus.

When everyone's attention was diverted, Fox fought hard to catch her breath, grateful her racing heartbeat had slowed some. Nerves, she chided, keeping her smile in place as she flipped to the pasta section of the menu.

The promotion she'd worked for all her life was hers. A pleasurable tingle followed quickly by a burning sensation raced through her chest again, as a wail of pain lodged in her throat.

"So, Ms. Giovanni," Mr. Chesterfield said on the heel of the escalating jolt, "How does it feel to be Vice president of Securities and Investments of Fields?"

She opened her mouth, but couldn't speak. Instead alarm bells crackled in her head. As a child they'd meant *Hide, danger is near!* Funny, she thought with a surreal vagueness, they still meant the same thing.

"It's an honor," she finally managed around the squeezing pain in her chest. "B-business economists are in demand, and I have some great ideas that if implemented, will change the face of how we gather data, thereby increasing the company business by at least thirty percent. As economists—"

"Ms. Giovanni." Chesterfield's gaze was tolerant. "I'd love to hear your ideas—tomorrow. Let me impart one piece of advice. There's a time to work and a time to play. It's time to play."

She didn't bother to respond as another arrow of fire ignited in the vicinity of her heart. It hurt like hell.

Hot, wrenching pain tore at her organ until tears blurred her eyes. That hurt worse. The tears. She hadn't allowed herself to cry in twenty years.

With all her strength, Fox pushed to her feet. "Be right back." As soon as she cleared the door, she allowed the agony to contort her facial features, and stumbling breathlessly, steered herself toward the ladies room.

A violent wave of nausea attacked and she clutched her belly, holding on to what she knew in her heart wouldn't have a dignified end.

The bathroom door loomed ahead. Fox recognized her own outstretched hand because of the sliver of gold that encircled her thumb. She reached for the handle as volts rivaling an electric chair's shock buckled her knees.

Unbecoming moans came from her body as she hit the floor and rolled to her back. A rush of people surrounded her. Shouts filled her ears. Through the haze of pain, sweat, and tears, coolness invaded. Fox struggled to open her eyes.

Andrew withdrew his hand from her forehead and his angelic gaze reached inside her body. "I'll help you, Madame."

Before she lost consciousness, Fox believed him.

CHAPTER TWO

Pushing air past chapped lips, Fox breathed on her own. Unmistakable surprise rushed through her that she'd awakened for a sixth day in New York University Hospital.

She tested her lungs. Air moved in, then out. She was alive.

The punctuated thumps in her chest cavity where her heart resided confirmed it.

Her doctor's words rang in her head again.

Inferior myocardial-infarction.

"Clarification."

She'd barely managed the demand through the anger and crushing pain in her chest while in the emergency room.

Dr. Caraway hadn't hesitated in his response. "You've had a heart attack."

Those five words had awakened her for the past three days. Would they for the rest of her life?

Fox breathed in and out again, anxiety climbing her nerves like a poisonous spider to trapped prey. How much life did she have left?

She mentally gave herself a shake and used the breathing and relaxation techniques the nurse educator had taught her yesterday. The anxiety passed.

Stinging tears brought relief to her overly dry eyes as she inclined her bed. Being sick was dangerously unproductive.

The door whooshed open and Fox hoped it wasn't yet another nurse on a never-ending round of blood pressure and temperature checks or worse, questions.

"Glad you decided to rejoin us, Foxy."

"I've been awake for a while. And it's just Fox. Another blood pressure check?"

On the slightly heavy side, the woman's pink pants simulated a wood saw when her thighs rubbed together. She loved wearing her hair high atop her head with decorative pins stabbed into the unmoving cocoon.

"No, it's time for your sponge bath. I'm glad you're awake. It'll be that much easier on me. Off with this blanket. Boy, it's hot in here. Can't see how you sleep under all this." Short, even teeth glowed a scurvy green when Sampson smiled.

Fox held the sheet firmly to her chest. "I believe you have incorrect information. I've been bathing on my own since the day after I arrived. There must be some mistake."

The woman continued pulling back the covers. "Your name is on this list so you get a sponge bath. Let go of the covers."

"Your list is wrong." Unaccustomed to being touched as much as having her requests ignored, her patience evaporated. "I want to see Dr. Caraway."

"Already made his rounds," she clucked. "Don't expect him back until evening."

"I need to see him right away."

Sampson flipped down the blanket on the bed and moved the rolling tray closer to Fox's chest. "Do you have a scar? Let's have a look. Got to be careful we don't get it wet." She cracked meaty fingers.

"Let's not." Fox gripped the hospital issue gown while Sampson tugged on the sheet. "Only Caraway is looking, touching, or inspecting me. This doesn't make any sense. As I've said, I've taken showers on my own since the day after I was admitted."

Anger warmed the soreness in her throat, making her words sound gutter-harsh when the woman gave her a disbelieving look. She tugged harder.

"The chart says bed B, Fox. You're bed B. I just need to touch it."

"You're not poking any scar on my body! Now I want to see Caraway, or draw up my discharge papers."

Sampson gave her a dead glare. "Our greatest pleasure is poking scars. It *must* be time for your pain medication."

Medical horror stories from the news bleeped through Fox's mind. Today it was a sponge bath, tomorrow an injection. She strengthened her resolve. "I want out." Her tone stopped Nurse Assistant Sampson who dropped one hand to her hip, raised the other, and pointed a fingernail in Fox's face.

"Foxy—"

"Get Caraway now. And if you can't get my name right, call me Ms. Giovanni." Struggling to hold onto the only thing she could control, she gripped the gown and met the woman's defiant glare with one of her own. She hadn't been able to stop the rush of people from surrounding her at the restaurant. Or the paramedics from stripping her down for all the world to see. Or the swarm of emergency people at the hospital who moved dispassionately, but efficiently, around her. But she could control how she was addressed.

"It's Ms. Giovanni. And a sponge bath isn't going to take the place of my doctor."

"It might improve your disposition," Sampson said, clearly ticked now.

Fox dismissed her sarcasm. "Don't count on it."

"I see you two are getting along." Doctor Louis Caraway

walked into the stalemate, his smile tolerant. "Feeling better today, Ms. Giovanni?"

"Immensely, since you arrived." Sampson's soundless exit riled her. "What kind of organization do you run around here? I was practically stripped!"

Dr. Caraway smiled. "The bath is supposed to relax as well as cleanse you."

"Under force? I can't take it anymore, doctor," she said, knowing she'd lost her cool. She brushed strands of limp hair out of her eyes. "Look on that chart and tell me I was supposed to get a sponge bath, and I'll apologize to Nurse Assistant Sampson."

He cocked his head as he read. "You are not supposed to get a sponge bath."

"See—"

"What I see," he said louder to get her attention. "Is a woman who's all worked up about a bath. A bath wouldn't hurt. Now an injection . . ." He grinned, trying to make her smile.

"You're not funny, doctor. But this place is driving me crazy." She smirked a grin despite herself and sighed. "I know I haven't been the easiest person to get along with."

"What gave you that impression?" He chuckled. Caraway's study of the chart gave away nothing. He snapped it closed, hooked a stethoscope in his ears and tapped his palm. "There's a pool going around," he said conversationally. "The loser gets to shove your food tray across the floor to you for dinner."

Finally, Fox smiled. The movement felt foreign and difficult.

"That bad?"

"Worse, my dear. Worse. Let's have a look." The doctor kept his tone light. "I'll rest my hand on your shoulder, listen to your heart through your back." Fox jumped when his hand touched her shoulder and she forced herself to relax.

"Easy. Breathe in . . . out. Now from the front. I'm counting the beats per minute, checking your pulmonary strength." He paused and she relaxed some. "Checking for signs of abnormality."

"Are there any?"

"No," he said, stepping away after examining her reflexes, eyes and throat. "You've progressed nicely. It's time."

"To go back to work?"

"Definitely not to work. You need rest. Lots of it. We unblocked the left circumflex artery. Without knowing your family medical history, I hesitate to say whether you inherited this problem or if the condition was brought on by bad lifestyle habits. I do know a twenty-eight-year-old woman shouldn't have a heart attack."

Long ago Fox stopped making excuses for the family she'd never known. She searched through a private detective for her parents and had found her mother in a small country cemetery. It was just as well.

"My eating habits, I'm sure."

"Whether it is or isn't doesn't matter. What's important here is that you change your lifestyle and become health conscious." His gaze continued to be level, professional. "You're a highly stressed woman. So much so, your blood pressure will need to be controlled with medication. No more red meat. No more smoking. You must exercise every day. And no work."

"What! Do you know what the French are doing right now?" She whisked her gold watch off the rolling table. "I need to go to France and finish my projects. My job is my life, doctor."

"Your work is meaningless if you're dead, Fox."

She shook her head, desperation creeping through her. "This has to be just a temporary setback. The company needs me."

"How do you think they've been functioning since you've been here?"

Dr. Caraway didn't understand. She had nothing else.

"Of course, someone is filling in for me. But I'm expected back. I'm needed." She exhaled an open-mouthed sigh, and vowed to change his mind.

He stood at the foot of her bed. "Where's your family?"

"I don't have any."

"Folks dead?" he asked, more gently.

"I'm a product of foster care."

"No known siblings?"

"No," she answered, irritated at the entire conversation. Who in their right mind wanted to be reminded they were alone in the world? "Is this inquisition going somewhere?"

"It gives me a better indication of your history. But you should take your own advice and go somewhere. Take a vacation, Fox. Try something new. Give yourself time to examine your priorities."

"They've always been clear, doc. I work. I wake up with the sole purpose of going to work. I go to sleep with the sole purpose of waking up and going back to work. I work weekends and holidays because I'm dedicated."

He shook his sun-streaked blond head. His natural tan said golfer. Probably got out on the links twice a week. His perfect life seemed to mock her. "You're a workaholic," he told her. "Those tendencies will be your death. Next time you come in here, you might not leave under your own power. I'm going to do you a favor and not release you for work for six weeks." He held up his hand. "Your insurance covers the leave. Take my advice, get a life."

Doctor Caraway pushed away from the bed and opened the door to her room. Six weeks? How could she not sit behind her desk at work for six weeks? Words spilled from her mouth. "What will I do?"

He returned, thrusting his hands deep into nicely pressed slacks.

"Travel if you can afford to. Teach yourself how to relax. It might save your life."

"But—"

"I'm not going to change my diagnosis or your treatment program."

"I didn't think you would. Actually, I wanted to ask about something else. Something personal." She looked away from his curious gaze. "Did I have any visitors?" *Coworkers? Neighbors?*

His smile was sad. "Your boss called from Hong Kong several nights ago. He sent his best. Nobody else came."

"Probably couldn't find this out-of-the-way hospital." The half-joke was so unlike her it fell flat, even to her ears.

She could hear her roommate being settled back into bed on the other side of the curtain. For once the woman was quiet.

"Fox, you've been given another chance." He patted her foot. Take it."

"Not for six weeks. Two?" The art of negotiation was something she'd mastered at Fields. She hated to do it now, but it was better than begging.

Caraway's blue eyes danced as he smiled. "This isn't a death sentence. Reconnect with a girlfriend from high school or college. I'll see you in my office in two weeks. Tomorrow you're going home."

The door closed, shutting out sound. *A girlfriend?* She hadn't been able to tell Caraway, but she couldn't even remember a single girl's name from Oswego State University.

The curtain separating the two beds whipped back like it had been snatched by a Chicago wind.

"I heard what your doctor said. What are you going to do?"

Overly curious and primed to chat, Maureen Gentry stared at Fox expecting an answer. Her freckled nose crinkled, while wild ringlets of red hair zoomed east and west on her head.

"I'd rather not discuss my medical condition, if that's all the same to you, Ms. Gentry."

"Heck, it's fine with me, but I'm worried about you. You

were crying up a storm last night.'' The fast talking woman waved a dainty hand. "I called your name. 'Fox, Fox,' I said, but you kept tossing and turning. Tossing and turning. I finally called the nurse. By the time they got here, the whimpers had subsided and you slept peacefully.''

Hearing the recount of the nightmare was almost worse than experiencing it firsthand. The dark dream, cloying fear, and cloak of death still haunted her. She tore her gaze away from the concern reflected in Maureen's eyes and tried to shut away the remaining memory of hovering over her own body.

Fox panted, fighting an anxiety attack. When her heartbeat slowed she turned back and found the woman still watching. "I appreciate your concern. But I'm going to be fine, Ms. Gentry.''

"Call me Maureen. I told you that. No need to be formal. We're roommates after all. Oh, I interrupted. I always do that. You just have to stop me.'' Maureen's eyes unglazed. She refocused on Fox.

"So, where's your husband? I noticed you don't have a ring line on your finger. You're not married? Gosh, how old are you?''

Fox eased against her pillow, closed her eyes and didn't answer. Why did the Fifty-first Street train have to crash, forcing the hospital to have no private rooms available? The incessant prattling was going to kill her before another heart attack could.

"Please, I'd like to rest.''

"You can rest at home. Isn't that what your doctor said?''

"Yes. But I'm tired now.''

"You're not tired. You're tired of me talking. Well, I'll stop.'' She paused long enough to take a deep breath. "Why doesn't a pretty woman like you have a boyfriend?''

"I don't need a boyfriend. Or a husband, for that matter.''

"But you've had a heart attack.'' Maureen ignored the

murderous look Fox shot her. "I'd cry if I had a heart attack, too. You poor thing."

Maureen's sympathy stopped Fox's downward spiral toward depression. Here was this woman, a virtual stranger and she cared.

"I hope I didn't keep you up all night."

"You didn't," Maureen said softly. "And your secret is safe with me."

"I have nothing to tell."

Maureen lay back finally. Her skin was translucent, tiny veins evident on her forehead. Staying in the hospital was taking its toll on her, too.

Fox wondered why she was there. She'd seen bandages on her leg, but that had been in passing from the bathroom, and she'd looked away to give the woman privacy. Maureen hadn't seemed to care.

She'd chatted away the days on the phone or with an endless stream of visitors. For a sick woman, she sure had a lot of company.

"How long are you staying?" Fox asked, feeding a sudden curiosity she never allowed herself.

"Until they tell me why my circulation is so poor. Doctor Grayson said I may lose my leg."

Fox grasped her chest, her fingers subconsciously covering her heart. "I'm so sorry."

"Thank you." Maureen wiped her runny nose with a balled tissue. "Anyway, I just thought you might have needed a friend last night."

We're friends? "No. I mean, I wasn't scared." Fox hesitated then said, "Thanks."

Last night she could have used a friend. The words echoed hollowly inside her. But what could a friend do that doctors hadn't? She was fortunate, she realized. At least she'd get to keep everything she'd arrived with. She'd still lied to Maureen, though. She was terrified.

"Are you afraid?"

"I'd be lying if I said I wasn't." Maureen's voice caught

on a sob. "I've got kids, and a husband, and a job in Manhattan. My life will change drastically. But at least I'll have my life." She dabbed her eyes with a fresh tissue. "Let's change this depressing subject."

Fox nodded in agreement. Maureen turned as much as her leg would allow. "If you don't have a boyfriend or husband to take care of you, you should call an old friend. Someone you can trust who will help you through this."

"I haven't spent a lot of time cultivating relationships."

"Well there's no time like the present. Somebody to help you through this makes it easier. You won't have to cry alone."

The door to the room swished open. A wheelchair pushed by a nurse banged the lower steel on the door.

"Ms. Gentry," he said, looking at the chart in his hand. His gaze swept Fox who'd gathered the thin sheet to her chest. Hospitals were the least private place in the world. The man finally looked at Maureen. "Time for more X-rays."

"Looks like I'm off, roomie." He assisted Maureen into the chair and swung her around. "Wait!" Maureen spun the chair around. "Push me over there, please."

The nurse pushed her between the two beds. Maureen picked up the phone and sat it near Fox's hand. "Call somebody. You're not alone." She patted Fox's hand and sat back and was wheeled toward the door.

"Maureen?" When she turned, Fox looked into Maureen's cheerful, but worried eyes.

"Yes?"

"Thank you, and good luck."

A quivering smile split the woman's face. "Thanks." The door closed softly leaving Fox alone. Ignoring the phone, she lowered the bed, and forbade herself to dream.

She awoke and realized she'd been asleep for two hours. She glanced over to Maureen's bed. Still empty. Why would a trip to X-ray take so long?

Slipping from the bed, her arms holding her ribs, Fox

gathered her meager belongings and stuffed them into a bag.

She climbed back into bed and avoiding the phone, reached for her brush. Her ribs had taken a beating and her muscles felt as if she'd lost a bad boxing match.

The thought of sitting in her condo for six weeks had her heart racing. Fox calmed down. Traveling held mild appeal. Her passport was active, but the length of time on an international flight dimmed the sudden idea.

She lay back, flipped on the television and watched a cartoon fade from the screen.

Her purse had been stowed in the bedside table and she reached inside and found her electronic phone book. The entries confirmed what she already knew. Every number listed was a business associate.

Except the last entry, which displayed a single name and a ten-digit number.

Before she could change her mind, Fox lifted the receiver and dialed.

CHAPTER THREE

Van Compton fumbled the phone, grimacing when it hit the counter then rolled across the newly sanded kitchen floor.

He retrieved it from a pile of sawdust, and blew one mighty breath to dislodge particles from the speaker holes.

"Yeah?" he barked more from frustration at the interruption than with the caller.

"I'd like to speak to Willow."

"She isn't here. Something I can do for you?"

"Where is she?"

It wasn't the demand so much as the accent that stopped him. The curl of the "R" gave away her geographic heritage. New York.

Van's lip curled distastefully.

New Yorkers weren't necessarily a problem. *Northerners* period turned Beef Jerky to stone in his stomach.

"Willow's outside," he said, brushing perspiration from his face with a dry towel.

"And the distance is too great for you to go get her?"

The woman's voice reeked bourgeois, high-class snob.

Just what he needed on this hot day. A headache from a
city woman.

Probably a realtor. Somebody was always offering to buy
his aunt's home and farm.

Van wiped his forehead again. What he wouldn't give
for a shower and an ice-cold beer.

"As a matter of fact, it is. If you're a realtor, she's not
interested in selling."

"I'm not a realtor," the northern voice said. "I knew
Willow long ago. I don't know if she would remember
me." The woman's voice faded into a helpless sigh.

His stomach clenched at the decidedly feminine breath.
Van frowned at his reaction. No surprise. It had been a
while since he'd detected real vulnerability in a woman.
Bracing his hip against the counter, he poured a quarter-
size of cleaner into his palms and rubbed vigorously.

"Age hasn't slowed Willow's memory a bit," he said
above the rush of water from the faucet. "What's your
name?"

"Fox," she said. "Fox Giovanni."

"Kinda strange, isn't it?"

He heard the sharp intake of breath. "Not to me. What's
yours?"

"Van Compton," he said, knocking the faucet off with
his wrist.

"You criticize me and you're named after a truck?"

The towel he'd used to dry his face fell off his shoulder
to the floor, and he scooped it up with a snarl. Who was
this woman with her clipped English and uppity attitude?

Another Perri. At the end of their marriage, his ex-wife
had always been quick to take offense to any comment
he'd made no matter how harmless. He couldn't say "Good
mornin' " without her asking "Who's it good for?"

Must be a Northern thing.

"Look, I've got work to do," he said, ready to end the
verbal sparring. "If there's a message, I'll give it to her.
She can call you back later."

"Oh, well, no. There's no message."

The earlier sizzle in her voice had been replaced with a hollowness he could feel. How could a woman's personality change so quickly?

Van banged his forehead with his still damp hand. Perri's "Exhale" antics of burning his clothes proved his theory since his divorce a year ago that most women were nuts. This lady's on again, off again attitude confirmed it.

He glanced out the screened back door. Willow's pink hat floated as she walked among the tall cornstalks. Except Willow. There was nothing crazy about her, but lately her tendency toward forgetfulness had begun to worry him.

"I was thinking." Fox expelled another breath. "Never mind. Just tell her I called."

"I'll do that."

She hesitated, as if she wanted to say more, then hung up.

Van replaced the receiver, and scribbled on the duck notepad Willow kept by the phone he'd given her for Christmas. She'd loved the phone and the many features it offered and had insisted on leaving it in the kitchen so she could show it off to all her friends. Throwing the pencil on the counter, he glanced at the display console, and stopped short. It displayed the number and location— New York University Hospital.

A volatile cocktail of guilt and concern hit him.

What if this Fox Giovanni was a sick relative on Willow's husband's side of the family? Although he knew most of his Uncle Ray's kinfolk, he didn't know all their children or their children's children.

He glanced out the screened door. Willow was half a mile down the road. She wouldn't be back until early evening.

Today she would feed the pigs, water her herbs, and go to the county jail to work with the prisoners in their garden.

Then she would come back and bake until late evening

while listening to old Sammy Davis Jr. records on her phonograph.

The baked goods would go to the church tomorrow. Willow couldn't stop taking care of others. Including him. She enjoyed the fact that he would stay on the farm until the remodeling on her house was complete. His presence gave her constant and ready company.

Van dug in the refrigerator and pulled out a plastic covered plate. A plump chicken leg caught his attention and he took a healthy bite, his thoughts returning to the caller.

Fox Giovanni sounded young. She was probably one of Willow's foster kids. A bad taste settled in his mouth. So far this year, five of her foster kids had passed through. All hadn't left with just their belongings, either. Willow's antique silver and several of her collector dolls had disappeared, too. And according to Denise at the bank, Willow's account had been depleted with several large withdrawals.

No, he thought with resolve, finishing his food. Another person with a sob story and sad face wasn't going to take advantage of his family.

Van jotted down the number, and left the pad on the counter where Willow would see it. He hoisted a plank of wood onto his shoulder and didn't break stride until he reached the drawing room. Efficiently he fit it in place.

Accustomed to working alone in the century old home, Van mentally listed the work that still had to be done.

The wooden floors in the double front drawing rooms had been replaced about thirty years ago and were still in good shape, so all they needed was a good cleaning and waxing. The carved marble mantelpieces for the four fireplaces throughout the house had been tended to already, and the original chandeliers would be returned cleaned and restored to their original luster and austerity within two weeks.

Taking the restoration class in masonry last summer helped him understand the necessity of care for the origi-

nal fourteen-inch-thick brick walls, but once he'd gotten
the hang of plastering the brick, the work had come easily
and quickly. Floors in two lower level rooms and the upper
parsons or travelers room had to be completed, as well as
papering and painting the walls in the lower level dining
area.

The phone rang and he snapped it up. "Yeah?"

"Hello, Van this is Denise from Slumber Community
Bank. Is this a good time to talk?"

"Yes, Denise. Is Willow overdrawn again?"

"Yes. Two checks were presented today that drained the
money in her checking account. Per our agreement, I
wanted to tell you we were going to access the money from
the savings account to cover the shortage. Okay?"

"That's fine." He sighed heavily. "Who were the checks
written to?"

"One to the church and one to the senior center."

Van shook his head. If she didn't curb her generosity, his
aunt's kind heart would land her in the homeless shelter.

"All right, Denise. Go ahead and accept them."

Her voice lowered. "Van, you know I don't do this for
everybody, but Willow is special. She's been good to my
family for many years when Mama and Daddy were struggling, but what are you going to do about all the discrepan-
cies."

"I've just got to stay on top of things until I can figure
out if she's just forgetful about her resources or if there's
a larger problem."

"Van, you know Daddy's gone on and Mama's senile. I
know it's hard to make decisions for your elders, but you've
got to. Even though you have Willow's power of attorney,
you're going to run yourself ragged trying to mind her
and her affairs."

A memory flashed in his head of Denise's mom and dad.
They were a fine-looking couple but when her mom had
been stricken with Alzheimer's, her father couldn't take
it and died a broken man.

Van stretched his neck. He wasn't sure what the situation was with Willow and until he knew what he was dealing with, he wouldn't jump to any hasty conclusions.

He didn't want to take control of his aunt's affairs and kill her and her spirit.

"Denise, I appreciate your concern and your help. Just keep me up on anything you find suspicious. Okay?"

"All right, Van. Be talking to you."

He hung up and resumed working.

The bright morning skies turned into dark rain clouds before he finally fitted the last plank of wood on the drawing room floor. Van closed the windows to the humid air and stepped back to admire his work.

No one could tell him a house built today was better than one built two hundred years ago. Willow's family had grown up on this plantation, first as slaves then as free men and women. Now she owned it. His thoughts were dragged back to the influx of freeloaders that had swooped down on them this year.

No one was going to scam, or steal the house, under the deception of needing a shoulder to cry on.

This Fox woman could talk to Willow, but his aunt wouldn't be taken advantage of again.

Willow's vision to restore the old house had become his dream after Cleophus Woods and his cousin, Bootsy, had taken more than enough of her money and hadn't delivered work for pay.

Van rubbed at a spot on the shiny floor until he'd buffed it away, anger budding inside him again. They were just another example of people taking advantage of the elderly. Not for the first time he wondered if his aunt's faculties were slipping. If so, decisions would have to be made for her care.

He sensed Willow's presence before he heard her, and glanced at his paint splattered watch. "I thought you were going to feed the animals?"

Her soft chuckle and bustle made him smile.

"The creatures of the forest can take care of themselves today. I needed some refreshment. Join me for some lemonade and cookies?"

"I'm too old for lemonade and cookies," Van said, swallowing a grin. This had been their first conversation, the day he'd come to live with Willow over fourteen years ago.

Living here had changed his life; it had given a troubled young boy a reason to live.

Willow hooked arms with him. "Until you're old as me, older than dirt on the ground, you'll never be too old for lemonade and cookies."

Together they stepped on the drop cloth protecting part of the kitchen floor. The place looked a mess, he knew, but it was an organized mess.

Van washed his hands and pulled out a chair for the older woman whose movements didn't reflect her seventh decade.

"You had a call. A woman named Fox Giovanni," he said, filling her glass with the pale juice. Rings of fruit toppled into the glass and his mouth watered in anticipation.

Willow stopped ripping into the plastic dish of cookies and touched his arm. "Did you say Fox Giovanni?"

He caught the glimmer of hope in her eyes. "The message is on the pad."

The container of cookies spun on the table where she dropped it and hurried to the counter. "How long ago?"

"A few hours. Who is she?"

"A chosen one." Van knew that meant a child who had become one of her own. This surprised him. He was a chosen child, also. Willow often said so.

But the people who were closest were often the first to betray. Finding his wife in the arms of another man taught him that. Naturally, Van's suspicion piqued.

"She might need to hear from you," he said to answer the guilt nagging at him. "She was calling from a hospital."

Willow's aged fingers shook as she dialed. "Fox? Willow

here. How are you? I'm blessed ... I got your number from Van." Willow looked at him. "You didn't give it to him?" The older woman's chuckle was gentle. "I've got one of those newfangled phones that shows your number. Why are you in the hospital?"

Van sipped his drink as he sat down, gazing out the porch door, pretending not to listen.

"Why didn't you call? I would have come to nurse you."

Van sucked an ice cube slowly. Years ago, Willow had vowed never to return to New York. She'd never explained her reasons. He'd always assumed it was because of a broken relationship or business gone bad.

"Of course, I got your Christmas card," Willow said, smiling again. "I get them every year. The money?"

Van ears lifted despite his best effort. "That money is for you. You won't give it back to me. I insist you keep it."

Another user! He'd put a stop to this once and for all. Willow's ringed fingers clinked when she clasped her hands together.

"Come visit me. Slumber is the best place for you. What do you mean 'why'? Because I'm here. And my warrior is here, Van. We'll take care of you ... I know you don't need help. You've always been self-sufficient."

Having warned her before about inviting every lost soul to the farm, he tried to cut off the impending invitation. "Willow, we don't have room."

"Of course, we do," she answered, waving him away. "Fox, I need you." Her voice dropped low. Van knew the woman on the other end was hooked, even if *she* didn't. "You're the strongest person I know, dear. I've always admired your strength. Come see me, Fox."

Willow had closed her eyes, and he knew even as she continued to have a conversation with Fox, she was also having one with God.

As her nephew, he had a great influence in her life, but even he left Willow alone once she started to pray.

Willow coughed, a dry wracking that shook her entire body.

"I'm feeling right fine, child. You know I'm in my seventies." She cleared her throat. Van moved toward her. "Shh, shh. You won't be a burden to me. Course I don't have forever to walk this earth."

Willow's loving gaze rested on Van when she opened her eyes. She winked to let him know she was fine. Chatter came through the phone but he couldn't make out the words.

"I'm glad you decided to come. Do you need directions?" Dread sank deep within him. How could he assess his aunt's faculties with another person around? Fox Giovanni was already a problem.

Willow's burst of laughter didn't relieve his anxiety.

"That's right, just point your car south and it'll come right to my door." Willow listened for a moment, nodding. "That's a good idea. Call when you get to Raleigh. Until I see you, blessings and peace."

As soon as she lowered the phone, her expression saddened.

"More than her heart needs to heal."

"What's wrong with her?"

"She had a heart attack. But she sounds empty inside. Slumber will be a good place for her. Just like it is for my other chosen children."

"Why do you insist on inviting everyone here?" Van gentled his tone. "Haven't you been taken advantage of enough?"

"You know that saying, 'God takes care of fools and children'?"

"You're nobody's fool." Van couldn't bring himself to say what was truly in his heart. But he could think it.

Willow was getting old. She was becoming increasingly forgetful and lackadaisical about business in a way he'd never seen before.

She stood tall and reached for the cookie container. "I

may not be a fool, but I am God's child. Honey, don't worry about my money, it's in good hands." She smiled and walked away.

Van rested his hands on his hips and prayed she was right.

"Where's my lemonade?"

He pushed a plate over and filled her glass. Galloping raindrops pounded the roof. "How old is this woman?"

"Late twenties. Very young."

"And she had a heart attack?" The idea was so foreign, he scoffed.

"Good health isn't promised to us all." They both reached for a cookie and by silent agreement split it.

"Where'd she get her name?"

"Ask her when she arrives. That'll make a nice ice-breaker for you two. Will the blue room be finished soon?"

Willow had risen to dig through the refrigerator. She returned with more lemons, which she cut and added to the lemonade pitcher. Two pieces remained on the cutting board.

Furniture in the upper four bedrooms had been repaired and refinished last month. He'd arranged every-thing with the help of several moving men in the blue room just last week. He didn't relish anyone being in that room and wanting to change it around. The furniture was large and heavy, more than one man could carry.

The rugs had been laid before the furniture arrived, and all he awaited now was delivery of the swing-frame Queen Anne walnut toilet mirror for the corner near the newly built walk-in closet.

"It should be finished tomorrow or Thursday at the latest. But it's very isolated. You recall I had the widow's walk torn down and replaced with regular roofing. She won't have access to the front balcony. Don't you want her down here with you?"

"Van." Willow pursed her lips around the lemon peel she'd popped into her mouth. "I know the widow's walk is gone. And I don't think she'll need the front balcony. Besides, she can come down here if she wants company. And if she wants privacy, she can use the back staircase and avoid whomever she wishes. Fox is a grown woman. She'll need her privacy. You never know, she may find somebody down here and decide to stay."

Fox's uppity attitude sailed through his mind like the torrential rain that poured outside. He swallowed his cookie and took a healthy gulp of lemonade.

"She's a city woman. She ain't hardly interested in a country man." The look in his aunt's eye sent him to his feet. "Don't go getting any fancy matchmaking ideas, Willow. You know I don't cater to city women. We're as different as night and day."

"Your mama and I would disagree. We think you should be married again by now. City or country woman don't matter to us."

Just the mention of his mother sent Van back into his chair. She was another one who needed watching. She was on her fourth husband. Most of the old men she married couldn't keep up with the energetic Zenobia.

Fortunately his brother Aaron was in Mississippi with her.

"Don't you read those magazines you bring home, Willow? People with things in common should marry."

Too much sugar was added to the pitcher. Willow stirred away.

"How would you know what's in them? You once told me reading was a waste of time."

"I pick up a thing or two when I'm at the dentist" was all he said.

"Thought so." She chewed another rind. His aunt wasn't going to change her mind, and neither was he.

City women were trouble. But freeloaders of any kind made him mad. He'd keep a close eye on Fox Giovanni. And when the time was right, she'd have to leave.

"I thought you had to go to the prison today?" he said,

his decision erasing all the pent-up concern that accompanied caring for an elderly relative.

"With this downpour, we won't get anything done. I've got other work to do since Fox is coming." She gathered a stack of furniture catalogues and strolled to her room on the main level.

Van didn't see Willow again and worked until after midnight laying new floor in the hallway leading to the parlor.

The original floor had been eaten away by time and termites. But this house now had someone who would care for it. Once complete, it would be a showpiece and a wonderful place for Willow to live her remaining years. If nobody stole her finances.

As he hauled the remaining wood to the storage barn, the phone call from Fox Giovanni popped into his head again.

Van hoisted himself into the driver's seat of his pickup, backed onto Willow's driveway and hurried through the rain to the remodeled cabin.

He stripped the clothes from his body and kicked them aside. Van longed for his house, his shower, his bathroom, his solitude. Instead he stepped on the cold tile of the bathroom and scrubbed the day's dirt from his body.

"Be civil," he'd heard Perri say to him about her corporate crowd of coworkers more than once. Fox would see his civil side.

The one that didn't take mess from anybody.

He turned the water as cold as he could stand it and let the spray bleat over his skin. Satisfied, he stepped out, shutting off the water as he did.

Thank goodness, Wayne, one of the hands, had taken care of the dogs.

As he lay in bed, still damp, he made himself a promise. If Willow were taking leave of her senses, he would care for her no matter what.

And Fox had better not get in the way.

As it was, a city woman in these parts would sure garner

a heap of interest. Possibly cause some infighting among the few eligible men. There were plenty of women around, but when fresh meat arrived, the natives went wild.

He hoped she could hold her own. He didn't have time to defend anybody's virtue.

Van got up and had a long-awaited beer.

CHAPTER FOUR

North Carolina stretched wide and flat and far. Interspersed among fields of dust were acres of brown people-tall plants, with full green trees providing a billowy backdrop.

Sun-darkened men of African-American and Mexican descent walked in rows swinging hand tools harvesting the state's number one crop, tobacco. Some sang, while others breathed through bandanna-covered mouths, too busy working to notice her slow the car and capture their progress with an interested, but tired stare.

So, this is how it's done she thought, as she accelerated, passing one field after another.

Fatigue had become her steady companion on the long drive, and Fox looked forward to arriving at Willow's—maybe then she'd be able to sleep.

The psychologist she'd seen before being released from the hospital had said fear of sleep was a normal reaction for heart attack victims. She'd made Fox practice deep breathing techniques and other stress reducers, but Fox knew she was the exception to the rule. She should have but hadn't slept in twenty-four hours. Any time she closed her eyes, the haunting dreams of death were still too real.

Fox fought to keep her eyes open and reached for her cup of coffee, then hit the radio's scan button. Settling on a station playing rap music—that would keep her alert— she adjusted in her seat and planned what she'd say when she saw Willow in less than an hour.

Needles of excitement prickled through her. It had been nearly twelve years. Willow had cared for her from her twelfth to her sixteenth year. Then Fox had been taken away because, according to state rules, she'd been with Willow too long.

Willow's valiant fight to regain custody fell on deaf ears. Then after losing the last battle, she moved south. But not before she'd taught Fox the necessary skills she needed to survive in the world.

Keeping her gaze glued to the trance-inducing white lines on the road, Fox sipped her coffee and chuckled as Doctor Caraway's parting words played in her head.

"I don't want to see you back until mid-summer. And under no circumstances will I release you to work. So have a good time in North Carolina, and check in with Doctor Norris Rawlins when you get there."

Attempts to bargain an early return to work date had been in vain, so she'd given up and was taken by taxi to her condo.

The place had smelled closed up, her bills had been piled neatly on the table near the front door and she was alone.

No Nurse Assistant Sampson. No cheerful greeting from her roommate who'd found the good in losing a leg.

God, she missed Maureen.

Without a second thought, Fox had packed and tipped the doorman to carry her bags to the underground parking lot and cram them in her convertible. She paid her bills, then drove out of Manhattan unable to glance back at the buildings that scraped the sky.

Horns blared, bringing Fox back to the here and now. Heart racing, she fought the steering wheel as the car spun, then swerved, missing a drainage ditch by several feet.

Finally her small car stopped, and Fox glanced up to see herself pointed in the wrong direction. A roar filled her ears while stars danced before her eyes.

She swallowed and breathed deep, fighting unconsciousness.

Somebody banged on the window with the force of a jackhammer.

"You all right?"

Panicked, she drew in a big breath and held it. Without looking up at the concerned citizen, she nodded, exhaling.

"Lady, roll the winda' down."

Fox did as instructed, panicked, and rolled it up again. The man straightened, shaking his head. He bent at the waist, his face coming level with hers. He was dark. Very, very dark with teeth the color of newly shucked corn. But honesty radiated in his calm, concerned eyes.

"Lady, we ain't tryin' to hurt you. Now, where you headin'?"

She hesitated not knowing what to do.

He stood. "Bert! Git over here!"

Seconds later, a tall woman with a baby attached to her hip knocked on the passenger window. "Miss, are you all right?" she asked through the glass.

Fox nodded.

"She's all right, Daddy. Can you drive, Miss?"

To her horror, Fox felt her chin tremble. She boned up her strength and nodded.

"Where're you going?"

Fox looked at the man and young woman and the baby who'd smeared her window with a slobber painting. She pressed the automatic controls and rolled the window down a quarter of the way on both sides. "I'm going to Willow's farm. She's expecting me."

"Daddy, she's goin' to Miss Willow's. I don't think she

can drive, though.'' Fox started to protest but looked at her still shaking hands and kept quiet. She was slowly losing control in every aspect of her life.

"Miss, we can take you. My daddy's car is back here. You come ride with me."

"No, I can't leave my car."

"Daddy will drive your car to Miss Willow's. You got all this stuff on the seat. I'm not goin' have him pile it on top of you. You just had a bad scare. Come on," she said, gently but firmly. "Miss Willow don't live but over yonder."

"Yonder?" Fox repeated the word that had never entered her extensive vocabulary. *Where exactly was yonder?* To the woman she asked, "How far is yonder in minutes?"

The daughter and father glanced at each other through the windows and burst out laughing.

"Where you from, Pennsylvania?" the father asked, reaching in to unlock her door. He helped Fox from the bucket seat with large but gentle hands. "Steady on your feet, now."

The young woman, Bert, who stood very tall up close, held Fox's arm firmly and steered her toward a relic of a car.

A Chevy of some kind. All the windows were rolled down and some of the cushion from the roof had begun to sag. Fox held it up as she slid in. Bert secured the baby in the rear car seat then got behind the wheel.

"Can your father handle my car?" Fox asked, not wanting to offend, but noticing how billows of white smoke blew from the tail pipe as the woman's father raced the engine.

Bert studied the dashboard of the Chevy closely and shifted the car into drive. "My daddy can drive anything." Confidently she added, "He drives every day of his life."

Fox settled back and secured her seat belt as they pulled onto the road. She stifled a yawn. "What does he do?"

"He's a forklift driver for Crenshaw Paper Mill."

Fox watched her car disappear up the road until it was a

dot on the horizon. "Doreen," Bert said over her shoulder, "look at Daddy havin' fun."

From the back seat the baby clapped and Fox's stomach sank.

After twenty minutes, she stopped wondering where yonder was, shut her eyes, and let her thoughts drift. If this family were dangerous, they'd found the perfect prey, because her eyes refused to open. Wherever yonder was, Fox hoped it was quiet.

Already a pain in the ass.

Van watched the ostentatious black convertible hurtling down the lane toward the house and shook his head. So much for feeling sorry for Fox Giovanni. She was driving like a bat out of hell.

The car screeched to a halt in a cloud of dust, and he stalked down the steps, ready to give her a piece of his mind. Willow wasn't home, so somebody had to do it.

Chickens flapped out of the way perturbed at the rude arrival.

Waving his hand, Van fanned dust and peered into the window with what he knew was an intimidating scowl.

"What the hell?" the two men chorused.

"Walter Braxton, what are you doing behind the wheel of this car?"

"Drivin'. Whatchu think?" The older man unbuckled himself, all smiles.

"Where'd you get this?" Van helped the older man out of the car and slammed the door.

"From a little girl who had a mite of trouble on the road. Said Willow was expectin' her." Van looked in the car and saw no one.

His heart beat wildly. "Where is she?"

"With Bert. Ain't you never heard of hospitality? Got somethin' to drink?"

"I'm not worried about your thirst, Walt. Where are they?"

"Over yonder," he waved. "How's about that drink?"

"Get it yourself. I'm waiting right here. Something happen to her, Willow would have my hide."

"Suit yourself," Walter said, heading up the wide bank of stairs. "I got to get a drink."

"Get it and come back," Van warned his decade-old friend. "I want to hear how you ended up driving her car."

Walter returned with a tall glass of lemonade and settled on the wide steps. "Me and Bert and Doreen was comin' from the farmers market and we saw her coming out of a spin and swing into a swerve. I thought she was goin' to take the drain, but she stayed on the road. She looked scared when I got to her, but I think she's right fine. After some rest, she'll be good as new."

Inexplicable relief flooded Van. "She's not hurt?"

"Whatchu mean?"

Van hesitated to speak of Fox's ailment. News would be all over town once Walter told everybody tonight at the paper mill. Small towns thrived on gossip. Strangers, the stupid, and celebrities were fodder for all the local gossip mills.

The state worshipped homeboys Michael Jordan and James Worthy, but held no-names like Abner Wilmont in some celebrity regard, too.

Ab, as he'd been known, had gone to the drive-thru bank for his mama, but instead of depositing her check, had given the teller a plastic bag filled with marijuana. When the cops pulled up to the drive-thru, Ab was still sitting there waiting for his receipt.

No matter how stupid some of the things town folk did, strangers were held in lower regard. A TV newscaster had recently been run out of town because she wore a too-short skirt to church.

The people of Slumber, North Carolina, weren't letting just anybody into their folds. And that suited Van just fine.

"There they are."

Van admired Walter's eyesight. He was just now seeing the cloud of dust, indicating the Chevy's arrival on the lane.

"Willow's crops are lookin' mighty good this year."

"Yeah." He kept a watchful eye on the approaching vehicle. Bertha pulled in beside Fox's car.

"Hey, Van," she said shyly. "How you doin?"

"I'm good, girl. How's Doreen?" He bent down and could see her sister slumped over her car seat sound asleep.

"Bad as usual. This lady ain't doin' too good, though." Bert indicated Fox, who slept with her head back and her lips parted. "Miss Willow in?"

Van peered over the roof of the car, wishing Willow's van would appear. She'd gone off this morning without a word as to when she'd get back. "No. I'm sure she'll be back soon. I guess we should wake her up," he said, gesturing at Fox with his thumb.

"She ain't wakin' up." Bert stepped from the car, and stretched. "She's out. I sleep like that when I pull an all-nighter at school. I don't think she'll know if you two strong men carry her in and put her to bed."

"I ain't carryin' nobody. My back is bad, Bert," her father complained. "This boy's got yout on his side. I'm old."

"Youth, Daddy."

"You know what I mean. Bad enough I got to haul Doreen everywhere I go. Her big ass is getting heavy."

Van grinned at Bert, who crinkled her nose, smiling. Everybody in the two connecting counties knew Walter and his youngest daughter, Doreen, were inseparable. He'd even switched to nights at the paper mill so he could work while she slept. Or else Doreen wouldn't sleep. And neither would anybody else.

Van sized up the comatose-looking woman and

decided—what the hell? She wouldn't get in the house under her own volition.

He walked to the passenger side and eased the seat belt away from her stomach and arms. It snagged on her breasts momentarily, and he glanced up to see Bert staring at him with a look of wonder on her face.

Van licked out his tongue, and she smothered a giggle with her hands. He didn't need it going around town he was lusting after an unconscious woman.

Sliding his arm beneath her legs and around her back, he guided Fox's body from the car and up against his. That's when things started going wrong. She molded her chest to his and wrapped her arms around his neck. The unsolicited sigh that seeped from her lips had all three adults staring in surprise at each other.

"Look to me like she need a lot more than sleep," Walter said and scooted away from Bert's shushing hand.

"You, shh, Daddy," Bert said softly. "We're going to take her in. I think Van might need a hand with her."

"I don't think he need you, Bert."

Van cleared the door and looked over his shoulder. "I'm gonna get you, Walt." The older man chuckled as he shuffled down the stairs to check on Doreen.

"Which way?" Bert asked, holding Fox's purse and a small paper bag.

"Up the stairs. Last room on the left." He groaned when Fox shifted. Her breast mashed into him. This wasn't how he'd anticipated their first meeting. In fact, he couldn't have imagined anything more erotic than holding a woman in his arms. He inhaled the faint scent she'd dabbed behind her ear and felt heat rising from the soles of his booted feet.

His reaction took him back ten years to the first time he'd held a woman. At eighteen, he'd been surprisingly stunned at the erotic view of bare womanly flesh, but immensely pleased. Holding Fox in his arms reawakened the innocence holding a woman once meant. Her hand fell between them.

Van focused on the caulking that needed to be done in the hallway and made it to her room without further incident. Bert studied him with a twist to her mouth as he gently lay Fox on the bed. They both watched the sleeping woman. She hadn't stirred.

"You think she's all right?" Bert asked.

"I don't know. We'll see when Willow gets here. Probably just tired." Van couldn't tear his gaze off Fox's smooth, cinnamon-colored skin. A thin gold chain circled her neck and the cross he'd seen at the end of the necklace had gotten lost beneath her shoulder-length hair and her cheek.

Dainty dark brown lashes sealed her eyes closed while little gold loops pierced her ears. Something in him connected with her and he felt as if he'd known her all his life. The feelings that unfurled in him weren't platonic either, and if he could have gotten away with it, he would have liked to watch her sleep for a few extra minutes.

The thought sobered him and he stepped back. This was Fox Giovanni—the city woman with the bourgeois attitude and quick tongue. Keep your head about you, he warned himself.

"I'm going to loosen her buttons so she doesn't choke to death. You staying?"

"No!" Van softened under Bert's watchful gaze, hooking his thumbs through his belt loops. "Naw, girl. You can handle that. I'll be downstairs."

The closing door should have been enough of a barrier for him, but Van found his body still primed. The brush of denim against his legs made them tingle as they'd never done before. His shirt suddenly felt too small and his chest tightened as if he had a cold. "What the hell is goin' on," he muttered, grabbing two cookies from the kitchen for Doreen. Glad to have a little hike ahead to catch up with Walt and Doreen, Van pulled himself together.

The farm stretched over one hundred acres of land that, although small in comparison to other surrounding farms, reaped great benefits for Willow. Every year she harvested peanuts, cotton, corn, and beans. She'd done so well over the years, she'd decided to refurbish the old house and surrounding cabins as well as build a proper driveway and entrance.

Walt and Doreen were standing by the gate, watching the hogs feed and slop around. Whenever the animals had an audience, they put on a show. Van watched, too. Buster, the hog, seemed to be making eyes at Charlotte, the sow.

Van averted his gaze and swung Doreen up to the second highest post.

"Where's Bert?" Walt asked.

"She'll be right down."

"You doin' good on this house. Better than Cleophus and his cousin, Booty."

"Bootsy."

"I'm just trying to get a laugh." Walt chuckled to himself. "I would have never let them boys out here if I knowed they were going to try to take advantage of Willow. I keep telling Bert to let that fool go. But you know how girls is. They make up their minds and it don't matter what you say."

Van gave Walt a reassuring pat on the shoulder.

"I know it wasn't your fault, Walt. Besides, Bert's got a good head on her shoulders. She'll make the right decision as far as Cleophus is concerned. Bootsy is another matter."

Walt looked back at the house to ensure their privacy. "Bet I could convince her to invite you over for supper."

"Bert doesn't want me, Walt. Besides, I got enough to do without a woman mixing up my life. Right, Doreen?"

The little girl frowned, balled up her fist and socked Van in the stomach. He grabbed his stomach dramatically, stumbled back and fell to his knees. "Please, Doreen. Don't hit me any more."

The invitation had been extended and the toddler

leaped off the fence and tore after Van who ran on his knees. The trio laughed until Bert came on the porch and clapped her hands once.

Doreen and Van froze. When Bert meant business, everybody knew it. They headed back to the house.

"In the car, little one," she said to her sister, who began to cry. Walt held the cookies Van had brought and coaxed his little sphinx into the car seat.

"Tell her if she ever need anyone to drive her car, call me," Walt called around a bite of Doreen's cookie.

Van saluted.

Bert met his eye level gaze. "You sure you going to be all right with her up there?"

He gave her a "come on" look and patted her shoulder. "I'll be fine. Ya'll take care."

Bert finally folded her six-foot frame into the car. "Call if you need anything."

"Sure will." Van waved until they'd disappeared from the lane, then turned and faced the thirty-room antebellum house asking himself, was this place going to be big enough for the two of them?

CHAPTER FIVE

The nightmare had returned. Fox felt her vocal cords vibrate as a scream ripped from her throat. Stopping wasn't within her power as she struggled from the confines of darkness.

Death threatened to claim her if she didn't outsmart it, so she ran, pumping her arms, propelling her legs, thrusting her body forward to escape its final lick. Her chest hurt and fear of succumbing made her run harder.

A crushing weight pushed her down and she fought, clawing, screaming until the pressure reversed and lifted her whole body high, then higher still, suspending her away from danger.

A violent force shook her, bringing her to her feet, and she stilled. She was free.

"Wake up, woman. You're shouting the roof down."

Death talked? Before comprehension settled in, her body jiggled again like a neglected rag doll. "Wake up, Fox."

The call of her name in a gruff but softer tone brought her lids up and Fox looked into the face of a man she didn't know.

"Who are you?" she managed to rasp, wanting to stop the tremors that shook her body.

"I'm Van Compton. We spoke on the phone," he said carefully. "You're safe. You're here at Willow's house."

His soothing tone and reassuring gaze walked inside her and uncapped relief in the form of tears. She tried to step away from his steadying grip, but he wouldn't let her go. To her horror, two tears slid down her cheeks.

"Let me go." Tears dripped from her chin like solitary raindrops. His eyes widened and she wanted to crawl under the sleigh bed and die. She wasn't a crybaby. Tears meant nothing. That lesson had been drummed into her years ago.

Extracting from his back pocket, a rag, surprisingly clean considering the state of his paint splattered clothes, Van caressed her chin with it, then her cheeks, then put it back.

He held her with one hand. "I would let you go if I thought you could walk, but you're tangled in the afghan."

She glanced down and sure enough, a beautiful, thick blanket wrapped her feet. Detangling herself took only a moment, and she stepped free of the blue-on-blue crocheted blanket.

Fox met no resistance when she tugged her arm from his hand.

The room she was in was vast and filled with richly lacquered walnut furniture from the eighteenth and early nineteenth centuries. The sleigh bed she'd slept in looked sturdy and large enough for an entire family. Evidence of the nightmare was everywhere. The sheets had been pulled away from the corners of the mattress, and the blankets and pillows littered the floor.

Fox couldn't believe she'd slept so badly. She didn't realize Van watched her until she met his intense gaze.

"How long have I been asleep?"

"Since yesterday afternoon."

"Oh, my. I didn't realize. Where's Willow?" Disoriented still, Fox looked around the room for her shoes and didn't see them. She made an attempt to straighten her wrinkled clothes and refasten the buttons on her shirt, but her trembling hands prevented the movement and she stopped moving all together. Her gaze was dragged back to Van.

"She came up and sat with you last night, but you didn't budge. She's already gone for the day, but said for you to make yourself at home. She'll be back later. She went to town."

Hiccups from her hysteria shook the quiet air. Her eyes stung and she heeled them hard with her hands. She wanted to cradle herself as she'd done as a child but this man was present and watching her like a hawk.

Why did he watch her so? Van's dark gaze followed her as she put distance between them. He seemed too able to assess her need of a gesture so simple it was as easy as a sigh.

She desperately needed a hug.

He stepped toward her.

Fox backed away, though no longer suspicious. The family resemblance between Van and Willow was striking. Although she hadn't seen her friend in years, Van reminded her of Willow, only in a masculine way. He was tall and broad like a bodybuilder and a deep golden brown from the sun. But his arms hadn't been thickened by weights at a gymnasium. Only hard work made his muscles bulge beneath his T-shirt.

Thick dark hair framed a face softened only by the lack of intensity in his stare. She got the distinct impression if Van wanted you to be uncomfortable beneath his gaze, you would be.

"Why didn't Willow wake me before she left?"

When he didn't say anything she eased farther away from him. "I told her I was coming yesterday. Was she here to greet me?"

"Willow is a busy woman. You said you would call from Raleigh, and you didn't. She had no idea what time you'd be arriving so she went on about her day. You can't expect

time to stand still for you." Her raised eyebrow met his
steady gaze.

"And just who are you, anyway?"

Although he didn't look much older than herself, Fox
wondered what his relationship was to Willow. He certainly
was strong and attractive in that defensive-back sort of
way. Faded, splattered jeans snuggled his legs and from
all indications, he must have been in the middle of some
hard, dirty work.

"Willow and I are family," he answered, prompting her
gaze back to his.

Fox kept her lips clamped shut. Who was she to judge?
He rapped his knuckles on the ancient walnut dresser.
The real brass handles rattled when his fingers slid up and
toyed with them. She watched his hand until she realized
he was pointing and she was definitely staring. She straightened her badly wrinkled blouse.

"The bathroom is out this door and down the hall.
There are six additional rooms located up here, but they're
vacant. Two aren't completely finished yet. You'll have
complete privacy up here. Willow's room is downstairs."

Her hiccups had stopped and she felt more in control
as the remnants of her troubled sleep faded. Wakefulness
beat sleep any day. "How far is town?"

"About twenty miles. Did you need something? I'm
going later this evening."

"No."

"When you're ready, come down. I'll show you around,
and help you with your things."

Fox met his stare evenly. "If Willow told you I was coming, she probably told you why." She smoothed her wild
hair with her fingers reaching for control. "I had a heart
attack, but I'm not an invalid and I'm not helpless. I don't
need you or anyone else running errands for me. Thank
you very much, but I can fend for myself."

His chest puffed some, and his brow lifted fractions.
"Suit yourself." The door closed quietly behind him.

Fox sank on the bed and listened to her heart hammering. She was alone, but not alone.

She'd been invaded by Van's presence. He was taller than the average man, exceeding her five-foot, seven-inch height by at least eight inches. His skin was the color of steeped tea, with a small scar marking his nose. His eyes were a penetrating deep brown protected by long dark lashes. Men in corporate America rarely wore mustaches, but his was thick and rich and black like the hair on his head. It wasn't bad. Not bad at all.

In addition to being halfway handsome, he possessed an uncanny ability to measure her thoughts with his dark brown eyes. And his matter-of-fact, not quite friendly demeanor made her want to defend herself against—what?

He hadn't said or done anything inappropriate.

She reached for her purse and a cigarette before she realized neither were available. Her purse was gone and she'd quit smoking.

Fox licked her lips, the urge building as she rose from the bed. *No cigarette,* she told herself sternly.

She searched the bed, dresser, and other far dresser with the bracketed feet. Her feet whispered across the floral printed rug and skimmed across the gleaming wooden floor. Her belongings were not there.

How did I get here?

A man had driven her car away!

Fox hurried to the window and pulled back the lace curtain, afraid at what she might not find.

But her car had been parked in the center of the paved lane and was surrounded by red beaked, white-feathered chickens. This was so different from the walk-up she and Willow had shared in New York so long ago, and so different from her condo and doorman now.

Fox let the curtain go and closed her gaping mouth. Cacciatore and Cordon Bleu would never be the same.

She opened the door and walked to the impressively wide, but in need of repair, staircase, hoping to avoid an encounter with Van. Unfortunately midway down, he stepped into the hallway, a tray of white liquid in his hands.

Van met her gaze. Anger and dislike radiated from the depths. Her gaze roved him, taking in his work clothes and the sweat on his brow. "Looking for something?" he asked, suddenly self-conscious about himself and the state of the unfinished house. Her eyes missed none of the dust that gathered on the unfinished floor or the stripped banister and stairs. She'd even shrunk away from the wall where large holes had been punched in the walls and patched.

"No."

"Good."

What a snob. Perri, his ex, used to look at him with that same expression on her face whenever he walked into a room. It was as if his work clothes and paint-splattered boots weren't good enough for her. It hadn't mattered that his labor fed and clothed them.

"I don't have time to chat around the water cooler. Some of us are not on hiatus." Her startled expression didn't fool him. "Willow will be back in an hour. She said to tell you there's chicken in the fridge if you're hungry." Her face twisted and she grimaced.

Van dropped the tray disregarding the plaster that splashed over the side and hurried up the stairs. "What's wrong with you? Another attack? What? Are you hurting? Should I call a doctor?"

"No." She walked down the stairs with the grace of a queen, chin uplifted, step sure. "I'm not having another attack, just a twinge of discomfort. I'm fine, really. I said I could find my way."

He backed down and retrieved his discarded tools and scraped up the spilled plaster. "Fine. I'm going back to work."

That's what you get for trying to be nice. She's no different from Perri.

Van worked in the large drawing room and slapped mud

on the seam of the wall, dragged the spatula down in one swift motion, and smoothed it out, angry with himself. What did he care what a stranger thought of him?

Fox was a stranger, and if he had his way, she'd remain that way. Besides, if he wanted a woman, there were plenty of them right here in Slumber.

The screen door banged, indicating Fox's departure and for a moment Van wished she'd drive off. Never one to ignore his instincts, he knew why he wanted her gone.

He was attracted to her. He'd never been able to resist a woman in need. The tears that had slid down her face had been hard fought. She'd trembled, she hadn't wanted to cry. But vulnerability wasn't something one could control.

Fox Giovanni needed somebody, and maybe Willow was just the person.

He slapped, dragged, and smoothed plaster down the long seam. The motions were familiar, his arm seeming to have a mind of its own. Van let his thoughts drift.

Objectively speaking, having Fox around probably wasn't such a bad idea.

Maybe Fox was a blessing as Pastor was fond of saying. She sure wasn't bad looking. She wasn't model beautiful, but had a certain special appeal in her wide-set eyes that would garner a second or third look. He slapped mud and smoothed.

While she was around, he'd get over his weakness for full lips. No, sir, hers wouldn't bother him at all. He licked his lips knowing how badly he still wanted hers.

Van slapped mud, then cursed, digging droplets from his eyes. The cloth he used to wipe her tears filled his hands and he stopped, threw it on the floor, and used his dirty shirt instead.

"Here chicken-chicken. Here chicken, chicken."

He walked toward the back door not believing what he was hearing or seeing. "Move chicken."

Fox stood at the bottom step while chickens rested on

the roof of her car. Fat lumps of beady-eyed white fur stared back at her like she was crazy. Van sided with the chickens. She sure looked crazy talking to them. He made a mental note to fix the hole in the coop so the chickens would stop getting out and messing up the driveway with droppings. For now he enjoyed the show.

"Get off my car, chickens."

"What are you doing?"

Startled, she turned, shading her eyes. "I've got everything under control."

He chuckled. "Sure you do."

"Don't you have something to do besides watch me?"

"I'm taking a break."

She hunched her shoulders, pushed up the sleeves of her silk blouse and turned. "You're wasting your time."

"My time," he conceded.

He could see by the rigid set of her shoulders that he'd aggravated her, but that was her problem. And so were the chickens. Van stepped onto the porch and leaned against one of the thirty-foot white pillars.

She took a tentative step forward, making kissy noises. "Here chicken, chicken."

The chickens did a better job than he of ignoring her.

"Move, now." She pointed with her index finger.

Bruce, the chicken on top of the car squawked, loud. Van couldn't contain his laughter when Fox dashed up the porch stairs, stopping almost inside the house. She definitely wasn't a country girl.

"What's so funny?" she demanded.

"You, city girl."

"What have I done to you?"

"I know why you're here. When are you leaving?"

"My comings and goings are none of your business."

"Anything that happens on this farm is my business."

"That may be, but I was invited. And since it wasn't by you, I'm not answering to you. Excuse me."

Van felt heat rising in his blood. This woman had a great act, only he wasn't buying it.

Not again. Fox Giovanni, bad heart and all, was on a schedule. She could stay a few days, then she and her flashy-ass car had to go. He stepped in front of her.

"Willow's place isn't a hotel. Don't forget it."

She dropped her hands on her hips.

"Obviously you have some kind of problem, but whatever it is isn't my concern. I'll say this much, Mr. Compton. I'm perfectly able to take care of myself. You came out here uninvited. I didn't ask you."

Van studied the fierce determination on her face. "You don't know what you're getting yourself into. I'll say this much, I'm dead set against any more people from Willow's past coming down here thinking they can have a free ride."

"I came here to relax, Mr. Compton, not run off with her silver."

"So you know she has some." He eyed her suspiciously. The fancy clothes were window dressing and he intended to find out what Fox Giovanni wanted and see to it she didn't take advantage of his aunt. "All year people have been coming around to take advantage of Willow. You might be here for one reason, but I see you just like I see the others, and until you prove otherwise I don't trust you."

She glanced around him to the chickens, then met his glare.

"I'm not here to bother anyone. I'll stay out of your way and you stay out of mine."

"You got yourself a deal, lady." Van descended the stairs. As long as they had an understanding things would be cool. He reached inside his pocket and fingered her car keys.

"Park your car around back on the grass under the Willow tree. Willow parks on the drive and so do I, and for future reference, 'Excuse me' won't move a chicken." Turning toward the car, he whistled and yelled, "Scat!"

In a flurry of feathers and protests, the chickens scattered. He opened the car door and emerged from the back stow away area with bags and a small case. He popped the trunk and dragged out two large suitcases then climbed the stairs laden with the packages.

"Got a lot of stuff for just a couple days, don't you?"

"I said I don't need—"

"I'm doing you a favor. Count it as my good deed for the year."

"I wouldn't boast about that if I were you," she said, holding the door open.

Van acted as if he didn't hear, but couldn't contain his surprise that she was holding the door for him.

"Now that's right nice," he said with an exaggerated drawl. "A woman getting the door for a man. I didn't think ya'll learned that upstate."

"Oh, yeah." She barred her teeth at him. "Manners are taught only in one tiny city in Rhode Island. The rest of us northerners had to learn from television."

Van followed her up the winding staircase to her room. Her hips seemed to swing in exaggerated motion as he labored with the bags. He averted his gaze and made the familiar trek to her room.

"I must have been absent when they offered live chicken removal classes," she said once he had dropped the bags in the center of the bed. "Obviously, you were present."

"It comes natural when you're raised in the country."

His pronouncement carried such pride she wondered why. Was he making some snide comment about being raised in the city?

"As does hailing a cab in New York."

"Touché."

They stood in the same spot as they had moments ago when she'd awakened from the terrible dreams. She'd been screaming, reaching for someone, anyone, to save her and he'd been there for her. He hoped she wouldn't need him like that again. Tears he could deal with, but helpless need was more than he could handle.

"I appreciate what you did for me earlier."

"No problem."

The sound of a car on the lane caught their attention. Fox hurried to the window and let out a relieved sigh.

"Willow's home." She hurried past him, her shoes hitting the wooden stairs with excited clicks.

Van held back, watching from the window.

Fox had run down the lane to Willow's car, then stopped short. She stood, head lowered, arms at her side.

Willow embraced her and only when it was clear that she wasn't letting go did Fox move to return his aunt's enveloping hug.

Van watched the women rock in the emotional embrace as he grew more confused than ever about Fox.

Moments ago, she'd faced him down with determination and fearlessness. Now she was humble, tentative in her return of Willow's affection.

His thoughts skittered back to the moments when he'd held her while she was in the throes of the nightmare.

He'd consoled her as he would anyone, but what could explain the attraction mingled with caution he felt already toward her? He'd thought it was from the dream, but maybe it had been his touch.

He let the curtain fall and walked down the stairs just as they entered the house. Willow's arm encircled Fox's waist, but she moved away and put the kitchen table between them.

Van felt her hot glare and knew she hadn't forgotten their conversation.

Willow looked between the two and said, "What's going on with you two?"

CHAPTER SIX

The hours since Willow had arrived home had rushed by in a whirlwind of constant motion. Willow had insisted on showing Fox the house room-by-room and sharing the history of how her ancestors came to own it and extensive details on the progress of the remodeling.

She regaled Fox with stories and anecdotes and refreshed her memory on family and friends Fox had met and forgotten. At times Fox just stood back and watched the woman who'd given her so many reasons to live when she'd barely needed one to die. Now the evening had faded into night and they rested on the porch. Willow stroked her hair again with the comb and caught another tangle.

"I don't think Van likes me."

"Oh, honey, he's a prince. Van likes everybody." The bubble of laughter that burst from Willow caught Fox by surprise, that along with the tug of the lock of hair Willow nearly combed from her head.

Initially, Fox hadn't minded when Willow had started to comb through her wet hair, giving her a chance to rest her extremely sore ribs.

Each stroke of the comb brought back good memories of the day Willow had taught her how to apply a home permanent.

So much time had passed.

To cap off a wonderful reunion, and in deference to her food restrictions, Willow had prepared a healthy, delicious meal. While the detangling conditioner had worked its magic on Fox's hair, they had filled their bellies with good food.

Only instead of Fox cleaning up the kitchen, like in the old days, brooding, watchful Van had cleaned it.

His silence had taken its toll on dinner, making conversation difficult at best. But that hadn't stopped Willow. She'd insisted the three of them retire to the porch to watch the stars twinkle in the sky.

Fox hadn't expressed the magnitude of her relief when Van had begged off and retired to the cabin. For the first time since meeting him, she finally relaxed.

Willow combed, catching another tangle. "Fox, Van is like a son to me. He's really my sister Zenobia's child. But in spirit, he's mine."

"I didn't realize that," she said. "I'll do it." Unable to take another stroke of the comb, Fox peeled it from Willow's fingers.

Earlier they'd doused the kitchen lights and now she saw only shadows of Willow who rocked in the cane-bottom rocker.

"The way he watched you through dinner, I thought—well I assumed, well, he said you w-were family." Fox stuttered, struggling to voice to her thoughts. "I thought you and he—I thought he was your main squeeze."

Willow's chuckle made Fox blush. Thankfully it was dark.

"Honey, all I been squeezing lately is lemons for juice. I wonder if I should tell this to the ladies in the women's ministry? They'd get a kick out of it."

Willow rocked, and Fox could hear how she enjoyed

her pecans. She spoke with some in her cheek. "You got somebody special in your life?"

"I don't need anyone," she said, to fill the lingering silence. "I have a good job. I own my home. I have a car."

"Things. You got a bunch of things. One catastrophe and all that *stuff* is gone. Things have no value when it comes to real commitment."

Fox snuggled Willow's old sweater around her and hugged herself. The gesture warmed her, but didn't give her the security familiarity brought.

A fish out of water, she thought about herself. The steady thump of her heartbeat made her breathe deeply. *But I'm alive.*

The wind whipped the sounds only insects and animals could make into a frenzy. New York was so different.

There was always a rush of cars, horns, and people. Even the sound a cigarette made when she smoked would seem foreign now.

Fox recognized the desire she had to live and nursed it.

"What's your medical situation, darlin'?"

"I had a mild heart attack." She shrugged making light. "Nothing serious. Everything is going to be fine."

"A heart attack was a pretty serious thing the last time I checked."

"I don't mean it that way. I mean, if I take the medication, eat right, and quit smoking, I'll be fine."

An accepting silence followed her words. There was no lecture, no harsh criticism.

"Willow, do you know what it's like to almost die?"

"I died a little when Ray did, I guess. But the kind of dying you're talking about . . ." She cracked a nut. "No. I can't say that I do."

"Yeah, well. I guess we all have to go someday." Fox denied an outlet to the well of riveting emotion that grew big and ripe like a tumor within her.

Fear she could overcome.

The other emotions that pressed at her lungs, she wouldn't acknowledge.

Everything was changing too fast.

The heart attack. Leaving New York. Slumber. Even the color of dirt in the south was different. She couldn't even smoke. Tucking hair behind her ear, she reached for her electronic calendar that was never six inches from her right hand. Too late she realized she'd left it on the desk in her condo.

For the next six weeks she had no appointments to keep.

Slowly she slipped her hand into the sweater pocket and caught hold of a loose thread. Her fingers wrapped and unwrapped the yarn.

"When I go, I don't want people to mourn for me," Willow said. "I want a party for my home-going. A beautiful celebration. I gave Ray a party. Second best one I ever gave."

"What was the first?" Fox asked softly.

"The day I got married, honeychild. M-mm, now that was a party."

Willow's cluck, the grin Fox saw on her face by the rising moonlight, and her tuneless hum as she rocked told a story all its own. Fox smiled, sadness eclipsing fear. Ray had been gone by the time she'd had come into Willow's life. Pictures were the only reminders of Willow's husband, but she'd never looked at them closely.

Sometimes it was difficult to look at something you couldn't have. Especially when it took so little to make up a family.

"We do have to go sometime." Willow continued oblivious to her musings. "But we have a lot of power in deciding how it'll happen. Are you happy, child?"

"Sure."

"I mean really happy?"

The attainment of professional stability was what most people wanted—strove for most of their lives. She'd accomplished the dream. "I don't think it gets better than profes-sional fulfillment."

"Some would say you could have all the money in the world and not truly be happy." Willow swatted away a bloated mosquito.

"They don't know what they're talking about."

Willow snickered. "Take my Van for instance. He thinks because I give a little money away I'm being taken advan-tage of."

"Are you?" Fox looked at Willow over her shoulder.

"No," she scoffed. "It makes me happy."

"Willow, I insist on paying my way. I don't want you or him to think I'm here to take advantage of you. Here." Fox got up and handed Willow three one hundred dollar bills. "I know it's not much, but I insist."

"Don't you dare give me money! My home is your home. Is that understood, young lady?" Folding the crisp bills, she shoved them back into Fox's hand.

"I can't stay here without at least paying for food. Nobody in the world lives somewhere for free," she said softly, reclaiming her seat on the steps.

Pecans spilled from Willow's lap, bouncing against the wooden porch floor. "I will not take your money! If you want to give it away, give it to somebody who needs it. You're my guest and I won't hear another word of it. Now what was my point? Oh, yes, my home-going. When my day comes, I plan to walk off, happy, like the Indian half of my ancestors and not come back. I'm going the way the Lord brought me here. I'm going home to the forest."

Fox turned on the step and abandoned scratching the mosquito bite on her ankle. "You were born in the woods, Willow?"

"Well . . ." Willow snickered, her humor restored. "No. I was born in a farmhouse. But it was a barn." Laughter rolled through Fox, matching the cadence of Willow's bub-bly chuckles.

Only Willow could make death seem funny.

"Willow, I was thinking of staying only a week." She braced herself, when a lapfull of Willow's pecans hit the floor again.

"This better not be about saving me money. I want you to stay for your entire recovery. Why do you want to leave?"

How could she say she'd already been told in not so many words her stay was temporary? Besides, it didn't make sense to disagree with Van. She was here to rest, not start World War III.

"I just figured with the renovations and remodeling on your home, you didn't need a bunch of company," she lied.

Willow shut her eyes. "You're hardly a bunch," she said, sounding tired. "Just barely one. You're so thin. No, this is the place for you."

A pecan shell cracked under Willow's strong fingers. Fox licked her lips, and ran her hands over her damp hair. Boy, she needed a cigarette.

"Heard about Walter driving your car while I was in town today."

"Good news travels fast." Cynicism laced her words. "Why would anybody care about that enough to repeat it?"

"Folks don't get a lot around here to gossip about. You're a hot news item." Willow chuckled. "It'll be worse when they find out about your condition."

Fox turned on the stairs. "You didn't tell them about that, did you?"

"No. Shh." Willow hushed her. "I'd never say anything about your heart attack. But Walter and Bert told everybody at the restaurant about the accident you almost had. You'll probably have visitors tomorrow."

"Visitors?" Wariness crept through her.

"People are curious. Some of the folks haven't ever seen a woman from New York City."

"And what do women from New York City look like?"

"Like everybody else, darlin'. Bear with them, Fox. Eventually something else will come up and you'll be old news. Honey, just enjoy the attention while you can."

Fox suddenly felt like a specimen. The curious and voyeurs were coming to see the latest attraction to hit Slumber.

Van had already expressed how he felt about her staying past a few days. Now people were coming to view her. Fox wondered if she would be considered a coward if she drove off tonight?

"Do you have plans tomorrow?" she asked.

"Oh, child." Willow struggled to get up. "I got to feed the animals, go to the prison, and water my herbs. Oh, yes, I've got to go see Sis Miller. She hasn't been feeling well. How about you? You planning on relaxing?"

To her horror, Fox chewed off the top of her acrylic fingernail. She inhaled, exhaled, fighting the desire of her addiction.

"I don't need to relax. Surely there's something you want me to do. I can't possibly stay unoccupied for six weeks. I'll go crazy." She held up her thumb, using the moonlight to guide her and bit down on a hangnail. She yelped when it stung.

"I thought you got over biting your nails when you lived with me all those years ago."

"I need a cigarette."

"Here, darling. Before you chew your finger off, have a pecan."

Willow got up and handed her a handful of nuts.

Fox gladly popped one into her mouth.

"Didn't your doctor tell you to rest? Surely you can't work right away."

"Yes, he did. But I can work. Some." Fox kept her gaze averted. "A little work won't kill anybody."

"Well I sure don't plan to have any dead bodies on my property. Not if I can help it. No work for you, young lady, until your doctor says so. When do you have to go back to the doctor?"

"I'm supposed to go to Raleigh and see a doctor named Norris Rawlins tomorrow."

"He's a nice fellow. Good looking, too. He does work at the clinic sometimes. And at the supermarket."

"That's novel." A humorless laugh burst from Fox. "A cardiologist-check-out-clerk."

Willow brushed shells from her long, flowing skirt and stood. Mid-length gray braids had been tied in a knot at the base of her neck and she freed them. "He works in a booth at the market. You know, like a kissing booth, only bigger. They do blood pressure screening and such." She shuffled closer. "I'm tired, child. You ready to turn in?"

Fox rose. "No, you go. I'd like to stay out here for a while longer."

"Don't stay up too long. Did your doctor give you something to sleep? You need a good night's rest after this morning. Van told me you had a terrible nightmare."

Fox gathered the sweater around her, strengthening her tone to brook no arguments. "They'll go away soon. The doctor said so."

"All right, darlin'. Just let me know. I've got some soother tea in there. Hold on a sec."

Willow banged inside the house and returned a moment later. She pressed leaves bound by a small string into Fox's hand. "Take these with warm water. Make sure you're close to a bed cause this tea works fast."

Gratefully she closed her hand around the natural concoction and stepped out of hug range. "Thank you. For everything."

Willow patted her cheek, then walked inside again. "God loves you, child."

"Good night."

Fox waited until she heard Willow's bedroom door close, then sat back on the porch step. Clouds covered the bright moonlight making her feel all alone. All she desired was a glass of wine, a good book, and a cigarette, and none were handy.

A gentle breeze whipped the ends of her sweater, and set Willow's rocking chair in motion. Fox rested her head on her palm as she turned to look at the slowly rocking chair. It had been way too long.

Fox listened to the rick-rock and was taken back to the day the child protection people had disrupted her near-perfect life. The day she'd been taken away from Willow had been the last time she'd sat in a rocking chair.

The chair swayed again, seeming to beckon her. She pocketed the tea and rose, approaching the sense of freedom she'd felt as a child while in Willow's care.

Life had changed that day. Hopes and dreams had vanished, and she'd become a woman with the click of the detention hall door. A childish desire stirred within her so she sat down, her back straight, and resisted the natural urge to lean back and flow with the motion.

Fox braced her hands on the arms, locked her elbows tight and slid back slowly to control each movement.

Propelled by the gentle breeze, the chair rocked on its own. She planted her feet firm, kept her arms straight, and glanced around. After a long moment, she let the chair rock a little. Boy it felt good. Lifting her feet, she relaxed more and rocked.

A grin creased her face.

"A person would think you'd never seen a rocking chair before."

The sound of Van's voice cut into her newfound pleasure and she rushed to her feet. The rocker toppled backward, crashing, the sound splitting the cacophony of bullfrogs, crickets and pig snorts.

"Why are you sneaking around in the dark?" she hissed, wishing she could close her hands around his neck and strangle him. Instead she massaged her thundering heart. "Are you *trying* to give me another heart attack?"

He emerged from around huge green bushes that lined the front porch. "You're the one acting like you've never been in a rocking chair before. If you hadn't been concentrating so hard, you'd have heard me coming."

She righted the fallen chair, wondering when the clouds had passed, giving the full moon permission to smile. "I-I was concentrating so I wouldn't fall over. Not that it's any of your business. Willow treats this thing as if it's a toy. She was rocking so hard, I was sure she'd fall over backward."

"Uh-huh. It's called having fun. Some folks do that." He tugged his ear as he climbed the stairs and sat down in the chair. Fox dragged her hand from her heart and dropped it to her hip.

"That's my seat."

A smirk creased his mouth. "Oh, I didn't think you'd be ready to take on the big bad rocking chair again so soon. Here you go." He got up and made a grand gesture with his hand.

Fox ignored the chivalrous gesture and took the seat. She braced her feet so the chair wouldn't move.

"Why aren't you in bed?" he asked.

Her brow shot up. "I don't have a mother or a father. I've been deciding my own bed time for a while."

"Are you afraid to sleep? Is that why you're sitting here in the dark? Alone?" His voice coaxed her, made her want to trust it, and Fox looked away, wondering when she'd become so transparent. *He's just guessing.* He couldn't possibly be able to see inside and assess her fear.

The darkness might catch her if she slept. She closed her eyes and rested her elbows on her knees. "I'm not tired. Slumber is pretty at night."

"You have to sleep sometime," he said, bringing the subject back.

"Why aren't *you* in bed? You seem mighty interested in it."

"It's Friday night. I'm going into town."

Glancing down at him, she noticed his clean jeans and almost florescent white shirt. His face had been shaved and his hair neat and freshly washed. Some woman was probably waiting in town, too. And who could blame her if she was? He looked great. A pang rattled in her belly. Fox recognized the silly emotion for what it was. Jealousy.

"What's in town?"

"People I've got to see," he said, the vaguest hint of arrogance thickening his voice.

"I might go into town tomorrow," she tossed out. "I have things to do, too."

"No, you can't. Willow said you were expecting company and besides, I don't have time to entertain your guests. I thought I made that clear?"

"People I don't know are coming out here and I'm expected to entertain them? They're not my guests. I didn't invite them and as far as I'm concerned I never have to see them." She closed her hand over her heart and hated the weak feeling that speared through her. It had been stupid to drive straight through.

The anxiety wouldn't go away.

Putting on the act of appearing unruffled and controlled would kill a lesser person, but she'd perfected it . . . only it failed her now. Her heart hadn't stopped its quickened beat since Van's voice overrode the sounds of animals and insects.

"That should be easy enough, humor them."

Fox lowered her eyes and gnawed on her nail. "Don't let me stop you from leaving."

He ignored her smart comeback and continued to study her.

"What time is your doctor's appointment?"

"What?"

"Woman, you heard me." She almost wanted to laugh at his teasing tone.

"Ten o'clock. Why?"

"Curious. Here." Suspiciously she looked into his out-stretched hand. Several pieces of wrapped hard candy lay in the center of callous worker hands. Despite her best stab at nonchalance, she took a piece.

Her taste buds jolted in response to the treat. "Mmm, this is good."

"Don't chew it," he said, when she bit down on the next piece. "You've got to savor it, take it slow, enjoy the pleasure it gives you. When you rush, you miss the tiny ingredients that make it delicious. You know what I mean?"

His gentle, persuasive tone made her want to agree, but Fox held back. His deep voice had evoked an opening in her head and chest as if she'd been laved with salve. She knew exactly what he meant, but her thoughts weren't on candy.

She devoured the treat and licked her lips. "Got another?" This time Fox picked a piece wrapped in green paper. "Thanks."

Her eyes rolled as she swallowed the tangy apple candy. The craving abated and she rested her elbows on her knees.

From his position on the stairs, he watched her with a mixture of curiosity and disbelief. Shadows passed over his face.

Van's snort of disapproval floated to her.

"Things done recklessly, can be enjoyed, treasured even." He shifted. "But despite advice to the contrary, you do things your way. Why is that?"

"That's the best way. I don't need a census bureau to make decisions for me." His gaze swept her and she felt the heat, yet ignored it.

"What about your family? Did they think it was smart of you to drive all the way down here after your stay in the hospital?"

"I think for myself."

Explanations to the handyman, even if he were Willow's nephew were unnecessary. As it was, the town folks would have enough questions. If he were that interested in her business, all questions would be answered at one time.

"Doc Hall makes a fine set of dentures," he said, popping a piece of candy in his mouth.

"My teeth are the healthiest things on my body."

"You'd be batting a thousand, if you messed that up."

She kept her tone light although the urge to snap presented itself. Obviously the only type of relationship they'd have would be adversarial. "Why are you under the misguided impression that you know everything?"

He laughed, coming toward her. He took the wrapper paper from her hands and balled them into a tiny dot before inserting them in his pocket.

His nearness was discomfiting, but heady. She suppressed a nervous giggle.

"As the oldest of six brothers and sisters, I've solved a lot of problems. Believe me when I say I know a lot about everything. For instance I know you smoke."

Startled, she lifted her foot and the chair rocked. "I quit," she snapped bracing her feet again.

"Under pressure from your doctor. But you still smoke in your mind. Candy is a temporary substitute." His smoldering gaze left her eyes for a second and landed on her hips.

Unconsciously, Fox contracted her thighs.

"Course too much of it could get you into trouble, too."

Amusement flickered, deepening the lines around his mouth.

She would not pull the sweater over her hips. Silently she dared him to say more. Heart attack or not, she would jump him.

He simply smiled and before she could react, braced the chair with his hands and tipped her backward.

A tiny yelp escaped her, and his face loomed inches from hers.

"You'll learn it's easier to let someone who knows more than you help rather than do it yourself. You might have a city education and fine background, but things are simple down here. There's nothing wrong with vulnerability and needing someone.''

"I don't need you," she barely managed to whisper.

The chair tipped back a few degrees. An unfamiliar flutter took flight in her chest. Saliva dried in her mouth and she wondered if he were going to do something crazy like kiss her, or make her fall.

His gaze hardened as he focused on her. "I think you could use all the help you can get. You came here because you claim to need Willow. If that's false, I'll smoke you out faster than a rabbit in hunting season.''

Fox wanted to leave, but suddenly staying mattered. "I don't have to prove anything to you, but I would never do anything to hurt her. Willow's been a friend to me for years. What about you? You act protective, yet you've gone out of your way to be rude to me. Are you more concerned for her interests or your own?''

He muttered something unkind beneath his breath, his eyes shining dark like the night.

"Don't ever question my intentions. You don't know me well enough.''

"Take your own advice," she shot back. "Now lower this chair.''

He brought the chair slowly back to its original position and adjusted the cuffs of his shirt. "I'll be watching.''

"Weren't you leaving?''

Fox wished she could run into the night, but didn't know if her legs would hold her. Van's closeness shook her to the core. For a moment when they'd been inches apart his jaw had tightened, the strength within unimaginable.

But he'd tempered it when he'd looked back at her. And she'd seen raw love. Its depth was incomprehensible.

Her leg cramped from the bracing, but she refused to acknowledge it in his presence. He stood too near. Good grief, he might even want to help.

Her gaze skated over strong, muscular thighs, past a full

chest and over a chiseled face. His cologne made her want to inhale deeply to absorb as much of him as she could in one breath. Fox hated herself for noticing.

"Got something you might be interested in." He held out his hand again. Two chocolate kisses sparkled like twinkling stars.

She drew back, folding her hands to keep from snapping the candy from his palm.

What was he trying to imply? Maybe she'd misread the signs. The feeling of naked vulnerability returned.

The chocolate looked good, very good, but she wouldn't give him the satisfaction. Fox looked away. "No, thanks."

Van started to laugh. The masculine chuckle tingled up her stiff spine and made the hairs on her neck stand up.

"You think because I'm offering you chocolate kisses I might want something in return." He shrugged, unwrapped the candy and popped one in his mouth. "I'm disappointed. I thought a city woman like you was savvy enough to know when someone was trying to help her, again. You'll learn. Oh, well, more for me. Good night."

His truck's taillights became pinpoints before she walked into the house. She tried to relax in the old claw-footed tub, but couldn't manage it with her long legs. She ended the bath, dressed for bed and tried to relax, but even the exercises the nurse educator taught her were ineffective.

Fox opened the window, lay on the bed watching the white blades of the ceiling fan as they sliced the moon, and couldn't stop wondering if Van had gone to town to meet a girlfriend or a special woman.

Gosh, who could stand him?

She was still awake hours later when his truck returned and she heard him and a woman share a passionate kiss in front of the house.

"Come on, before you get me into trouble," he said with just the mixture of need and longing she found could trigger deep jealousy.

Feet shuffled against the side walk until the wind and billowing grass drowned their footsteps.

Fox turned over, punched her pillow and curled into a ball.

The fetal position should be good for something.

Before she blacked out from exhaustion, she chewed off another nail and wished she'd taken the damned chocolate.

CHAPTER SEVEN

Van lay in his bed, head beneath the pillow, but still couldn't completely block out the sound of his younger brother, Troy, and his wife Trina, making love in the room next door. Mating horses were quieter.

Tiny cries sounded from the floor and he shook the cardboard box with his foot before realizing what distressed the puppies. Their heartbeat had stopped.

Getting up, he wound the old fashioned ticking clock and snuggled it between the three orphans. One nipped at his finger but the other two were concerned about the false mother they'd come to depend on. He tucked in the corners of the old baby blanket and wondered when he'd gotten so soft.

Must be old age, he thought as he reclined on the king-size bed. The puppies were supposed to be on the lower level in the back hall until they were old enough to be given away. But with each week since their birth, they'd moved closer and closer to his room, until they'd ended up beside his bed. That's why next Monday was their last day on the farm.

Van waited for more complaints, but the ticking satisfied their needs. Crisis abated, he closed his eyes, hoping to sleep.

Trina and Troy started again.

"Aw, hell." Van flipped over and gave the wall a smack with his fist. "Shut up in there."

They quieted in response—long enough for Van to catch his breath—then resumed the party with the added insult of heels banging the wall with each thrust.

Van sat up wanting to curse, but held it instead. The puppies would take the interruption as an invitation to play. His black-banded watch revealed the late hour and he vowed to have words with Troy first thing in the morning.

Finding him and Trina in Cleophus' bar with no money and no place to stay hadn't been the highlight of his dull evening. No, they'd milked a free meal and endless bottles of a honey-based lager from him before dropping the bomb of their current living situation, or lack thereof.

Fortunately, Trina had gotten a one-article assignment for a travel magazine, and they would start early in the morning on their cross-country trek. Van cringed at their chosen topic—traveling the country on two hundred dollars or less.

The highlight of the evening had been to pay their eighty-five dollar taxi bill, pick up the tab for dinner, and bring them home to Willow's. It had been one thing to bring them back to the farm, but quite another for them to behave like farm animals.

Van lowered his feet to the floor, not wanting to confess to being jealous of his nineteen-year-old brother. He knew his sexual deprivation wasn't a forgivable excuse for murder. Although going a few rounds with his brother might make him feel better.

He gathered his pillow, slung on his pants and strode out the cabin. The cool air felt good against his bare back and shoulders. He'd worked hard this week, harder and faster than even he could have guessed.

Finally, progress loomed.

And Willow was happy. Especially since Fox had arrived. Dinner conversation had been stiff with Willow dragging the reluctant woman down memory lane. Fox had been very quiet, speaking only when spoken to and eating very little. But her eyes never left Willow. His aunt hadn't seemed to mind her scrutiny. And even when he'd caught Fox watching him, he'd returned her stare until she lowered her gaze. Her reason for being here wasn't purely to get better. He sensed more, much more.

Temptation brought him to the house and fate had her on the porch. He'd wanted to kiss her, feel her supple lips beneath his, but he'd held back. The surge of feelings were too new to act on. Battling trust against distrust was too difficult.

Unlike his brother, he could control himself.

Van took his time enjoying the night. It was late and he had to work early, but whenever he could, the secrecy of being in the dark, in an open space and yet alone had always intrigued him.

He settled in the rocking chair on the porch to enjoy the solitude, when he heard the muffle of a struggle. Once inside, the pillow he carried landed in the vicinity of the table as he headed first for his aunt's room. Bursting in, he stopped short. Willow was sound asleep in her bed.

Silence floated soft as air, but his tension hadn't eased. He balled his fists ready to do battle when he heard a thump and whimper again. Crime in Slumber was as uncommon as a sushi bar, but things change.

In long, galloping strides Van took the stairs, barreling through Fox's closed door.

He glanced around, but no one tortured the woman except whoever chased her in her dreams. He pushed the switch on the table lamp, prepared to shake her awake, but in the flicker and flash as the light expired, he saw her face.

It was contorted in fear, her eyes squeezed shut. She was

terrified even in sleep. She thrashed, tears rolling from her tightly shut lids, her long legs flying as she ran in her dreams away from whatever haunted her.

Van hit the wall switch in the tiny closet and hurried back to her side.

Her pink silk camisole top was drenched from perspiration and exertion, and her legs shined like those of an Arabian after a fast race. He touched her arm and she grabbed his hand calling out in a weak, starved voice, "Save me."

His heart wrenched and he shook her with an urgency he could feel to his toes. "Fox, wake up. You're safe. You're safe," he said in soothing tones reserved only for children and injured.

Fox *was* injured, he realized. Whatever plagued her had followed her into sleep. Even there she wasn't safe.

In truth, she'd destroyed the bed and he could see how the tangled sheet on her foot might be manifesting itself into her dreams.

He freed her foot and sat beside her. Van gently held her shoulders realizing how frail her body was.

"Come toward me. Reach for my hand."

He laced his fingers with hers and squeezed, hoping he could reach into her dreams. Her legs pushed against his hip and he ran his hand down the smoothest skin he'd ever touched. The thrashing subsided.

Precious seconds were spent getting a cool cloth from her bathroom, but he returned and dabbed the moisture from her head and neck, careful not to break the dainty chain and cross at her throat.

Her hands batted at his. "No, I don't want to die." Sobs shook her chest. "Don't take me."

The desperate plea broke the control he fought to maintain. He dropped the towel. She had to wake up.

Van took her arms and rubbed vigorously. "You're safe, Fox. Come to me. Take my hand." Their hands gripped and he pulled her up into a sitting position. Her damp skin touched his, setting off a slow burn where their bodies connected. Her head against his shoulder, her lips to his neck, his chest to her chest.

Van yielded to a tender part of himself, gathered her in his arms and rocked. His eyes slid closed as he warmed her, held her as he'd held the newborn puppies, but it was different because she was all woman. Hip lips automatically pressed against her hair and cheek, and he rubbed the back of her neck. She was so vulnerable.

Vulnerable woman. It would have been so easy to take advantage of her. Kiss her mouth, taste her. But he wouldn't. Not under these circumstances.

Instead, he cooed in her ear and rubbed her back until her heartbeat slowed, her breathing evened, and he was sure she had returned to a restful sleep no demon could penetrate.

Then he lay her back down on the bed.

"How is she?"

Willow whispered, watching her nephew and the daughter she could only claim by love, and knew she couldn't let them slip away from each other.

"She's asleep." Heavy concern marked his voice.

"Should I call the doctor?"

Van caressed Fox's arm and maintained a grip on her left hand. Willow noticed how even in her sleep Fox hadn't released him, either.

"No. It's just a bad dream."

He looked at Willow for the first time since she'd spoken as her hand rested on his shoulder.

"You're doing just fine, son. She'll probably sleep for the rest of the night."

"Did she say anything about having nightmares to you before she arrived?" Worried that he'd misjudged Fox, Van searched his aunt's face for the truth about Fox Giovanni.

"No, never." Willow whispered. "When she goes to the doctor tomorrow she should tell him about it. Maybe he can give her something to help her sleep."

"All this can't be good for her heart."

Willow smiled at her nephew as they both gazed down at the sleeping woman. Fox didn't look tough now. The razor sharp eyes were closed and the toughness that radiated from the woman had been buried under a sea of emotional exposure. If Fox knew they were seeing her like this, she'd be furious.

Fox whimpered and her face creased. "Willow?"

Willow sat down in front of Van on the side of the bed. He tried to let Fox's hand go, but she still gripped his.

"Shh, darling. You're safe here with me."

Van sat behind his aunt who rubbed Fox's bare arm. He shook his head at the two nail-bitten fingers next to the other manicured tips.

She moaned, her fingers tightening against his. "I really am glad to be here, I'm so glad to see you," she said on a broken sob.

For a brief second he and his aunt looked at one another. "I'm glad you're here too, darling. Rest now. We'll talk in the morning."

"Don't leave, yet."

"I won't darling. I'll be right here."

Van rose and tried to disentangle himself from Fox's grip, but found himself caught in her hold.

Willow caressed Fox's cheek, closed her eyes and prayed silently. When Willow smiled at him, he felt an odd pressure in his chest as if she expected something from him.

The longer he held her hand, the more his defenses weakened. How could she hurt Willow? She appeared to be what she claimed. A sick woman in need of rest. If that were so, he was sorry he'd misjudged her.

"What?"

"You're fine." Willow smiled.

Van had everything in hand. Literally. If only he and Fox could find their way to one another. They were a perfect match. However, a little nudge might help them along, and she had six long weeks to help guide them together. Warmth tickled her chest. Ray approved.

Quietly, Willow propped the pillows at the head of the bed and draped the covers over the foot, before backing quietly away.

"Goodnight, nephew. I'll see you for breakfast."

"Wait!" Fox continued to sleep through his demand. "What about her? Aren't you going to stay?"

Willow doused the closet light, her finger to her lips. "You're doing just fine. Good night, son."

Van's head whipped from Willow to Fox and back to the fast closing door. The click sealed his evening's fate.

At that moment, he hated the shimmering moonlight, he hated Fox for wearing sheer pajamas to bed, and he hated himself for noticing.

"Damn, damn, damn," he muttered, noticing the dark centers of her breasts that pressed against the damp camisole. "Woman, you're a pack of trouble if I ever saw one."

His tongue stuck to the roof of his mouth and the snap of his unfastened jeans brushed his arm as he covered her from her head to her knees with the blanket. Fox hadn't awakened again or let go.

There surely wasn't a God, he thought grimly, when she turned, pulling him closer.

With nothing left to do, Van propped a pillow, lay on the bed, kept as many inches between them as humanly possible, and wished he'd stayed in the cabin.

"Good morning."

Van sent his aunt a turbulent glare. "Mornin'? What's so good about it?" he asked, borrowing a line from his ex-wife.

"You didn't sleep well?"

"You know damn well I didn't."

Willow simply smiled and heated water for grits. She diced potatoes, adding red and green peppers along with onions. Fat slabs of bacon were lined up on a pan and dropped into the heated oven while she tossed the home fries into hot oil.

Soon the kitchen filled with the smells to make any mouth water. She was trying to bribe him out of a bad mood, he thought incredulously. It wasn't going to work.

"Why did you leave me up there? I didn't get a wink of sleep, and I have plenty of work to do today." He rose, refreshed his coffee, and sidled up to his aunt who gazed out the open screened back door. The house was filled with the smell of sunshine and wildflowers.

"You know what I think? I think my aunt has something up her thick sleeve, and I don't think I like it."

"Are you accusing me of something sinister, nephew?"

"Yes, as a matter of fact, I am. You knew I wouldn't leave her by herself, so you conveniently disappeared." He shook his head and bent down to look directly into his aunt's eyes. "I'm not interested."

His body had had other ideas, but Van prided himself on his control and kept this to himself. Sometimes he craved the cigarettes he'd once been addicted to, but his mind knew better, just like now.

Willow folded her hands in front of her and walked to the stove.

"Vanderbilt, I'm not doing anything other than fixing a nice breakfast of bacon and home fries. A little grits won't hurt so you'll have energy, and some coffee so you won't fall off my roof. I'm doing all this for my favorite nephew." She twirled the spatula in the homefries, then turned off the range.

"Course if you don't want my good cookin', I'm sure somebody in town will appreciate my efforts. I wouldn't want all this good food to go to waste."

Van gave her a hollow look. "No more disappearing acts, Willow. If she has nightmares, you deal with her. I've got my hands full with finishing the house. I'm not a baby-sitter. Do we have an understanding?"

She tapped her jaw. "A long time ago, I had the pleasure of having my nephew come live with me. He wasn't always in the best mood or the easiest to get along with, but I opened my arms and loved him anyway. Now he's a successful businessman who buys houses, fixes them up and sells them. He even has his own big house less than an hour from mine. Such a handsome devil, with his bright smile. I wonder if he'd have turned out the same if nobody loved him?"

"You think using syrupy words will make me fall for whatever silly plan you've concocted?" He brushed her forehead with a kiss. "I'll help as much as possible, but I draw the line at baby-sitting. Any more nightmares, you handle them. In fact, I'll move a chair up there so you'll be comfortable. Deal?"

"You're so responsible, darling," she said with a smile.

He chucked his aunt under the chin and moved on. "Speaking of responsible—Troy is here. If he asks for money, say no. Never mind. I'll tell him myself."

The family had decided a long time ago to leave Troy and Trina alone. The couple was obviously meant to be together. As neither had worked a steady job in two years, it was inconceivable to think of them conceiving a child.

"Troy, Troy, Troy. A lost soul if I ever saw one." Willow shook her head. "Don't you worry. Before I hand over anything to the likes of that scoundrel and his wife, I have a few words for them."

"Don't *hand over* anything, and lock up when you leave or things will start walking out of here."

Van worked out the kinks in his neck. Lying awkwardly for four hours may have left him permanently impaired. His head felt as if he'd slept in a fish bowl.

"Did Fox have any more nightmares?"

"No." Van sat down and rested his elbow on the table. "She slept soundly for the rest of the night."

But she'd never released his hand. In fact, it had nearly taken a surgical procedure to extricate his fingers from hers at dawn. Each time he'd tried to remove them, she gripped harder. Especially when their bodies had touched. She'd frozen and her breathing hitched, then a long, too sexy sigh exhaled from her lips. Van had wished more than once he was back in the cabin listening to Troy and Trina put jackrabbits to shame.

He'd finally slept, but not well. As soon as he felt her bottom pressed to the spoon of his body, he'd shot off the bed.

There was only so much a man could take.

The phone trilled, breaking the memory, and he realized his cup had been poised at his open mouth far too long to be natural. Van gulped and choked on the hot coffee.

Willow cast a glance his way before answering. "Hello . . . Oh, Denise, dear. How are you? Well then, I'll have to come right down and straighten that out. Wonderful. See you in an hour."

"What's going on?" he asked, suddenly concerned about his numb lips.

"Seems as if I can't balance my checkbook lately. Denise said Bootsy cashed two checks today and I can't for the life of me remember writing them." She puttered around the counter straightening the appliances. "I'd lose my head if it wasn't attached. Well, I'm going to town, and I might as well stay there and catch up on my visits to the senior citizen's home and the homeless shelter." She turned off the stove and dished him up a plate of hot food. "Some of those old folks don't need to be in a home. Some of 'em just like being old."

Willow smiled and looked at her nephew. "I personally don't enjoy it as much. If I were forty-eight again and Ray were here—honey, honey, honey."

Her youthful cluck and giggle was more than he could handle.

"Don't, Willow," he said dryly. "Yours and Ray's private business should stay a memory you don't share with me."

She grinned and winked as she often did when she'd embarrassed him.

Van winked back.

Willow's eyes were clear and bright, no hint that she'd perceptively picked up on his concern over her ability to care for herself personally or financially. As a rule she was perceptive, eerily so. How often had he accused her of talking the rabbits out of her cabbage patch when everybody on the surrounding farms were being eaten out of business? Once she'd confessed, not to talking, but to communing with the animals and nature.

But the call from Denise had more than distressed him especially if Willow couldn't recall if she'd written the checks. He had to get to the bottom of things.

"Give me five minutes," he said, halfway out of his chair. "I'll drive you to town."

Willow scoffed, wrapped her shoulders in a shawl and donned her pink hat. "My business at the bank isn't going to take more than a few minutes. I need you to drive Fox to Raleigh to see her doctor. She wouldn't admit this, but she's not supposed to be driving. When Ray had his heart attack, the doctor ordered him not to drive for six weeks. Didn't stop him, though, and probably won't her, either."

Willow gathered her keys and checked the stove again. "I swear I don't know what possessed her to drive across the country in one day anyway."

His heartbeat had quickened at just the thought of being in Fox's company. A day and a long night were enough.

"She won't have a problem going up the road thirty minutes to Raleigh, Willow. I, uh, need to go to the bank, too."

"Van as amazing as I think Fox is, she's not supposed to be driving! I need your help, nephew. Just this once. All right?"

Not waiting for an answer, Willow dropped her cloth bag on the kitchen table so she could dig through it.

"Here's a list of things I need from the store. Just put

it on my account at the Wink and Star. I'll see Buford-Sam tonight and settle up.''

Van scooped a portion of home fries into his mouth. Slowly he reached for the list, again knowing Willow was confused. She didn't have an account at the Wink and Star.

The account system had died along with Buford-Sam, Sr., ten years ago. Burfod-Sam, Jr., wasn't having any of that "buy now pay later" for groceries.

Dread worked its way into a headache. Had Willow been leaving the store with food she hadn't paid for? Van mentally added one more stop to his list.

But he'd have gladly gone shopping just to avoid Fox. He'd already spent half the night in her bed, now Willow expected him to spend half the day in her car?

No way was he folding his body into a pretzel to fit into that death trap.

Anybody who didn't drive a truck was—in his mind—dumb.

The potatoes grew cold in his mouth. Van chewed quickly and swallowed the lump of congealed starch.

"Willow, I can't take her to the doctor. I've got too much work to do. The drawing room needs to be painted as well as the dining area. Anyway, I ordered a nail gun from the hardware store and it's in.''

"Vanderbilt Compton, surely you can do this one favor for me after all I've done for you. I'm going to have to call my sister and tell her how she raised her son and how he's forgotten all the manners she drummed into his head. Then I'm going to tell her . . .''

The speech Willow would tell his mother already rang in his ears. "Fine, Willow! Fine.''

Her eyes sparkled in victory.

"You didn't get away with anything, so wipe that grin off your face. Once per year you can emotionally blackmail me." He sipped his coffee, taking his time. "I'll take her.''

Willow walked around the table and kissed him on the cheek.

"You're a good boy."

"I regret that sometimes."

"You're going to make somebody a very special husband."

"I've had my chance, so don't go getting any ideas about me and Miss City. She's not my type." Last night, her body fit to his like a glove, or a noose.

"Whatever you say."

Willow headed out, and he finished his breakfast in scowling silence.

CHAPTER EIGHT

Fox surged from sleep into a sitting position. Her head snapped from side to side as she searched for the heat that once enveloped her. At one point last night, it seemed to cover her whole body offering protection and safety from the darkness.

Nothing seemed out of place in the room. Flowers on the blue wallpaper saluted the sun with shimmery greetings. Her shoes were still lined against the wall where she'd put them yesterday, and her suitcases still stood by the door so she could inquire as to the best place to store them.

Yet something was different. Running fingers through her straight hair, Fox turned and stopped short. Each of her pillows was indented as if there had been more than one person in the bed. Hesitantly she picked up the pillow farthest from her and stared at it.

Who had been sleeping in her bed?

Bringing it to her nose she took a tentative sniff and let it blossom into a full-blown inhale. The pillow smelled of soap and shampoo and fragrance. Masculine fragrance.

A tingle slithered up her spine. Had she slept with Van? Her mouth dropped open. *Had he slept with her?*

Certainly not, she reasoned. Why would he? He could barely stand to talk to her, much less sleep with her. The idea was so foreign she dropped the pillow back on the bed and got to her feet. There was only one way to find out if he was in her room and that was to ask. He'd deny it, and she'd know that the blanket on the floor had somehow become that warm body next to her.

Fox hurried through her shower, curled her hair, chose her most conservative casual outfit, and got dressed.

She noticed the extra three minutes she spent on her makeup, and couldn't even meet her own gaze in the mirror. Challenged, she stared back at herself.

"What?" she asked her reflection, "I'm crazy. It was the blanket. He didn't sleep in my bed." She dabbed mascara at the tips of her lashes and studied the full effect. Just the right amount of color and style. Very professional.

She cleaned up the powder that had fallen to the sink and wiped everything clean. At least he couldn't accuse her of being a slob.

Fox took the stairs with determined steps. She would find out what happened last night.

The wood flooring in the drawing room had dried and Van buffed it to a high gloss. The push and pull of the manual buffer and the exertion required to get the job done correctly kept his mind off Fox Giovanni, her nightmares, and their recent sleeping arrangement.

Last night wouldn't happen again. Thankfully she'd stayed asleep and his hope was that she wouldn't remember his ever being in her room . . . ever.

He and Perri had gone the distance as far as relationships went. But in the end, their differences had outweighed their similarities. She was a city woman to her heart. And he loved the sights and smells of the country.

No two ways about it, if he ever—and that was a big ever—got hitched again, it would be to a down-home, country woman.

He pushed and pulled the buffer again, sweat falling from his brow. Love be damned, he thought, pushing the machine again. Compatibility was the key to the world. Love was for greeting card companies. He paused as a drop of sweat hit the floor and beaded.

Too much wax. Damn, the buildup would be outrageous.

He parked the machine, then toweled dry in the lower bath before walking to the kitchen for a drink.

Van downed the first glass of water, and had poured a second when Fox walked into the kitchen, refreshed and dressed to kill in a blue silk blouse and creased ivory pants.

His bad mood slipped into place.

"Good morning," she said.

"It's afternoon."

One look at her face and he realized she looked more rested than he'd ever seen her or than she'd been since she'd arrived. Yesterday the sallow look only exhaustion could conjure marked her face and jerked her movements. Today, though still frayed at the fringes, she looked rested.

Her hands shook when she picked up the coffee—the only sign of her difficult evening. He took the pot, poured her a cup and sipped his water.

"I can't believe I slept this late. I haven't slept—" She caught herself on the edge of a confession and reined herself in. "Where's Willow?"

"She had to go into town on business."

Her nose lifted in the air, and she looked down on him. "Do you know when she'll return?"

"Once she's finished at the bank, she said something about going to the senior citizen's center and the homeless shelter."

Her gaze turned cool. She braced the counter with one hand, then slid her arm across her stomach as she sipped her black coffee.

A scarf with a fancy knot was tied around her neck and she'd accented the ensemble with silver earrings and bracelet. The twinkle of gold around her thumb caught the sunlight.

Fox lowered the coffee mug and twisted the bracelet on her arm. Briefly he wondered what it would be like to embrace her now while she was fully awake. A pulse of desire beat inside of him still, and he tried to ignore it, unsuccessfully. It strummed away.

"She mentioned that yesterday, but I thought, well—I just thought she and I would spend some time together. I need to ask her something."

"Maybe I can help you."

Her eyes shifted then came to rest on his. For an instant Van felt trapped. "Do you know if Willow was in my room last night?"

"Yes, she was." He answered quickly, hating himself for not stating the truth. "You had a nightmare and asked her to stay with you for a while. She did."

"Oh," Fox gave him a brief smile of relief. The pace of his heartbeat quickened. "That explains the dent in the other pillow."

"I guess it does." He looked at her closely. "That's not exactly farm attire. We're not formal here."

"What? Oh, right. Well how does one dress for a day at the farm?" Her glance swept him. Van was in his typical work clothes. Worn jeans, work boots, grunge T-shirt.

She shrugged. "I don't have anything that falls into that category." He opened his mouth to snap, but she cut him off.

"I wasn't sure what to bring. Maybe I could stop in town and get some jeans." Her hand waved toward him. "And a T-shirt."

"You don't have a pair of jeans?" he asked, knowing he'd fallen just short of laughing aloud.

"No. I don't. It might be fun to buy some."

"Sure. The excitement is killing me," he grumbled and contemplated taking a pill for his aching head and his racing heart. A cold shower might be better.

She turned and leveled her hard, dark gaze at him. "Why do you have a problem? I haven't had time to commit any dastardly deeds. What, did things not work out in town last night?" she asked coyly.

His head snapped up and he met her piercing gaze with an ill-disguised growl.

Finding Troy and Trina hadn't been the way he planned to spend his evening.

As a matter of fact they hadn't.

But he'd spent most of the time thinking about her. Lying with her. Imagining doing things to her he hadn't done in awhile.

"My evening in town was fine."

"Maybe I'll go with you sometime. If you can get lucky, well—the possibilities are endless."

"Lucky?" Van shook his head, laughing, releasing some of the pressure of his headache. "I didn't get lucky. Besides, the places I go are not a place I'd take a lady."

"I'm flattered. But if that's the case why do you go there?"

He drew up. "Because I'm a grown man."

She cocked her head to the side. "Do you have children?"

He drained his glass, set it in the sink. "No."

"A wife?"

"No," he said more firmly.

"I'm surprised. You strike me as the type of guy who's at home bossing the little lady around. You should get a pet."

"Listen," he said, tired of the verbal sparring. "Willow's very concerned about you. You weren't supposed to drive down here so soon after your attack and now you're talking about going into a no-name bar. You can have a death wish if you want, but take it back to New York. Willow has enough on her mind.''

And he'd about had it with the both of them.

''Van, I came down here to rest. Not be a burden on Willow. She needn't worry about my driving. I've been driving for fifteen years. I can take care of myself.''

Suddenly the plate clattered on the counter and she slapped her pockets. ''Where are my car keys?''

In a panic, she seemed to go into overdrive as she dug through the pockets and unearthed neatly folded tissues. Before he could stop her, Fox took off up the stairs.

''Do you think Willow picked them up by accident?'' she called, her feet resounded overhead.

Van didn't answer, instead he poured himself a cup of coffee and sipped. He could hear her tearing up the room as she demanded the keys appear.

Reappearing moments later, her cool was completely gone. Strands of hair had gotten staticky and jutted out. And she'd smeared her lipstick. For some reason he was pleased with this turn of events.

''Have you seen my keys?''

''You don't need them. I'm taking you to the doctor.''

She planted her hands firmly on her hips. ''No, you're not. I already said I didn't need any help. If you just provide directions I'll be on my way.''

If only she knew what he'd endured last night, she'd realize how wrong her words were. She stepped close and extended her hand. ''My keys, please.''

''Look, you weren't supposed to drive down here from New York the day after you were released from the hospital. Doctor Caraway called this morning inquiring if you'd made it.''

''Caraway called?'' She shook her head. ''Doesn't matter. I can damn well do what I please. I'm grown, too,'' she said, throwing his words in his face.

"Boy do you have Willow fooled. She ranted last week about how responsible you are. So far you've proven to be anything but, and a whole lot of work."

"Since I arrived, you've treated me like some undesirable. I don't appreciate it. I came here to rest, not argue like an adolescent."

Fear and dread rolled from her forehead to the bottom of her feet, as she massaged in the vicinity of her heart. Fox tried to identify the tightening, against her ribs, chest and throat, but couldn't. Maybe this was another heart attack. Scared she reached out and Van caught her hand.

The crushing pain from the first attack wasn't present. Still she felt as if an elephant had plopped down on her chest.

"What's the matter?" His cup clattered to the sink, the noise making her jump.

"Give me a minute." She let him lead her to a chair as her breathing quickened.

Van sat beside Fox, afraid of what might happen, terrified he wouldn't be able to help her if it was a heart attack.

"I'm calling an ambulance," he finally said, when she dropped her hand on his arm.

"Wait," she said, her look desperate. "It'll pass."

She breathed deeply in an odd rhythm and he caught the plea in her whiskey colored eyes. "Three minutes, or I'm hauling you there myself."

She breathed deeply, her fingers closing around her knees as she struggled to regain control. Her chest heaved up and down and perspiration beaded on her brow. She closed her eyes, her dark lashes flattening against her cheeks. Van found himself not only wanting to draw her onto his lap and reassure her, but he wanted to press his lips to her eyes and kiss her.

Disgusted with his misplaced desire, he controlled it.

Three minutes transpired to fifteen as he watched her focus, breathe, and slowly calm herself.

Finally her brown eyes slid into view.

"I'm better. Thank you for not overreacting."

He dabbed at the perspiration on her brow before she took the towel and tended to herself.

"What happened just now?" he demanded, angry. The woman could have died on the kitchen floor and he wouldn't have known what to do. He drew her a glass of water and put it on the table. Her hand shook when she lifted the glass, but steadied under her intense focus.

Her control had surpassed that of most men he knew if they were faced the such a dangerous situation. His view of her was more confused than ever.

"I had an anxiety attack." Her voice was rusty and where she seemed alert awhile ago, she now seemed tired, lethargic.

"The doctor said they were common occurrences and the nurse showed me how to control the attacks with breathing and relaxation techniques. I guess I haven't mastered control yet. I'm sorry."

"No more than me." Van hovered.

"Don't do that. I'm going to be fine."

"How can you say that?" His anxiety burst in the form of anger. "You almost had another—could have had another attack."

She shook her head. "Believe me the real thing feels a lot different. The nurse told me to identify the source of the anxiety and eliminate it. I don't need anyone telling me what to do."

He picked up her trembling hands. "Then what do you need? To get behind the wheel of a car and black out? Come on, Fox," he coaxed. "Let me drive you to the doctor."

She resisted his offered arm. Van wanted to shake her until sense dropped from the sky and landed on her head. "I've already missed my appointment. It was for ten o'clock."

"After what just happened, do you think I'm letting you

stay on this farm without seeing a doctor? Think again, City."

Struggling, she got to her feet, gripped the table with one hand, her head with the other.

"See what I mean?"

"I'm just a little lightheaded. No big deal. And don't call me City."

Despite some reluctance, he guided her toward the door. Van would have preferred to drag her into his arms and carry her as he'd done only forty-eight hours ago. But today she was awake and would probably put up a fight that would go down in North Carolina history.

"Fine. I'll decide what to call you when I know you're all right."

She walked down the porch steps, squinting in the bright sunshine. "I can't believe I slept late. That's a change," she said almost to herself.

Guilt for not telling her their sleeping situation gnawed at him, but he didn't let it slow their progress. He only hesitated when heat-seeking-missile Trina sped toward them.

Fox glanced up and tried to straighten. She tried to lift her hand to shield her eyes, but winced and brought it back down to her ribs. Despite her mantra about not needing anyone, he supported her, holding her against him.

"Van, I want to know when you're coming back to the cabin. I need to talk with you, privately."

"Later, Trina. I'm busy."

The nineteen-year-old had dressed with the maturity of a preschooler. None of her clothes matched, and every conceivable hole visible to the naked eye was pierced. Yet the girl had an excellent education and was a brilliant travel writer.

"When, then?" she demanded. "It's getting late. When you didn't come back last night, I began to wonder what happened." Her mouth drooped into a pout only his brother could love. It annoyed the hell out of Van. "Sorry about the noise."

Fox uncurled her hands from Van's arm. "Look, I see you've got a situation that needs your immediate attention. I can drive myself to Raleigh." They'd reached her car, and Van's control snapped.

"You're not driving anywhere! Trina, go back to the truck. I'll deal with you later." Van steered Fox toward his van with an increased step and a firm grip on her arm. Trina trailed them. "I—"

"I—" Fox said.

"Enough!"

The women stopped talking. Both looked angry, yet Fox held her cool while Trina resorted to what would surely send him over edge. She whined.

"Van? What are we supposed to do? We're hungry. Did Willow cook? Something sure smells good. Can you bring back some money? Can we bunk here for the weekend?"

"No! I'll get you something to eat. And stop whining." To Fox he said, "Don't move."

He stalked inside the house, followed by his brightly dressed sister-in-law and tore containers and packages from the cabinets. Shoving them at her, he did something he hadn't ever done. Once on the porch, he locked the door to the house.

He growled in her ear. "Tell that punk brother of mine, next time, don't send his wife to do his dirty work."

Trina bopped up and pecked his lips. "He's very sensitive, Van." She backed down the steps. "Thanks. I can't wait until you get back."

"Go back to the cabin, Trina and stay out of trouble."

Quickly he walked to the truck and opened the door for Fox and slammed it once she got in.

"Who's your doctor?" he finally asked once they were on the highway.

She finally dragged her gaze from him and looked out

the windshield. "His name is Doctor Norris Rawlins, and he's on New Bern Avenue."

Questions and distrust narrowed Fox gaze. He knew she was wondering about Trina, and what type relationship they had, but Van didn't feel compelled to reassure her. He had too much other stuff on his mind. Let her wonder.

CHAPTER NINE

Doctor Rawlins's waiting room wasn't unique in decor. It sported the usual doctor's office beige with maroon chairs and short flat coffee tables. Aged magazines lined the tables, and a fish tank with uninspired fish occupied a corner.

Van walked her to the counter and greeted the nurse with a friendly smile that caught her by surprise. A tiny part of her wanted to be the recipient of his attention. She turned away when he gave her a quizzical look, and concern replaced the heat.

"I'm Fox Giovanni," she said to the woman. "I had an appointment for ten, but I overslept. If now isn't convenient, I can make another appointment."

"We're not leaving," Van said confidently.

"If they don't have any availability—"

"You had an anxiety attack not less than an hour ago. We're not leaving until you're checked out by a doctor."

Had his manner been confrontational, she'd have jumped all over him, but his approach was so smooth, he left her unable to speak.

The nurse looked between them and smiled. "We can fit you in, Miss Giovanni. Just take a seat."

Fox waited for Van to choose a seat, then sat across the room from him. He pointed to the chair next to him.

"You sure you don't want to sit here next to me?"

"No, thank you. I'm fine right here."

He shrugged, gathered magazines onto his lap and began to flip through them, ignoring her.

She watched as he read articles intently, his large masculine hand gripping the pages of a woman's magazine. He turned each page slowly, smoothing out any creases, and her imagination ran away replacing the magazine with her body, the pages with her breasts.

Fox gasped at the surge of desire that swept through her.

Van looked up and caught her staring. "Everything all right?"

The magazine hit the table and he stood.

Her gaze riveted up and she shook her head. "I'm fine. Really."

"Miss Giovanni, the doctor can see you now."

Hurrying from under Van's watchful gaze, she stumbled, righted herself and walked through the door.

Rawlins's exam was thorough, and afterward she was ushered into his private office. Relieved he didn't have a replica of a human heart floating in a jar on his desk, she sat back in the buttoned leather chair and listened to the list of don'ts Doctor Rawlins's read aloud.

"Don't smoke, don't eat fat, no red meat, no hard liquor, a little wine won't hurt, but no driving. Low-cholesterol foods only and get plenty of rest."

The man's smile changed his face, pulling his mouth into a generous welcome. He was handsome in a Black Sean Connery kind of way.

Fox stared at him. "There's not much to live for after you hear that, is there?"

He appreciated her sarcasm. "Doesn't seem like it at

first. However, there are some good recipes and seasonings available that everyone in your household can benefit from. Cutting cholesterol prevents heart disease and we both know you don't want to have another attack." His bushy eyebrows shot up for affirmation.

Fox shifted in her seat. "When can I go back to work? I'm much more rested when I'm busy."

"Dr. Caraway said you were a workaholic." The folder slid closed. Fox didn't like that. "I'll make you a deal. You lay off cigarettes, fat, and salt and I'll think about letting you do something in . . ." He shrugged, considering her with an intense professional gaze.

"When?" she pressed. Before she realized it, Fox was leaning against his desk, her hands mashing his. "When? I have to know."

"Three weeks. Very light duty."

She straightened in her seat, a blush warming her cheeks. "Thank you very much, that's satisfactory. Will there be anything else, doctor?"

He flipped the chart open. "Oh, yes. No sex."

Her smile dropped. "No problem."

"How are you sleeping?"

A chill raced through her at the thought of the haunting nightmares. Last night the dream had returned, but had been chased away. She had wanted to awaken, she recalled vaguely, but an unidentifiable warmth, doubled with reassuring strength had surrounded her and she'd slept.

Though tired this morning, she'd gotten her first good night's sleep in a long time.

Unable to stand the confines of the chair, she rose and walked the room. "I'm managing."

"Do you have nightmares or just restless nights?"

"What's the difference? If I can't sleep, I can't sleep."

"If you're restless, you may need to exercise to burn some energy before bed. It could also be anxiety from not wanting to sleep." She couldn't shrink from his strong gaze.

"It's common to have nightmares after a heart attack, Fox."

Fox sat, crossed her legs and folded her hands around her knee. "Why is that?"

"You survived an important and life-altering experience. And while it's common for a person to suppress a healthy amount of fears or insecurities, yours were compounded due to the nature of your situation. Your subconscious can only handle so much. Fear often manifests itself in the form of a dream. How bad are they?"

"I can handle them."

He withdrew a pad from a side drawer. "Look, I'm going to prescribe a sleep aid. If you don't need it, fine, but don't let the dreams get too bad before you address them."

He scribbled illegibly, glanced at his calendar, marked the chart, then handed her the prescription and chart. "I'll see you on the sixth of next month. If the dreams continue after three weeks, I want you to come back and we'll get set up with a therapist."

The prescription magnified her weakness. Fox Giovanni, vice president of Securities and Investments at Fields, Inc., did not need sleeping pills. Or therapy. She walked to the door, gave the doctor a look she knew could burn a hole in steel and gripped the doorknob. "That won't be necessary."

He rose, too, and she had to give it to him. Lesser men had shrunk under her gaze, and her leadership, but Doctor Norris Rawlins was in a different class. He wasn't in "business" but in the business of saving lives, and his type of arrogance was fostered by playing god on a daily basis. The wall beside her with framed degrees and commendations supported the confidence he needed to face her.

"Fox, the only way I'll let you do light duty is if you rest. I'm going to help you get on the right track to building a better life for yourself. Sleep late, get good exercise, and get to bed early. Start with a half-mile of walking next week, and at Craig's, the pharmacy, ask for my book, *Love your Heart*. Try some of the recipes. You'll enjoy them."

His brown eyes roved her face. "This isn't the end of the world. Take the time now to learn a new way to live."

"That's easier said than done." She wouldn't allow pity a moment of her time. Fox squared her shoulders, acquiescence filling her. "I'll do whatever it takes to get back to normal."

"Good. Call if there are any problems or if you have concerns. I see you're at Willow's in Slumber. How is that working out for you?"

"It's an adjustment of disproportionate belief, but fine, thank you. I won't take up any more of your time. Good day, Dr. Rawlins."

"Goodbye, Ms. Giovanni. Enjoy North Carolina."

Fox hurried through the bill paying, rushed from the inner office, and past Van who sat in the waiting room flipping through another magazine.

Oncoming traffic forced her to stop briefly, but she didn't focus on the pedestrians who meandered along the sidewalk and lingered in the window of the formal wear store. Nor did she focus on the curious stares that followed her as she stepped from the curb and crossed against the light.

She was away from Norris Rawlins and his gaze. Back at the truck, she caught her breath, ran a hand over her flyaway hair, and dabbed at her face with a tissue. It was so hot. New York this time of year was rainy and gray, but she'd never minded. Rain washed away the last of the dirty snow, readying the ground for spring and warmer temperatures. Since she'd arrived here though, it seemed the temperature always hovered near seventy. Her body hadn't adjusted yet.

Van's grip on her arm startled her. His touch was foreign, yet familiar. It warmed, comforted.

She looked up.

"Hey, what happened in there?" he demanded.

"Nothing," she said, removing her hand from the door handle. "I'm just glad to be outside."

He released her. A suspicious gleam sneaked into his eyes. "That's it? He said you were okay?"

"Yes, as a matter of fact, he said I could start work in three weeks. I knew there was a doctor somewhere who would see things my way."

Van's gleam shifted into a look of disbelief. "Three weeks? You just had a heart attack!"

"Make an announcement, why don't you." She glanced over her squared shoulder at the woman and daughter who had been ogling lingerie in a nearby shop.

Van angled closer, blocking her view of the women. To his credit he did lower his voice. "Three weeks hardly seems appropriate since your doctor in New York said six weeks off. Right?"

"Right, but everybody is different."

"This guy sounds like a quack."

"Quack?" Her purse slid home under her arm. "But he's my quack, isn't he? He's got degrees from here to kingdom come, Van. Besides, he was referred to me by my physician in New York."

Five o'clock shadow darkened his jaw and she wondered if he and Trina had been at it all night. She shoved the offensive thought away, disgusted she was even remotely curious.

"You can claim him if you want. I think he's making a big mistake."

His body language projected closeness when he reached out and tapped her waist, moving her aside for a group of teenagers. For a moment she was protected from the world with his chest and arm as shield and staff. Sinew and muscle rippled, getting lost under a bright red T-shirt. She soaked in the rest of his profile from the neatly brushed tips of hair that darkened his head to the corded muscles in his neck.

"Why would you care what the doctor said?"

"I don't want to see you hurt by following bad advice. If I had anything to say about it, you'd be resting for six weeks exactly."

He stared down at her, eyes intent, mouth firm and unsmiling. His protectiveness reminded her of an ex boy-friend, William, who'd cared too much, too quickly. He'd become suffocating in his demands of love in return and they'd broken up because she wouldn't commit.

"I guess we'd better get back," she said. "Your girlfriend must be tired of being banished from Willow's house."

Suddenly tired, she glanced around, absorbing her sur-roundings. A gray building with odd angles and planes stood opposite her and the yellow banner draped across the front announced it was a museum. The town seemed only minutes big. She could find it again alone.

Fox started around the truck.

"Trina isn't my girlfriend." His words stopped her short. He took her arm, guiding her away from the truck. "What gave you that idea?"

"You did. She did. She said she would wait for you to come back. If she's not your girlfriend, then who is she?"

His hand didn't leave her arm as they walked down the pathway. Fox drew her arm back.

Inexplicable tension gathered in her chest. The question invaded, pried into his life. Asking a question of that nature would make Van think he could reciprocate. She mentally kicked herself. No matter how innocent her presence at Willow's, Van still believed she'd come to take advantage of his aunt. And until that was resolved, he would pry. She knew he would.

"You don't have to answer that."

Van slowed, looking in storefronts and at local sidewalk vendors. Stopping at a small intersection, he took her hand and urged her into a trot until they were safely on the other side of the street. She immediately separated their palmed hands.

He didn't appear in any hurry to return to the farm

with the demanded money. Or comment about Trina. She wished he would answer.

"Trina is my brother's wife."

Fox tripped on a small patch of stiff grass and tried to maintain a level expression.

"You all right?" He gripped her arm and she kept her gaze averted, embarrassed. "I keep forgetting you're not well. We'll eat and get back so you can rest."

"I'm perfectly all right," she maintained, although she wasn't. Her heart pounded from the exertion of running and knowing she'd misunderstood what she'd heard last night. Obviously Van hadn't been kissing anyone. A thrill of happiness bounced within the empty chambers of her soul.

Fox looked up at him as he led her into a cafeteria style restaurant and wondered how she'd made such a mess of things. The air-conditioning cooled her face and the aroma of cooking food stirred her empty stomach, but nothing could mask her embarrassment.

She straightened, lifting her chin. "We should just go back. Obviously you have to deal with them and I don't want to delay you any further."

Van acted as if he didn't hear her, grabbed a tray, loaded it with silverware for two, napkins, and two unsweetened teas.

Although she hated unsweetened tea, she kept quiet.

"You still trying to mind my business, City?" He slid the tray along the counter making selections as he went.

Keeping in mind the list of don'ts from Dr. Rawlins, Fox selected a salad and a bald piece of chicken.

"Not at all." He continued to make selections, a self-satisfied grin plastered on his face.

"That's all you want?" He eyed her plate distastefully.

"I don't want to eat. I want to leave." The growl emanating from her stomach proved her a liar. His tray was piled high with a delectable feast, while she could barely stand to look at the lonely lettuce on her plate. "I'm just a little hungry, but I can wait. I'm sure there's something back at the house I can have for lunch.''

"Well, I'm hungry so you can watch me eat, even if you're not going to.''

He stepped to the cashier and offered money for their lunch. She didn't even try to reach for her wallet. He'd probably pass out if she tried to pay.

She selected a table for two by the window and sat down near a couple flanked by two empty baby carriers. The infant the woman held on her lap wiggled, catching his mother's attention, while the other napped quietly in the father's lap.

The young mother couldn't have been any more than twenty years of age, yet she looked older. And tired.

Is that how my mother felt before she gave me away at two? Fox shook herself. Her mother was dead, and all the answers had died with her. While families worked well for some, for her, they were unnecessary.

Van sat down, and she averted her gaze when the woman opened her shirt and began to breast-feed the child.

He dug into mashed potatoes, greens, cornbread and grilled chicken. Fox eyed her boring lunch, set down her fork and watched Van as he seemed to savor every bite of food. Involuntarily her tongue glanced along her lips.

Suddenly he focused on her and her heart skipped.

"Don't tell me you're one of those women who doesn't eat when she's out with a man.''

"I eat,'' she said to hide her agitation. "This diet isn't worth the time it would take to chew. I'm restricted on everything.''

"Like what? You can have food, can't you?''

She gave him a sidelong glance. Van waved his fork, smiling. "Go on.''

"He suggested I read a book he wrote on healthy eating. Craig has it.''

"He's the pharmacist.''

She nodded. "He specifically said I can't have salt, fat,

red meat, or hard liquor. I can only have foods low in cholesterol. I can't drive and no sex." She threw up her hands. "I'd rather not bother at all."

"That's pretty bad."

Their gazes met and held. Somewhere in the background a Toni Braxton song crooned and Fox was sure Van could hear how hard her heart was thundering in her chest.

The attack of awareness that soared through her made their surroundings seem to disappear, leaving his gaze and her words hanging between them. Longing leaped into his eyes, then curiosity, followed by surprise.

"That's not exactly what I meant. I meant to say that the list covered every aspect of my life. Not just food."

Van began to chew slowly. "Freud wouldn't agree."

"He's not sitting here either."

Immediately she spotted people in the smoking section and gnawed her lip. Maybe somebody would blow some her way.

"Give it up," he said in a low conspiratorial voice. "It'll kill you."

"So what?" she hissed, embarrassed at her obvious craving. "I smoke. And don't lecture me. All I need is one cigarette."

She'd never known a man who could smile so quickly. But his face creased into a wide grin, then graduated to a full-blown laugh.

She couldn't help but chuckle at herself, too, but still kept a tight grip on herself.

Van was proving to be too complex to be taken at face value. He still suspected she would commit some heinous act against Willow and until he changed his mind, she'd have to show him how independent and self-reliant she was.

Proving herself had become part of who she was. A woman without the benefit of a family or a family name to build on had to create her own track record.

Fox noticed the dessert bar full of delicious treats and turned her back to the goodies. Instead her gaze was dragged back to Van as if he were a magnetized target.

Van ate his food, and watched pedestrians who strolled by the window. Fox eyed the greens he ate, hungrily. To her dismay, he noticed.

"Did Rawlins say you could have grilled or broiled foods?"

"I'm restricted to foods low in cholesterol, salt, and fat."

"Here, try this." He carved a piece of his chicken and laid it on her plate along with some of his greens.

Fox pushed the food around with her fork, but hunger won out. Jolts of flavor erupted on her tongue and she savored the tender meat. When it was gone she eyed his speculatively.

"Here."

Fox cut the meat he'd laid on her plate into small pieces and relished each bite. The food was outstanding.

"I can't have this." She ate another bite. "This is so good it has to be bad."

Van had eaten his vegetables and had started in on some fried turkey and macaroni and cheese.

"It's just chicken with seasonings and a little gravy. Some chicory pepper, cayenne, garlic salt. The cook gets down in here."

Fox ate until her stomach threatened to burst. Hunger satisfied, she assessed. Why was he being so conciliatory? He reminded her of Mr. Chesterfield eleven years ago when she'd had to prove herself to get the job over two hundred other applicants. Perhaps if Van glanced at her bank account, he'd know she had no need to spirit away the silver or anything else.

But she wasn't an applicant looking for a job. She was a person healing from a heart attack, and the last thing she needed was a to start World War Three with a man who could make her temper soar.

Fox excused herself, made a selection from the dessert

bar and sat down, glad to have been able to distance herself from him at will.

She sat down and munched on her dessert. "How long have you lived with Willow?"

"A month. I have a house about an hour away."

"You do?" Surprised, she frowned. "Do you ever go home?"

"Of course. What did you think, a grown man like me can't live on his own?"

"No. You just act like you——you own the place, that's all. I assumed you lived there."

He eyed her speculatively. "I look out for Willow. She's getting older and needs somebody around to take care of the house and someone who cares for her best interests."

"That's very commendable." She felt the heat of his gaze assessing the hidden meaning behind the words. How often had she wished for someone to care about her in just that manner? To cheer her accomplishments and ease the sorrow of her failures?

There had been no one. Except Willow. And that had been nearly twelve years ago. The time to recapture that feeling was gone. Jello slid down her throat.

"How long do you think it will take to finish the remodeling?"

"Two months, part time." He laid his fork down, reached for his iced tea and sipped. "Long enough to get everything decided."

"What has to be decided?"

"Get things done," he corrected, his gaze sliding from hers. "It gives me time to finish the house. Period. Are you ready?"

His abrupt change in attitude brought her defenses up, and she dug in her purse for a tip and dared him with a glare to object.

They got into his truck, and rode in silence. At their first stop, she purchased shorts and tops, and her first pair of jeans before heading to the supermarket. Fatigue nagged at her as she waited on the bench outside the store. As soon as she climbed back into the truck, she fell fast asleep.

"If this don't beat all."

The sound of Van's voice brought her out of her restful sleep. She raised her head from his shoulder and rubbed sleep from her eyes. The fact that she was beside him shocked her. Bags covered the seat and the back of the truck was filled with a chair, lumber, and a large round machine.

"Where did all this come from?"

"I had a couple of stops to make after we left the grocery store. You were asleep." He gestured and she looked up at the house, her eyes widening.

"Looks like you've got a heap of company waiting on you." Her attention shifted to the porch where six men ranging from old to young sat with small bouquets of flowers in hand.

"H-how do you know they're for me? You know them, don't you? Maybe they're here to see you." Panic seized her as she checked out each man. They all stood and put on their brightest smile. Her stomach ached.

Van shut down the engine and looked at her. "A man better not ever bring me flowers."

"Would they be here to see Willow?" She hated the hopeful tone to her voice, hated that Van could see her weakness. She especially hated that he seemed to want to be rid of her company.

His gentle laugh sang a soft melody in her ear.

"Not by a long shot. They're here for you. Come on, I'll introduce you."

"Wait!"

Van kept his hand on his door and leaned back toward her. "What's the problem now?"

"I'm not in the mood for company. Can you get rid of them for me?"

"Some of them have come a long way. Especially Bender. Come on, Fox. Willow said you should be expecting company." He nudged her playfully. "At least the expecting part is over. I might not get a chance to give this to you later. Here."

A bag of wrapped apple candy landed in her lap.

"What's this for?" she asked, surprised and pleased at his thoughtfulness.

He grasped her hand and showed her the badly chewed nails. "Anything's got to be better than your nails."

Despite herself, she smiled. "Thank you."

Van swung open the door and helped her down. She pulled her hands from his wide shoulder and turned to greet the smiling, eager men who'd gathered around.

"Rufus, Wayne, Royce, Bender, Lil' Jim, and Sal, this is Fox Giovanni." He glanced at her. "A friend of Willow's."

His words stung as he stepped aside, leaving her with her admiring fans.

CHAPTER TEN

Three hours later, Fox ushered the men to the door.

"Goodbye Rufus, Royce, Wayne, and Sal, thanks for stopping by. Goodbye Lil' Jim and Bender, nice to meet you."

She closed the door, only to lean her head against it muttering, "Goodbye, goodbye, goodbye."

Van hurried away from the doorway leading to the kitchen and headed back to the drawing room. The shiny floors muffled his footsteps and he was glad he'd have a few minutes alone before she would find him.

Stopping in the entranceway, he admired his accomplishments. Completing the floors throughout the lower level of the house had taken two months, and he was glad that job was just about finished, but painting the walls would be a huge undertaking. The twenty-foot by twenty-four-foot drawing room with its high ceilings and ridged molding was the best place to start.

State meetings used to be held in the once handsome room, and when he'd undertaken the task of remodeling, he'd vowed to restore the room as well as the house to its former loveliness.

Working from pictures Willow had found years ago, he'd begun the arduous task of recreating the room and painting the high baseboards a sunny yellow. Sunshine reflected off the glossy paint and he walked over to a five-gallon can and pressed until the lid sealed.

Fox's determined footsteps headed straight in his direction. He didn't turn, but knew when she stopped in the open doorway. Her energy touched him from twenty paces.

"I thought you'd appreciate the company, that's why I left you alone." Van listened to his own voice echo off the wide walls, and waited for Fox to comment.

"Has everybody in Slumber lost their minds? Why would I want to marry Bender, Royce, Lil' Jim, Sal, or Rufus?" Her voice rang loud and clear, heels clicking against the lacquered floors as she closed the distance between them.

"Between Lil' Jim and Sal they had twelve teeth and they were at least, what, eighty? And Royce, he claimed since I looked like I came from money, why couldn't I take care of him and his six kids for a change?"

"Fox—"

"Oh, no, I'm not finished. And Bender—he just got out of jail and is on parole for spousal abuse."

"He's rehabilitated," they said in unison, mocking the man's constant proclamation. Bender hadn't stopped making demands until she'd closed the door in his face only a moment ago.

Van glanced at Fox from the corner of his eye.

A smile tugged at her mouth, catching him by surprise, her laugh making him turn completely toward her. Deep, throaty bubbles of laughter rippled from her, and Van joined her until the two were breathless.

Hours ago when it was clear her company wasn't planning on leaving, he'd quietly gotten a snack and set up a small area against the back wall of the drawing room. Old furniture pads made a nice soft seat and from their positioning, gave him a view of the countryside. His thermos of iced tea was still on the floor.

Fox headed to his make-shift table and plopped down onto the pads. Remiss of her ivory-colored slacks she folded her legs Indian style and gazed at him.

"How are you feeling?" he asked, turning away from her.

"Can we make a deal?"

"Sure."

"Every time you see me, you don't have to ask how I'm feeling."

Van lifted the cans of paint from the center of the floor and moved them to the cart in the hallway. He reentered, taking his time coming closer, liking the way she looked in his environment.

"On one condition. You tell me if you're feeling poorly. If I have to guess like earlier, you might find yourself on the way to the hospital in an ambulance when all you have wrong is a hangnail."

"Deal." She rubbed her arms briskly. "No more ambulances for me." Fox's earlier anger had been replaced with a gentle quiescence he found unsettling. He liked her better when she was feisty. At least then he could tell she was feeling fine. He realized he was staring, gathered the paint brushes from a sheet of plastic by the door and stored them in an empty can so he could clean them later.

He wanted her to retire to her room and leave him to sort his confusing thoughts, but she hardly seemed tired. The long day clearly marked her face, but he decided not to tell her just now. She seemed ready to talk.

"How did it happen?" he asked.

Gathering her knees close to her chest, her gaze followed him as he checked the baseboard foot by foot.

"I went to a luncheon for a promotion and on the way to the bathroom, fell down with a heart attack. Fast forward," she glanced at her watch. "Nine days and I'm in Slumber talking to you."

"That simple," he asked, taking his time inspecting the wall he'd just painted barn red.

Her chin rested on her knees and she spoke with her eyes closed. "No. But who discloses the details of their most humiliating experiences? Certainly not a dignified person."

"That's all it was to you, humiliating?"

She took her time, her cheeks reddening. "Of course. I'm here, aren't I?" Fox's attempt to disguise her feelings behind saucy words was a defensive maneuver he knew all too well. Perri had been an expert at burying issues, and he'd been an expert at packing emotional garbage around the problem until neither could speak freely.

If he'd learned one thing from reading Willow's women's magazines, it was that men had to ask more questions. He opened his mouth. Nothing came out. He tried again.

"What was worse? Being humiliated or being undignified in public?" He waited for that professional "Back off" armor to slip into place.

Her gaze slid from his and she ran a hand through her bouncy hair. "I was splayed all over a Manhattan restaurant at lunch time. Everybody who's anybody was there. I can't think of a more humiliating *or* undignified experience. I'm a vice president. I'm not supposed to lose my cool. Ever."

He shifted toward her, unhooking the paint roller from the pole. "Could you have prevented what happened? When it happened? Where it happened?"

"I could have had the damned thing at home." She chuckled hollowly. "Alone, where no one would know except maybe the doorman."

Her reaction stunned him. Her voice wasn't filled with pity, but anger. The smell of the fresh paint permeated the room, but she didn't seem to mind. In fact, he found her to be right at home sitting on the floor, talking. He wondered if she knew how beautiful she looked right now.

"Do you like being alone?" he asked.

"It's a state of mind. I learned a long time ago not to

depend on anyone but myself. Independence doesn't often inspire close relationships.''

Her speech was too well rehearsed. Too pat. He bet if she spent an hour in the company of his raucous family, she'd change her mind. His family's closeness was hard to resist. "When I think about not having my brothers and sisters, I don't feel right. They can be a pain in the butt sometimes, but we're all close—a family.''

Van peeled tape from along a wall he'd painted. "When I was little, my mom was always pregnant. I can't imagine a summer when she wasn't going to the hospital and bringing back another brother or sister.''

She rocked a little with a half-smile on her face as she stared out the window. He couldn't help but wonder if her thoughts were on her family. Or if she even knew them.

In his lifetime, he'd run across independent thinkers, people who were loners by nature. But if that were truly Fox, she wouldn't be sitting in this room with him talking about an experience that changed her life forever.

"I like people,'' she finally said. "I interact with people from work all the time. It's sophomoric to think a person living in the heart of New York City can truly be alone.''

He shrugged, gauging her reaction. "If you'd been alone when you had the attack, you might not have gotten help. Chalk up being in a bad situation at the right time and can your embarrassment. You're letting your dignity take a beating for nothing. What's more important,'' he asked when he caught a glimpse of her unconvinced frown, "pride or a little indignity?''

"Pride. Someone can strip away your dignity. But you control your pride.''

Inwardly he cheered and more of his initial suspicion slipped away. He continued to pull tape away from the wall. "I'm living proof that even in the face of lost dignity, you will survive.''

"I don't believe you," she said around a small smile. "You've got too much ego to sink as low as I was."

"You want to compare?" He sank down on the folded tarp beside her, balling the tape into a tight wad.

She inched away and studied him from the corner of her eye. "Yes. I want to hear your sad, sad story."

"All right." He turned some, capturing her undivided attention. "I can't tell you if you look at me."

"You're full of it," she said, moving to get up.

"Be still." Van caught her hand. "This is a little embarrassing, and a little painful."

Fox turned her head from him and stared out the window. Her shoulder-length brown hair had been tucked behind her ear and he noticed the glisten of her silver earrings matched the shimmer in her eye when she smiled.

She was beautiful in a conventional way he'd always admired. And he especially liked that she wasn't too tiny. Several times he'd already imagined his hands roving her body and had to stop himself. Instead he settled for appreciating her classic style. Her skin was healthy and the color of walnuts with dark brows and a curved nose.

She shifted and turned her back to him. "I won't look. Just say it," she said.

He followed her gaze out the window. "You asked me earlier if I were married. Well, I used to be, but things didn't work out."

"How long had you been married?"

Van nudged her a little. "This is my story, right? Don't interrupt."

She had beautiful teeth when she smiled. "Sorry."

He waited for her to settle back. "Anyway, my ex had one idea how she wanted to live her life and I had another. I was young and hadn't learned how to compromise, and I knew she wasn't happy. But I forced my way of life on her and when she'd had enough she issued an ultimatum."

"What did you do?"

"Are you interrupting again, City?"

"Would you spit it out? What happened?" Her gaze reflected interest.

"When I saw her packing my stuff, I finally reacted." He leaned closer, his voice sinking low. "I pleaded with her to give us another try. Everyday for a week I bought flowers and candy, and I made promises I knew I couldn't keep. Finally I got on my knees and begged . . . in front of her coworkers. But it was too late. The relationship had deteriorated too much and couldn't be saved. In the end, I said some things that were meant to hurt her and they did. In retaliation, she burned my clothes and got the best lawyer in town and between the two of them, took everything else I owned. I started my own carpentry business after that, buying homes, fixing them up and selling them. I worked hard day and night just to remake myself."

Van rose, sticking the wad of tape in the trash bag that was near the door. "So you see, we all have a threshold for indignity, but we survive. I think realizing I couldn't talk my way back into her heart was the worst for me. But you're right. Pride is important, but then there's love."

This time when he looked into her eyes he expected to see the reaction of a seasoned woman. He expected her to be coy, smart-assed even, but not plain.

Fox looked as if he'd announced ducks float on water.

Outside the trees rustled and far away he could hear the clink of metal from the barn door being closed. But inside, the house was quiet.

He wanted her to say something. "There's love, Fox," he repeated.

"Yes, there is. But I've often wondered, what is love?"

"A feeling, a commitment between two people." Silence hung between them. "Can I ask you a personal question?"

She shook her head no, but said, "Sure. I reserve the right not to answer."

"Have you ever been in love before?"

"Look at the time—" She attempted to rise.

"Come on, City." He challenged. "Have you?"

"I'm twenty-eight. What do you think?"

Without hesitating he said, "No. I think you've been too stubborn or too scared to allow yourself to let go." Inside he knew he was right. But having this knowledge wasn't all it was cracked up to be.

This time when she attempted to rise, he didn't stop her.

"Fox—"

"Van, did you bring the money?"

His brother Troy walked in, bare chested and oblivious to what he'd interrupted. Again Van had the notion to clobber him over the head. He looked into a face that mirrored his own in so many ways. Only Troy's hadn't been hardened by heartbreak and longing, or softened by love. He and Trina were still playing house as far as Van was concerned. Neither had taken responsibility for being a grown-up yet.

Fox attempted to leave. "I'll leave you two alone."

Van blocked her path, not ready to lose the closeness they'd shared. It had been so long since he'd talked to a woman. He realized how much he had missed it. "You don't have to go."

"I'm tired." He tipped up her chin, but she slid from his touch. "If Willow returns soon, tell her I'm taking a nap." Van stepped aside and let her pass.

"What's her problem?"

"She's had a long day." He fixed his brother with a mean look. "I thought you and Trina were leaving today?"

"What's the rush? We're going to be gone for at least four months if this travel thing plays out."

"Hey, Troy?" Van pressed the roller pole with a painter roller at the end into his brother's hand and guided him to a hallway wall with it. "You ever heard of getting a real job?"

Troy's pearly white teeth shined at Van. "Why? Trina's got a gig. When she's done, I'll do my thang."

An important message from the ARABESQUE Editor

Dear Arabesque Reader,

Because you've chosen to read one of our Arabesque romance novels, we'd like to say "thank you"! And, as a special way to thank you, we've selected four more of the books you love so well to send you for FREE!

Please enjoy them with our compliments, and thank you for continuing to enjoy Arabesque...the soul of romance.

Karen Thomas
Senior Editor,
Arabesque Romance Novels

Check out our website at
www.arabesquebooks.com

SPECIAL OFFER!
4 FREE BOOKS

ARABESQUE ®
A PRODUCT OF
BET BOOKS™

3 QUICK STEPS
TO RECEIVE YOUR "THANK YOU" GIFT
FROM THE EDITOR

Send this card back and you'll receive 4 FREE Arabesque novels! The introductory shipment of 4 Arabesque novels – a $23.96 value – is yours absolutely FREE!

There's no catch. You're under no obligation to buy anything. You'll receive your introductory shipment of 4 Arabesque novels absolutely FREE (plus $1.50 to offset the costs of shipping & handling). And you don't have to make any minimum number of purchases—not even one!

We hope that after receiving your books you'll want to remain an Arabesque subscriber. But the choice is yours to continue or cancel, anytime at all! So why not take us up on our invitation to receive 4 Arabesque Romance Novels, with no risk of any kind. You'll be glad you did!

Call us
TOLL-FREE
at 1-888-345-BOOK

THE EDITOR'S "THANK YOU" GIFT INCLUDES:

- 4 books absolutely FREE (plus $1.50 for shipping and handling)
- A FREE newsletter, *Arabesque Romance News*, filled with author interviews, book previews, special offers, and more!
- No risks or obligations. You're free to cancel whenever you wish... with no questions asked.

BOOK CERTIFICATE

Yes! Please send me 4 FREE Arabesque novels (plus $1.50 for shipping & handling). I understand I am under no obligation to purchase any books, as explained on the back of this card.

Name _____

Address _____ Apt. _____

City _____ State_____ Zip_____

Telephone ( ) _____

Signature _____

Offer limited to one per household and not valid to current subscribers. All orders subject to approval. Terms, offer, & price subject to change. Offer valid only in the U.S.

Thank you!

AN041A

Accepting the four introductory books for FREE (plus $1.50 to offset the cost of shipping & handling) places you under no obligation to buy anything. You may keep the books and return the shipping statement marked "cancelled". If you do not cancel, about a month later we will send 4 additional Arabesque novels, and you will be billed the preferred subscriber's price of just $4.00 per title. That's $16.00 for all 4 books for a savings of 33% off the cover price (Plus $1.50 for shipping and handling). You may cancel at any time, but if you choose to continue, every month we'll send you 4 more books, which you may either purchase at the preferred discount price. . . or return to us and cancel your subscription.

THE ARABESQUE ROMANCE CLUB: HERE'S HOW IT WORKS

ARABESQUE ROMANCE BOOK CLUB
P.O. Box 5214
Clifton NJ 07015-5214

PLACE
STAMP
HERE

Van put pressure on his brother's shoulder until Troy moved across the room.

"It's time to grow up."

"You took your time finding out what you wanted to do with your life. Why is everybody rushing me?"

"You have a wife, Troy. You can't live off her forever. How far do you think this travel writing is going to go?"

"I don't know. But I want to travel. Trina and I are having fun. Isn't that what I'm supposed to be doing at nineteen?"

"You're supposed to have fun, while growing up. You're a man with a wife." Van shook his head at his brother, his youth, and his innocence. "Troy, she won't support you forever. Keep that in mind when your two hundred dollars runs out. Trina's family was as opposed to this marriage as us."

Van headed into the kitchen and tossed his brother a couple of apples. "But you did it anyway. Now start acting like the man I know you can be."

"I will, in due time." Troy grabbed some food from the refrigerator and the cupboard beside the stove. Van folded his arms, watching him stockpile fruit and food in his baggy pants pockets.

"By the way your puppies are real cute." Troy walked onto the porch. He'd heard the advice. "I think Trina and I will head out in the morning. Do you think you could find somewhere else to stay tonight and give us some privacy?"

Van knew if he tackled and hurt his brother, he'd have to nurse him back to health. "Sure," he agreed. "But make sure you're gone before I get back."

Van gathered the brushes and took them out back. A long water hose ran from the house to the far cabin and he took the opportunity to scrub the pans and brushes clean.

The hot sun beat down on his wet back and he walked over to the old water well and pumped. Water splashed and he soaked his face and head, relishing the coolness.

A rustle caught his attention and he looked up at Fox's window. The blue lace curtain flapped in the breeze and he wondered if she were sleeping or hiding.

Guilt wound through him at their misunderstanding. Correcting her misconception had been simple, but pressing her for her personal thoughts hadn't been fair. His family was expressive, but she wasn't used to being asked personal or invasive questions, and she'd frozen when he'd hit one of her personal bull's-eyes.

Instead of shrugging it off, she'd walked away. Fox was the most unusual woman he'd met in a long time, and that unsettled him.

He laid out the tools to dry, then pulled down the chair he'd gotten in town for Willow. Sometime today he'd have to put it in Fox's room so if his aunt were ever up there at night, she would be comfortable.

He wouldn't spend another night with Fox. It was too risky an endeavor. Two days in her company and he already knew more about her than he needed to.

Beneath that tough exterior, he sensed a softness that had been carefully guarded for a long time.

As he carried the chair up the porch stairs, it suddenly occurred to him, Fox might not have even be aware that softness existed.

Knowing something so private about her made his chest a little tight and his loins ache. He backed through the door, when dust kicked up as Willow's car approached. Nestling the chair beside the refrigerator, he met her in the driveway, automatically taking bags from the passenger seat.

"Hello," she puffed, breathlessly.

"Where have you been all day? I expected you back hours ago."

He followed his aunt's progress as she took the stairs more slowly than usual. She held open the door so he could maneuver his way inside, then began to empty bags as soon as he laid them on the table.

"You know how it is once I get to town. I find things to do. The one-eyed Susans are beautiful this time of year."

Everybody knew the best place to see those flowers was at the Packer's farm.

"What were you doing across the county?" Van stared at his aunt. She was seventy-plus years old, she didn't need to be driving all over the world visiting. Especially since she had company.

"I'd planned to come back earlier, but I was needed. How's Fox?"

"She's been upstairs for about two hours. Willow, I told you I'm not a baby-sitter. You invited her here and then you disappear."

"She didn't need me to go to bed, did she?" Willow emptied a cloth bag filled with fresh corn on the cob onto the table.

Van didn't feel like being helpful and putting the vegetables away. He wanted answers, then he wanted out. Just for a while.

"No, but she asked where you were. What did Denise say at the bank?"

"Poo. Things are fine." Willow shuffled over to the cabinet and stored the dried herbs from the garden. "She just needed me to sign some papers. You know the bank. They get your money and then have a problem giving it back."

His aunt hummed as she checked the knobs on the stove that hadn't been used, wiped the table and counter of nonexistent crumbs, and put her goods away. She never stopped moving.

Van weighed whether to confess he'd been checking on her banking transactions, but decided against it. Denise had assured him Willow's business was under control. Bootsy had cashed two checks and the signatures had been suspect.

But Denise had said Willow couldn't remember whether

she'd written them or not. She wanted Willow to find the
checkbook first.

For now he'd keep quiet about his research and focus
on finding Willow's checkbook to see if any other checks
were missing.

"How was Fox's doctor's appointment?" Willow asked,
breaking his contemplation.

"The guy's a quack. He told her she could go back to
work three weeks from today."

"That's ridiculous," she complained. "How am I
expected to do anything if I don't have time?"

Confused, he stopped, too. "What are you talking about?
Time for what?"

She fumbled parsley and fresh onions in her hands.
"Three weeks isn't enough time to heal from a heart attack.
That's what I mean. I'm going to have to call that Doctor
Rawlins and give him a piece of my mind. Did she talk to
him about her nightmares?"

"Willow, I don't know," Van said, suddenly exhausted.
This was exactly what he wanted to avoid. Being responsible
for another person. Willow was enough and now Troy and
Trina. In addition to the fact he'd have to spend the night
out of the cabin if he wanted to get a moments rest. Van
shrugged his shoulders, responsibility weighing heavily on
him.

"Did you eat darling? You look so tired."

"Yeah, I got something in town. Her prescriptions are
filled and . . . I'll be back."

"Where you going?"

"I just need to be alone. I think I'll ride up west to the
old house. If you need me, call on the radio."

"Be careful." Balefully, she watched and he could feel
the unasked questions, but he didn't desire an inquisition.
Tonight he needed peace.

"Yeah."

Van slipped into the darkness and walked to the truck.
He wished he still smoked; sometimes a man had to have

something for himself. Instead he slid inside the truck, opened the windows, popped in a tape, and drove. The pickup bumped over the open pasture, gaining speed until he couldn't go any faster. Wind whipped around him, washing him, freeing him of the exhaustion and tension that coursed though his body.

He cut the wheel quickly, taking to the deserted roads, and loved how the trees whistled by and the smell of pine that scented the air. Far into the pasture he saw the first signs of the dilapidated house Willow and Ray had once called home.

It leaned like a tired rectangle to the right and had been nearly taken over by tall grass. His headlights brightened the faded house and he left them on, getting out and approaching.

Van sat on the stairs.

But loud wind whipped through the aged clapboards of the century-old house, as raucous as his thoughts.

He rubbed his head, stretched his neck. And thought of Fox. How often had he peered into the kitchen where she'd kept her six gentlemen callers? Ten? Twelve times?

She'd handled the men well, giving each a personal thank you for his flowers, then arranging them nicely in a vase. She'd even served cookies and punch, and although she declined the oldest male, Lil' Jim's marriage proposal, she still took the time to spare his feelings and make a joke at her own expense.

Perri wouldn't have done any of that.

The entire time they were there, he'd waited for an explosion, a rocketing burst of anger to bubble from Fox at the intrusion, but she'd kept it in until she faced him, then took him totally by surprise and laughed about the entire incident.

He chuckled, knowing what he feared most was happening. He felt more than a passing attraction in Fox. Sometime over the last few days, she'd planted a seed of love inside him and it had sprouted and begun to grow.

He couldn't curse the surprise away, so he laughed.

When the wind picked up the chuckles, carried them to the trees and brought them back as an echo, he laughed harder.

Here, away from the confusion of Willow and Fox, he let his restless spirit free until the wind died down and the insects climbed into bed. Then he drove back to the house and slept in the rocking chair beside her bed.

CHAPTER ELEVEN

Fox leaned over her wet toes and blew on the fire engine red polish. Carefully inserting the brush back into the bottle, she twisted it closed, lay back on the sleigh bed, and eased her feet over the high back to dry.

Boredom settled in again.

Thinking of her steel desk at work, the reports that smelled faintly of the computer room, and the printer that always jammed made her nostalgic for the simple joy of being productive. She missed the efficient office she called home more than her expensive condo, and she hated more than anything being idle.

How in the world did people survive doing nothing?

Since she was here in Slumber, North Carolina, languishing away a perfectly good workday, who would fix the printer she had developed an intimate relationship with last summer?

Somebody, she thought sadly. Somebody with a job.

Even Mr. Chesterfield hadn't seemed bothered by the fact that she'd be off for six weeks. When she'd talked to him right before leaving the hospital, he'd encouraged her to take more time if necessary.

Her thoughts took on a brooding quality uncharacteristic of her usual even-tempered mood, and she wondered what else the heart attack would change?

Her thoughts returned to Van as she wiggled her toes and looked at the rocker that had mysteriously appeared in her room one day while she showered.

Willow couldn't have carried the chair up the stairs, and the room was completely furnished already. So why had Van taken time out of his busy schedule to bring it to her?

The fact that she'd been naked in the other room sent tendrils of longing up her raised legs and she wiggled her toes hoping to dislodge the urge for pleasure from her body.

It didn't work. Desire pooled between her legs leaving her breathless for satisfaction.

She hadn't faced him in over a week when she'd drawn the wrong conclusion about him and Trina, and admitted she'd never been in love before. Knowing they weren't a couple had cleared a path for her unrequited needs, but it was no more than she deserved, she thought, for trying to mind his business.

Staying out of Van's way seemed small payment for interfering in his family.

The side staircase she'd discovered on one of her exploring expeditions provided easy access to the kitchen and aided in her effort to remain out of view. The tiny room where the staircase ended now held canned foods, the extra mop, and a broom.

The thought of food made her stomach rumble so she swung her legs to the floor and decided to see if she could get something to eat without running into Van.

Fox descended the narrow staircase, running her hand along the green flowered wallpaper when she heard Van moving about the kitchen. She considered retracing her steps, then thought herself foolish. Why fight the inevitable? They were bound to run into one another. After all he lived on the farm, too.

Fox walked into the kitchen. Their gazes locked, held. "Good afternoon," he said.

"Hi." Awkwardly she glanced past him to the pile of books on the table and recognized them as picture journals of old houses that had been on the desk in one of the numerous rooms occupying the first floor.

The one on top was open to a page that showcased a magnificent room with shiny floors and beautiful red walls. The similarity to the drawing room was startling.

"How have you been? Sorry," he said abruptly.

She shook her head, secretly glad to be talking to someone. "I'm fine. You?"

"Fine."

Fox tried not to move so stiffly, but his eyes followed her as she walked toward the table. Wanting to fill the silence, she said, "How's the work going in the drawing room?"

"It's going." He shoved his hands in his jeans pockets. "You want to see?"

The handle on a drawer became very interesting. "I wouldn't want to disturb you."

"Come on," he urged softly. "I don't mind. I could use a break."

He gathered the large book in his arms, allowing her to pass in front of him. "Hold this," he said giving her the book outside the room. She held it in her arms while he slid open the doors.

All the walls had been completely painted red and pictures were hung, breaking up the bright color. The floors gleamed like fresh rain, and he'd even begun to place furniture around an intricately designed cream and red floral rug.

The room resembled the picture in the book exactly.

"How were you able to recreate this? This room looks just like this one."

"Willow did most of it. She finds furniture from the eighteenth and nineteenth centuries and has it refurbished in town. My job was simple actually. All I did was follow the picture as closely as possible and try to recreate what I saw."

Walking the length of the room, she made comparisons and Van was right.

Willow and he had done a remarkable job recreating a period indicative of the antebellum house.

For the first time, Fox noticed the elaborate white cornices and carved marble mantelpiece. "This is so incredible. I've been in this room before, but I didn't see this fireplace. Can I touch?"

Her hand hovered over the hand-carved cornices and he gestured with his shoulder. "Sure, enjoy yourself." Fox memorized the intricacies.

"The fireplace was covered the other day when you were in here. I wanted to surprise Willow with how well they turned out, so once all the fireplaces had been restored, I covered them."

"It's beautiful. I'm impressed, Van."

"I'm glad you're easily pleased," he said.

Fox closed the book, and licked her lips. She noticed how easily she responded to his flirting as her breathing quickened and a flush ran like tiny fingers all over her body.

"You should be very proud of yourself to have accomplished something so grand. I'm sure Willow is quite happy."

"She hasn't seen it yet. You're the first."

She blinked him into focus and studied his face to see if he were pulling her leg. The truth was clearly written across his handsome features. He'd wanted her to see his accomplishments first.

Words of praise lodged in her throat and she wished she could convey what lay on her heart. It didn't seem unnatural to feel a closeness with Van.

She, who rarely touched anyone, wanted to caress his cheek and tell him without words how she felt. Her hand trembled, but she didn't move closer. Instead she smiled and walked between the strategically placed furniture suddenly glad her feet were bare. Scuff marks would disgrace such a pretty floor.

"So what's next? Are you almost finished down here?"

"Not quite. There are two additional rooms on this level that need to have the floors buffed, the banister and staircase need to be rebuilt, and the floor in a room upstairs needs work.

"There are some odd things like the roof and an overall coat of paint for the exterior, but that won't take too much time," he added, "I hope."

"Why do you work alone? Can't you hire workers to help? You'd get finished a lot sooner."

"True. But we tried that and it didn't work out. I chose to do the house myself so I'd know it gets done right. But I will hire some people to finish the painting."

"Such a perfectionist," she said sizing him up, having heard the same thing about herself.

Could two people who came from such different backgrounds be the same? She took in all the tiny details he'd thought of and liked what she saw.

Behind her Van clapped his hands. "I can't wait."

"For what?" she asked, turning.

"For the house to be finished, of course. I told you before I have other things to do."

"Like what? A neglected relationship?"

In an attempt to cover her mouth, she nearly dropped the book.

He gingerly took it from her. "You seem very preoccupied with my love life."

Her face heated. "I'm not. I just—It's not important." Fox stopped for a moment, realizing the uselessness in denying it. "About the other day, I do seem to have formed an unusual interest in your family. I've just never been around people like you. That's a compliment." She turned and walked to the door.

"Anyway, I was sorry to see your brother and sister-in-law leave. I'd better go back upstairs now."

"Why? Haven't you been avoiding me long enough?"

His low-spoken words reached her, and she squared her shoulders before she turned. "I'm not avoiding you. I was ordered to rest. That's what I've been doing. Resting."

"How much rest do you need? You sleep more than a newborn baby. You sleep peacefully without nightmares. You should be rested enough for ten people."

"How do you know how I sleep at night?" Suspicion curled through her. Until now she hadn't given any more thought to the indent that had been in the pillow next to hers, assuming it was Willow's head that lay next to hers and that Willow was being kind in not mentioning the nightmares.

But she hadn't had any nightmares lately, and she hadn't once taken the prescription sleeping pills. The fear of dying had faded, and even when she'd jerk awake sometimes from a daytime nap, it wasn't because a cloaked figure chased her.

Sometimes desire awoke her. The desire to be held and made love to would drag her from sleep.

But each time she'd awaken, she would be alone.

"How do you know about my nightmares?"

He carefully laid the book on a table, and with a familiarity she found alluring, tucked a lock of hair behind her ear. His finger lingered near her bare lobe.

"I was here the first night and helped you when you were struggling against whatever scared you." He hesitated then said, "And I was in your room the second night."

"I knew it! When I asked if you'd been in my room, you denied it."

"Willow arrived not long after I did. You were crying in your sleep, calling out for someone to save you."

"And that had to be you?" Embarrassed, she turned

away, wishing hunger hadn't driven her from her room a while ago. This whole conversation could have been avoided.

"It didn't have to be me, Fox." His voice was very near her ear. "But I was here. You needed somebody and I stayed with you. What's so wrong with that?"

His strong hand rested on her arm. She shook it away. "Nothing. I just don't need your help. I don't need anyone."

"That's bull and you know it. Everybody needs somebody sometimes. How much do you think you can do on your own?"

"I can do anything I set my mind to."

"Some things are better done with a partner." Double meaning snaked through her.

"Not necessarily," she said, intentionally ignoring the innuendo.

He took her right hand in his and caressing the finger without the acrylic tip said, "It's more fun with a partner. Trust me."

Fox eased her hand away. "Making love isn't everything," she said, though she often wished it had a more prominent place in her life.

"Sometimes it's enough."

"Not for me."

"Me either," he said. He reclaimed her hand and studied her fingers. "You surprise me, though. I can't believe you didn't learn about how much it could mean to have someone care for you while living with Willow."

"I did learn. For so long it's just been me. Before I was sent to live with her, I had already learned how to survive."

His gaze penetrated her. "You're not alone now."

"What are you saying?"

"You've needed me since the day you got here." He caressed her cheek. "You've used me and I haven't asked anything in return."

"I've kept away from you." With each stroke of his fingers a layer of emotional protection dissolved. "I've kept away intentionally." Their gazes locked. "Yes, intentionally. I think you're making this up," she whispered.

His fingers glided down her neck, flicked the gold cross necklace, then caught her around the waist. He turned her ever so slowly and drew her back to his chest.

The familiarity blazed within her, especially when she could feel his arousal against her back. The final straw was when he laced his hand with hers.

"Monday you wore short pink silk." His voice lapped at her need. "Tuesday, white lace, Wednesday, summer blue cotton, and last night, black."

Fox drew her hand up to her breast. He turned her to face him. "That's right. The ties wouldn't stay closed." He inched closer. "Every night you start to cry and I'm there for you. You haven't had a nightmare in a week."

"I didn't come here for this." Frozen in place, she spoke almost to herself. "I came here to rest." She struggled against the blazing feelings inside and looked into Van's eyes. "What do you want from me?"

His fingers stroked the back of her neck and she floated until their chests met.

His lips sank down on hers and he murmured, "Satisfaction."

She didn't know what to expect. It definitely hadn't been passion. But that's what she got. Breathless, urgent, naked passion passed from Van to her and back. Her will bent under the assault, softening as acceptance snatched the last rod of steel from her defenses.

Her legs and back and chest and head were flooded with heat, stimulated beyond her wildest imagination from a kiss. An insincere kiss, she realized before she allowed her heart to follow the route of her head.

Fox broke away, taking two steps back. "I've been here for almost two weeks and I don't know whether you trust me or even like me." His eyes clouded and his answer took too long. "You're moving too fast for me, Van. We need to slow it down."

"You've had space for two weeks. I can't deny my attraction to you. Can you?"

"No." The whispered word slid from her mouth and she caught the glint of unrequited passion in his gaze. "But that's not everything."

"It's not enough for me either."

His sincerity made her eyes sting with tears. Suddenly she appreciated the sacrifices he made to look in on her and not answer his physical needs at her expense. His sparring emotions, not her had kept his desire unreleased. Fox knew she couldn't claim the same control. As soon as his lips had touched hers, she'd answered with so much ardor, she'd surprised herself.

On an afternoon breeze that whipped through the sunny room, Fox acknowledged the flowering of love. But how could she overcome his concerns that she might hurt Willow? She loved her, too.

Her hands fluttered helplessly as her heart thrummed against her chest, and she knew he'd have to come to his own conclusions.

"I think it would be best if you didn't come back to my room."

"Okay." He spoke quietly. Fox was sure he could hear her heart breaking. "Will you take the pills?"

She shook her head. "I can manage without them."

"And without me?"

His gaze moved up her body and before she knew it she'd backed against the wall. He'd followed, but didn't touch her, yet his body was poised so intimately, Fox thought she would lose her balance and tumble into him.

"You'll adjust." She swallowed. "And so will I."

"We didn't sleep together every night. Most nights I'd sit in the chair."

Her sigh tickled the afternoon breeze. "I guess I didn't

want to know why you'd put it there. One part of me wanted to believe it was for Willow.''

''Is the idea of me being attracted to you unbelievable?''

Her heart flipped as a slice of joy and fear raced through her. Fox breathed in and out trying to catch her breath.

''Yes, it is.'' *Because I'm falling in love with you.* Standing tall, she moved from beneath his gaze. With his mouth so close to hers, she'd wanted an encore to their kiss, but knew Van had to understand the depth of feelings that had welled within her. ''I can't be intimate with someone who doesn't trust me. And I can't convince you to believe me. That's a conclusion you're going to have to come to on your own.'' The further she stepped away, the more her heart protested, but Fox knew she was doing the right thing. ''I'll see you later, Van.''

''Compton!'' Wayne yelled from the back door. ''Got a message for you.''

Wayne's voice floated through the walls of the house and echoed between them.

''Come on in,'' Van answered, moving toward the door to talk to Wayne.

Fox walked deeper into the room to give the men privacy, and hoped Van would forget she was there. Then she could slip back upstairs to her safe haven and decide if she should leave.

Her lips still stung from his kiss and she dragged her hands from her mouth to the back of her neck and stretched, her body on fire. Absently she fanned herself, no longer even hungry.

Reconstructing her control took longer than usual, but when Van returned, Fox had managed to cool it to simmer. She kept her distance and avoided looking at him at all.

''I need your help. Come with me.'' He started for the kitchen, not slowing once to see if she were behind him.

Fox let her curiosity get the best of her and followed Van, who was already outside and halfway to the cabin.

She walked through the door of the one story house and noted the similarities and differences.

The cabin frame was a rebuilt replica of the main house, but the interior had been upgraded with twenty-first century amenities like air conditioning, electrical outlets, and a television.

She hadn't seen TV since leaving the hospital.

"Where are you?" Fox walked around the table and headed for a short staircase in the back. Van appeared with something wrapped in his arms.

"What is that?"

He looked down. "This is a puppy. Fox, meet unnamed puppy. Puppy meet Fox."

She took the furry bundle in her arms, looked into its sweet little black eyes and fell in love.

CHAPTER TWELVE

"Why are you giving her to me?"

Wonder in Fox's eyes and the gentle, almost tentative way she held the puppy reassured him he'd done the right thing by bringing the two together. Van guided her to the sofa and helped her sit. She cradled the puppy close to her chest.

"This little bundle is a him," he said. "And I'm not giving him to you. That's why Wayne stopped by. He just gave away the other two. A couple wants this little guy but they're on vacation right now and can't pick him up for another two weeks. I have too much work to do on the house that I can't tend to him, so I thought since your schedule isn't crowded at the moment, you would baby-sit."

The way she supported the puppy took him back to a time after his divorce last year when his family had embraced him and soothed his hurts. He wished he could share his feelings with Fox, and reassure her of the love and passion he knew lived within her. She'd kissed him with an unchecked fire, but he, too, was glad she'd broken

away. Because as much as his attraction to her had blossomed, he didn't trust her. Early in the week he'd found
three one hundred-dollar bills on the porch wedged
between two slats of wood.

Willow had claimed they weren't hers, but money she'd
given back to Fox. He'd held off asking her about it, as
she'd taken to staying in her room and keeping to herself.
He had to admit she was a beautiful mystery, but he needed
to tread cautiously, although every instinct in him
screamed otherwise.

The puppy squirmed and licked at the blanket, crying
softly. Fox's eyes widened in fear. "What's wrong with him?
Here take him, I don't want to hurt him."

"Hold on a minute. Relax. You're not hurting him."
Van tried to ignore how dainty her hands were next to his,
and took the blanket from over the puppy's head, where
it had burrowed. "It's a dog, okay? You don't have to hold
him so tight, but he's a baby and likes to feel secure. Just
like a human baby."

Tentatively, Fox stroked the fur in long whispering
caresses, until the puppy's eyes closed. A jittery smile parted
Fox's mouth. "I can't remember the last time I held a
baby," she said, sounding as if she'd missed something in
her life by not remembering. "I probably held one of my
foster brothers or sisters, but it's been so long."

"There's nothing to it," he said sliding closer. "You can
lie him on your lap like this." Demonstrating with the tiny
creature, he spread him on Fox's thighs. "Or like this.
This one is so spoiled, he likes to be held."

Van slid the puppy into the crook of Fox's arm and
watched the woman's eyes grow large when the animal
burrowed next to her.

"What a friendly dog. But I'm afraid I can't take care
of him. I'm sorry."

Van looked up into Fox's earthy dark eyes and got lost
for a moment. Well-rested after a week of self-imposed
solitude, Fox's color was more radiant than ever. She'd

pulled her hair away from her face but let it hang loose to her shoulders. The khaki shorts she wore were slightly wrinkled, but still had razor sharp crease lines in them. Of course her top was color coordinated as if the clothes were made only for her.

But what turned him on were her dusty, bare, bright red toes. They mirrored her kiss-swollen lips.

"Why can't you take care of him for me?" he circled her shoulder, running his thumb along her arm. She fit next to him perfectly.

"For you?" She looked away and tried to rise, but the sleeping puppy kept her captive to the couch. Van didn't want her to move either. "I thought this was for a family."

"It is. But for now he's mine and I can't take care of him and finish the house."

"Where's his mother?" she asked softly.

"Samantha was in an accident a week after the litter was born. All the other pups have homes. He needs you, Fox. Can't you do this one favor for me?"

"I wish I could, but I don't know anything about taking care of a puppy. I'm afraid—"

"That's the problem, isn't it? There's nothing to be afraid of. He doesn't bite."

Their gazes were dragged back to the snoring pup. He cried again and Fox rocked him. "What's wrong, puppy?" she asked in a hoarse whisper. "This is exactly what I'm talking about," she said directing her comment to Van. "He could be suffering for all I know. Here, take him."

Van captured her hand and gently stroked the puppy's small floppy ears. A tiny gasp escaped Fox, but he kept up the soothing pets, loving the feel of her hand beneath his. Parting her fingers, he tickled under the puppy's chin, and Van got lost in the intimate gesture and began to imagine her hands against him again.

A groan escaped him. His body hummed wanting her, needing her.

He drew his hand up to her face and guided her head

back until it rested against his shoulder. He captured her chin between his thumb and forefinger. Her lips parted and he got the briefest peek of pink tongue when he lowered his head and sought completion.

This time he savored the pleasurable mating. Her warm, sweet mouth tasted faintly of apple candy and he took a tentative nip before delving deeper, then he stopped.

Fox's lips were still. She hadn't responded.

Van released his hold on her chin and blinked hard with regret as he pressed his lips together. He tried to smother the anger he directed at himself as she opened her eyes.

Desire glowed fierce and hot from the deep brown depths. Her painted fiery red fingertips glazed her lips before she caught her top lip between her teeth, and pushed to get up.

"Take the puppy." Laced between each word was a thread of disbelief.

"Fox, wait," he said, trying to stop her hasty rise.

"I can't do this." The choppy words beat against his ego.

"You don't have a choice," he said, suddenly angry. "The chandeliers will be delivered today, and I can't look after the puppy, too."

She was almost to her feet when he bumped her arm. The puppy protested and Fox let him go.

Landing with a plop on the sofa cushion, he scrambled around trying to get his footing, barking in tiny puppy yaps.

"See what you made me do!" Fox reached for the animal and scooped him into her arms, turning her now angry eyes on Van. "We could have killed this animal, and it would have been all your fault," she said, cuddling and talking to the puppy.

"He's fine, just scared, like you."

She acted as if she didn't hear and brushed past him with barely a backward glance. Van gathered the sleeping box, the bowl, food, and toy and caught up to Fox before she got in the house.

Clearly he'd misinterpreted her signals. He'd never kissed a woman who hadn't wanted to be kissed by him and he wouldn't start now. He felt like an inexperienced adolescent on a first date.

"Let me help you get him settled."

"I can manage on my own," she said. "Come on, Andrew," she said to the puppy.

The screened porch door slammed shut behind her and Van dropped the box and wondered when had he gotten in over his head. When he kissed her? He walked down the steps like a lost man. Or had the drowning started the day she arrived?

As he stood in the center of the lane, the feverishly hot sun beat down on his head, but failed to dehydrate the longing that burned within him. He lifted his face to the sun, closing his eyes and thinking how desire and hunger for food were so much alike.

A bead of perspiration ran down his forehead, over his nose, and wet his lips.

Hunger had to be fed before it was satisfied. So did desire.

Unfortunately his aunt chose that moment to come tearing up the lane. Her front fender stopped two feet from his knees.

"Willow, what's wrong with you?"

She struggled to get out of her van. "The town elders are going crazy. I swear if I weren't afraid they would drink up all the money, I'd resign as president and let them have the whole kit and caboodle!"

Gray braids jutted every which way and Van offered her a steady hand. Guiding her to the porch, he got her seated in her rocker. "Stay put. I'm going to get you a drink."

Pressing the glass into her hand, he waited until she drank. "Now tell me what happened."

"The town council wants to buy two tractors with the

rest of the money in the bank instead of paying to have all the children in the county immunized. You know it's only for Jim Sandlers' and Cleophus Woods' fields. A plow isn't going to help them, nephew. Only the man upstairs will redeem those unsaved heathens."

"All right," Van said, wiping his face and praying for patience. "This disagreement has been going on for two years. Why are you getting yourself all worked up now?"

"Because they have enough votes to make it happen. I won't have it. As president of the council, I won't have it."

"Willow, you're only one person. Take it back to the people and if they want to buy tractors let them. Besides, you spend too much time in town anyway. Lately you haven't been home at all."

"Van, there's a world revolving around out there. You should join in sometime."

"I know there is. But you don't have to be everyone's savior. You're in your seventies."

"I'm well aware of my age, young man. That tree over there was planted the day I was born. That's how I got my name. Does it look like it or me is ready to give up?"

"No, it doesn't."

"Well then, I'll let you know when I'm ready for you to start my home-going celebration." She shook her head and set her mouth in a firm line. "Oh, do I have a surprise for those elders." Willow drained the glass and ice clinked against the sides. "Where's Fox? Every time I come home she's hiding upstairs in that room. You haven't said anything mean to her have you, Van?"

"I've been nice to her. In fact, I gave her something to do while she's lazing around."

"Van," Willow admonished, finally calm. "You can hardly call the chil' lazy. She cleans the house like somebody is after her to do it, and yesterday I had to chase her out of the garden for pulling weeds with her bare hands. For somebody that's supposed to be resting, she's doing way too much."

Van stretched out on the porch, ignoring the nagging guilt of the kiss. But he had to be true to himself. He couldn't lie and pretend he trusted her when he didn't.

His aunt rocked in her chair, her eyes closed. "How are you two getting along?"

"We get along fine." Her taste lingered in his mouth. A flash of her face, flushed then closed with defiance, slammed into his gut. "She stays out of my way, and I don't bother her."

"Is she sleeping better?"

Van cursed under his breath. He'd hoped Willow didn't know of his nightly journey to Fox's room.

She'd been restless last night and he'd rubbed her back, held her hand. It was more than past time for him to deal with his feelings and decide one way or another what to do with his escalating attraction.

"She's sleeping," he finally said. "The nightmares come less frequently. They'll probably stop altogether soon."

His aunt opened her eyes. "Why?"

"I gave her a puppy."

"What! Van, how could you?"

Pressure of watching over Willow, taking care of the house, and the distraction Fox provided switched on his temper. "How could I? You're the one who was supposed to be tending to her, not me. But you'd let her shout the roof off before going up to her. Why'd you invite her, Willow?" he whispered hoarsely, aware Fox's room was right above them. "Why'd you ask her to come here, when you seem to be preoccupied with other things?"

"Just because it rains don't mean everything gets water. You understand what I'm saying? I've got work to do. Besides I wanted her here. Fox needs me as much as I need her. She was the daughter I never had." Willow's voice grew strong.

"Those bureaucrats snatched her away from her home. If I have my way, she'll never leave!"

"Then you're setting yourself up for heart break."

"Don't you worry, nephew. This old ticker might have a few cracks, but it ain't never been broke."

The phone rang and Van walked inside the house. "Don't move, I've got it. Yeah," he barked into the phone. When he heard the bank representative's voice, he immediately took the phone out of the kitchen and headed up the stairs for privacy. He didn't want Willow to overhear.

Van listened grimly as she reported news of Willow's depleted checking account.

"What shall I do, Van? The signatures are Willow's or very good copies. I've sent everything to Raleigh to be examined, but that takes a couple of days to verify.

"How much money is she short?" He whistled at the figure. "Four thousand dollars?" He sighed, his patience stretched thin. The responsibility of being the oldest and years of taking care of others gave him a raging headache. Willow obviously couldn't take care of her finances. "I'll handle it in the morning."

"The bank is investigating this. Unfortunately Bootsy Woods went to a new teller who didn't think to get another approval before she cashed them. I'll tell you what," she said chattily. "If he came in, I could question him and speed up this whole process."

Anger flooded him. He would cover Willow's losses, but if the checks were forged, he would take it out of Bootsy's behind.

"So it was Bootsy Woods. I think I'll have a talk with him myself."

"Somebody should," Denise said grimly. "If it's confirmed he forged the signatures, the bank will take a lot of pleasure in pressing charges against him. In the meantime, come on in and we'll work out the rest of the details tomorrow."

"All right, Denise. I'll be there when the bank opens. Don't mention this to Willow, all right?"

Hearing a noise behind him, Van turned and locked eyes with Fox.

"Thanks a lot," he said and then hung up.

"Was that about Willow?" she whispered.

"I've got it covered," he said evasively.

"Van, I have four thousand—"

"Look, City," he snapped. "We don't need your money, all right? Why don't you just go hole up in your room like you've been for the past few days and leave me alone?"

She stumbled back. "I'll be gone in an hour."

Guilt drove Van up the stairs two at a time. He didn't stop until he'd taken her into his arms, crushing her to him. "I'm sorry. I'm frustrated and I don't mean to take it out on you." He tipped her head back. "Stay. Willow wants you here."

Fox pulled away. "What about you?"

His gaze raked hers as he guided her closer. Memories of their kiss assailed him.

"I want you to do what's right for you."

Where only a while ago desire licked in her gaze, pain radiated now. She turned on her heel and walked slowly back into her room.

The click of the door closing was like a bullet piercing his heart. Van exhaled a curse and considered knocking on her door. Stepping to the imposing barrier, he raised his hand, then stopped.

What could be said? The impulse to kiss her had been followed so quickly by the reality he hadn't been able to stop himself. How often had he wanted to taste her mouth while keeping watch over her late at night? One time? One thousand? He couldn't keep track of how often he'd thought of it.

Kissing her had fulfilled a wish. But he'd blown their tiny steps of progress by confessing he didn't trust her. Van rubbed his head with his hand and realized the magnitude of his misjudgment of Fox. If she offered four thousand dollars, surely she didn't need three hundred from Willow.

Van stared at the thick wood that separated them, but

knew the door wasn't the only thing that would keep him and Fox apart. Their lives and lifestyles were too different.

He was at home in a truck and she a convertible. She ate fruit and cream in a cup, and he meat and potatoes. And she was bored living in the country. It had been written all over her face.

Van backed away from her and returned to the drawing room, nearly knocking Willow over.

"Sorry, Willow. I didn't see you. You doing okay?" He stepped around his aunt and gathered the garbage bag and book.

"I'm much better, honey. Van, I think I'm going to ask Fox to talk to the town elders and maybe she can offer ideas on how to manage the budget."

Willow swept her gray braids away from her cheek. He took a moment to study the woman who'd been a second mother to him and planted a kiss on her forehead.

Low rumbling jostled the air outside and Van hurried to the door with Willow behind him.

"Just in time. These guys will hang the chandeliers, then I think I'll go into town." He led his aunt by her shoulders and knew he'd take care of her no matter what. "Did you give Bootsy checks totaling four thousand hundred dollars each?"

"I don't think so. I recall giving him a check for materials, but that was so long ago. I'd remember a thing like that, wouldn't I? Just the other day I was in the store and confused Buford-Sam, Jr., with his daddy. His daddy's been dead for years. Funny what age does to a body," she sighed.

Van watched his aunt, wishing he could slow age and time. She smiled at him sweetly.

"Don't wait up for me," he said.

"Okay. Hey, darling. Why don't you take Fox with you? I'm sure she'd like to get out."

Van waved to the men who'd jumped down out of the cab of the truck. "This way fellas. Need any help?"

"We got it," the tall thin man said.

Heading back inside he nearly bumped into Willow again, and realized he hadn't answered her. "No," he said averting his gaze from where he'd seen Fox standing this morning. "She needs to stay here and visit with you." He held the door open and followed the men to the drawing room.

"As soon as they're gone I'm leaving. See you in the morning."

"Peace and blessings."

The thick black tires of Van's truck spit dust as he drove down the lane not five minutes after the men who'd restored her lovely chandeliers.

"You can't run, nephew," Willow said under her breath, having heard the last of the exchange between Fox and Van.

"You and Fox are already committed to one another. Right, Ray?"

Willow giggled when her body warmed, dug a pecan out of her pocket, then started dinner.

Van slid onto the barstool in the shack Cleophus called a bar and lifted his finger for service. Royce drew him a beer. "How's it lookin', man?"

"Cool." Van dropped money on the counter, then took a couple of pulls that drained the glass halfway.

Royce was in a chatty mood tonight, but Van ignored him. He felt the bartender following his gaze as he looked for Bootsy.

"What brings you to town, Van? Everything all right with Miss Willow?"

"Willow's fine. You seen Bootsy?"

"Naw." The man's eyes darted from one end of the dark, half crowded bar, then back to Van. "You ain't lookin' for trouble, are you?"

"I'm not ever looking. Sometimes it can't be avoided."

He turned his back and rested his elbows on the edge, effectively shutting down the conversation between him and Royce. Bootsy had brought him to town and it was Bootsy he would deal with before he left.

The air in the nearly condemned bar was stale, and the floor covered with betting slips from who knew when. They were the only things that kept people from slipping in spilled beer.

Some of the betting was legal, but 99 percent of it wasn't. People had been known to walk into Cleophus's bar on two perfectly good legs and be carried out, broken up after having a bad night gambling.

The only upscale thing about the dive were the state-of-the-art televisions that were hooked around the ceilings, tuned to various sports channels.

Across from him, Van watched two men bet whether an ice skater would do a triple or double jump. He'd turned back to the bar, when the skin on the back of his neck stood on end.

"Well if it ain't Van, the handyman."

The remainder of his beer slid down flat as Van swallowed and lowered his glass. At least he wouldn't waste a drop if he had to crack Cleophus over his head.

"I'm looking for your cousin. You know where he is?"

Cleophus was burly, with a high-yellow complexion that used to get him lots of attention when he was a professional wrestler. He'd been banned from the sport two years ago for breaking a man's neck and had gained a steady twenty pounds per year since.

His work in the community was self-serving, which in Van's mind was the only reason city officials looked the other way on the illegal activity in the bar. That, and his daddy was on the town council.

Today, Cleophus's stomach bulged from the bottom of a T-shirt that had once been black but was now an unap-

pealing gray. "Bootsy." He sneered. "He's gone. Heard
he came into some money today and you know a fool and
his money. How's that saying go, Royce?"

"Don't know, Cle." The older man wiped the bar with
a filthy rag.

"You know it. It happens to you every Friday. A fool and
his money are soon parted."

Cleophus took that opportunity to slap Van on his back
with more force than joviality.

Van captured his arm easily and subdued him. All noise
in the room ceased. Diana Ross stopped belting her tune
from the jukebox, leaving only the muted television screens
as entertainment. Everyone's eyes were fixed on them.

"You tell your cousin I'm looking for him and when I
find him, I'm going to beat out of him every dollar he
stole from Willow. You got that *Cle?*"

Cleophus struggled and for once his size was to his disad-
vantage. He couldn't maneuver and get a good hold on
Van. "Man, you done messed with the wrong brother."

Applying more pressure, Van waited until Cle's face
turned beet red, then released him with a shove. Cleophus
fell back against the bar, dropping the television remote
he'd gripped in his hand.

He surged forward only to find himself facing Bertha.

"What's going on, Cle?" Her voice was deceptively soft
and conversational. But Van and everyone else including
Cleophus knew not to mess with Bert.

"He started it, I'm finishing it," Cle said, furious and
humiliated in front of the other patrons.

Van headed for the door. "I'm not fighting you, Cleophus. I'm looking for Bootsy. When you see him, tell him
what I said."

"Go on home, Van," Bert said. "Tell Miss Willow I'm
going to stop by the meeting with some food."

"Night, Bert."

"This ain't over," Cleophus managed to say before the

door to the club shut his voice in. Van was already outside, searching the area for any signs of Bootsy. His raggedy car wasn't parked in the nearby lot, so Van got in his truck and headed to Raleigh.

Eventually Bootsy would surface. As sure as Van was of that, he also knew he'd have to deal with Cleophus, too.

CHAPTER
THIRTEEN

Fox lay on her bed watching Andrew sleep. His tiny chin rested on an even tinier paw and she marveled at the miniature dog, failing to suppress a happy sigh.

Andrew was hers. Her first pet. No matter how temporary, he belonged to her. And Van had given him to her. She licked her lips again. They still tingled from his kiss.

What had come over him?

One minute he was angry at the world, taking it out on her and asking her to leave. And in the next moment, he was lifting her to her toes with a heart-stopping, earth-shattering kiss. Her stomach quivered, still in shock.

Fox slowly lowered her feet to the floor and slid off the bed. The room she'd spent the better part of two weeks in suddenly seemed confining. The blue walls closed in on her as she paced. She wanted to go outside and feel a nice warm breeze and take a long walk. Maybe even go into town and get a massage or a facial to relax the tension that suddenly radiated through her bones.

She considered asking for a ride into town, then decided

against it. She was supposed to be resting, not running up and down the road into town.

She licked her lips again, the tingle an ever present reminder of Van's lips against hers.

"What have I done," she murmured, circling two straight back chairs and table chest so she could catch a look out the window toward the cabin.

Andrew's ears perked to attention and he yapped at her.

"Hello, there," she cooed, then stopped. Fox Giovanni didn't coo. She issued directives. Andrew's tail thumped the bed. He hardly seemed capable of following an order. She scooped up the little bundle and cuddled him in her arms.

Softly she spoke to her new friend. "You're not going to be sleeping in my bed, so don't get used to it." He lowered his head accepting her gentle rub. "And don't get the idea you can go to the bathroom on my fresh sheets. I just got these off the line yesterday. Have you ever heard of a dog bathroom?"

Andrew didn't answer, but his tail thumped against her palm. "We'll have to ask Van where to take you."

Mentioning Van's name took her gaze to the closed door and she wished she hadn't closed it completely. But how could a handsome man like Van, who was surrounded by family and friends, desire someone he hardly knew? He seemed so set in his ways, and certainly took being the head of the family seriously. Despite the fact that Willow had her own life, Van took care of her. He'd handled Troy with respect and patience she didn't know existed, while teaching the young man how to repair and paint the walls in the house.

Troy was lazy and talkative, two characteristics that would have landed him on the sidewalk outside of Fields.

Fox had to admit Van even took care of her, and she'd thought he disliked her, but he desired her, too. She reached for a piece of apple candy and popped it into her mouth.

A heady rush surged through her followed by a cold wave of uncertainty. She clasped Andrew to her chest and scooted back on the bed.

"Van always takes care of things. Willow said so," Fox told the sleepy-eyed pup. "Do you think Van and I make a cute couple, Andrew?"

Andrew yawned, shaking when he was done.

"I don't know either. He looks good dressed up. Did you see him in those jeans?" Fox sighed. "He's too autocratic, though. Two bossy people in one house is too much, let alone two in a relationship." She touched noses with the puppy. "I'm glad we had this talk. Since you've spent the last two hours sleeping, I guess I have to look out for you, too." She propped him in her palms. "It looks like it's you and me kid." Andrew wiggled and began to fill Fox's hand with nice warm liquid.

"Andrew, you naughty dog!" She scrambled off the bed, the guilty party thrust straight ahead of her.

Fox descended the stairs, a basket hooked on her arm, Andrew snuggled inside. The smell of food brought her closer to the kitchen at an increased pace.

"Hi, Willow," she said, resting her basket on a chair.

"What you got there, darlin'?"

"This is Andrew."

Willow peeked into the basket and nudged the puppy under the chin. She was rewarded with a wide-mouthed yawn. "I thought you were supposed to be puppy-sitting, not acquiring a pet?"

Fox shrugged, setting his basket on the porch. Andrew continued to sleep.

"Well, everybody needs a name. If for some reason they don't want him, I think I might like him to stick around."

"Well, now," Willow said around a chuckle. She bustled over to the stove and checked on her baking chicken. Fox wondered if the bird cooking was the difficult one that had perched on her car, then decided she'd rather not know.

"I remember a day when you wouldn't claim anything as yours. I'm proud of you, Fox."

Contemplatively Fox picked at her nail polish, unaware she was destroying the neat coating. "When I was in foster care I couldn't afford to form emotional attachments. One day you're happy with a family, and the next you're in the back of a sedan leaving a place you called home. But I'm all grown up now. People can't take things from me without a fight."

"Good for you."

Fox struggled to sound casual as she washed her hands and dropped them in homemade dressing, imitating Willow's kneading. "Where's your nephew?"

"My nephew." Willow tore bread, mixed in chicken livers and added corn meal to the bowl. "Hmmm. Does this nephew have a name?"

"Willow, you know who I'm talking about."

"I have plenty of nephews. There's Tyrone, Michael, Edgar, and Will . . . I could go on."

Fox checked on her basket o' puppy, then began to knead again. "You know who I'm talking about, Willow. Van. Where did he go?"

"Oh, that nephew. He went to town. Why didn't you go with him? He was upstairs a long time, but didn't decide to go to town until he came down. I assumed he was upstairs talking to you."

Fox's cheeks heated at the mention of the stairs. What had happened wasn't exactly something she wanted to talk about.

"He must have been in one of the rooms. I only saw him for half a second. Oh, well. I guess I'll take Andrew to the bathroom." Fox washed and dried her hands, gathered her basket and stopped at the back door. "Where should I take him?"

Willow's laughter was contagious as it reached inside

Fox and tickled her. Smiling was getting easier around her dear friend. And having Andrew was bringing out a side of her she never knew existed, especially since she'd only had him for a few hours.

Knowing she belonged to something was incredible.

"Take him outside. Train him to go far away from the house, that way you don't walk in with any surprises attached to the bottom of your shoe."

"Okay. When we get back, I'll help you with dinner."

Andrew didn't tinkle again, but yipped at butterflies and ran from a frog, but Fox didn't mind. She enjoyed spending the better part of the hour chasing him and laughing as he tumbled over his feet, ran sideways, and panted with his infectious smile.

They walked until the house came back into view an hour later and when they got home, he converged on a bowl of special milk for puppies. Glad with his preoccupation, Fox slid into a kitchen chair, trying to catch her breath.

"You didn't overdo it, did you?"

"No," she said to Willow, who now stirred a wonderful-smelling mixture in another mixing bowl. "I can't believe he's so busy. I need to get in shape," she said, reaching into her pocket, then remembering she'd given up the slim brown cigarettes. She did find a piece of hard apple candy Van had given her and popped it into her mouth.

"Leave his basket on the porch, then after you catch your breath, peel these potatoes for me."

"I'll do it right now." Fox scrubbed her hands and set to work. They worked in silence for a while. "Willow, are you in some kind of financial trouble?"

"No, whatever gave you that idea?"

"Your nephew."

"Van told you I was in financial trouble? What utter nonsense." She stopped kneading, a frown creasing her brow. "I have plenty of money. Don't worry yourself. Why did he tell you?"

"He didn't exactly invite me into the conversation. I overheard him talking on the phone."

"And he was talking about me?" Willow's voice rose, and Fox drew back.

"I think so. Just be honest with me. I have money tucked away for a rainy day and I'd be glad to help you if you need it." Fox looked at the woman she realized was the most important person in her life and knew she'd lay down her life for Willow. "After all you've done for me, I could never repay you."

"I bet he was talking to Denise. She's always stirring up something. What does Van think? I can't take care of myself anymore?"

Fox pushed the knife and bowl of potatoes onto the table and went to hug her friend. "No. He cares and doesn't want anything to happen to you. That's all." Finding herself in the position of defending Van was new, but deep in her heart Fox knew he was looking out for Willow's best interest.

Willow looked into her eyes. "Are you sure?"

"Yes. Yes," she said wanting to wipe the fearful look off Willow's face. Her friend didn't deserve to worry. Fox took Willow by her shoulders and slowly slid her arms around her. The hug lasted for a longer moment than she planned. "I'm sorry I brought it up. Everything is going to be fine."

"I believe you, darlin'. I know you would never lie to me." Willow grasped her hand. "Let me explain something. I give money away because I think it will help others. If they do wrong with it, they're only hurting themselves, and if they take advantage, nothing good will happen for them until they right the wrong. I don't have to worry, Fox. A higher power is taking care of me."

"I know," Fox reassured. "Come on. Let's finish cooking."

Fox got out her own mixing bowl and imitated Willow by not measuring her ingredients and made her own cake. She didn't even cringe when Willow's cake came from the oven a swollen golden brown and hers sunken in the middle. She and Willow ate it anyway.

"Fox, I need for you to do me a favor."

Thinking it was about money, Fox readily agreed. "Anything."

"The town elders could use your expertise in a matter of our finances. In a nutshell, they're about to bankrupt the entire town by being foolish. They've made bad decisions over the years and won't listen to anybody, and need an impartial outside party to come in and offer some sound advice."

"Willow, I don't know." Even as she said those words, a thrill sailed through her. To be working again would be heavenly. She still moved cautiously. "Sometimes people are set in their ways and don't want to hear what an outsider has to say."

"But you're the only one who doesn't have a vested interest in how things are run around here. Please say you'll at least look at the books. We're a small town. We have one policeman and a volunteer fire department. Our needs are simple. But we can't let the same people who have never been able to find solutions keep looking. We need expert help. Please, Fox."

Willow's hand pressed into hers and Fox couldn't say no. "Of course. I'll try."

"Thank you, darlin'. I knew I could count on you. Let's clean up so I can retire early. I've got lots to do tomorrow."

Later that night, Fox congratulated herself for hardly thinking of Van. He'd crept into her thoughts only when she used the back staircase to return to her room, and then when a truck had headed up the lane. It turned out to be Bender and she'd sent him away after a drink of lemonade and a piece of mashed cake.

For some reason, Fox doubted he'd come back.

Willow had turned in early, leaving Fox to her own devices, so she walked the halls of the house getting to know items in each room. Finding a stack of magazines, she leafed through them, then raced up the stairs when she heard the engine of Van's truck pulling up on the driveway.

Andrew looked up as she dove under the covers, but otherwise didn't move from his makeshift bed on the floor.

Fox forced herself to stay on the bed when Van's heavy footsteps landed on the top step, and she pretended to be asleep when he knocked on her door. He knocked again.

"Who is it?" she finally asked.

"Me."

"Yes? What is it?"

"Can I see you in the kitchen?"

She hesitated. "Sure. I'll be right there."

Fox donned silk pants in a soft lavender color and an oversized cream silk jacket. Before she could stop herself she'd pierced her ears with silver earrings and was poised to apply her lipstick when she stopped herself.

"A little won't hurt," she said to Andrew who watched with definite curiosity.

"Let's go see what he wants."

Van sat at the big block table with his hands folded behind his head.

"Hi," she said, glad to see him. His dark brown eyes assessed her in an up then down fashion. He'd changed clothes from the work outfit he usually wore to fresh jeans and blue button-up shirt. He looked good, delectable even, and Fox knew she was headed for trouble. She raised her head and tried not to fidget with the ends of her hair. "What did you want to see me about?"

"I just wanted to say I was out of line this afternoon for kissing you."

Anxiety worked its way into her chest and tightened. Fox spoke past it. "It's okay. Was that all?"

He dropped his head for a moment and clasped his hands together, then looked at her. "Yeah, that's it."

"I just want to know one thing." Fox took the seat to

his right and settled Andrew on her thigh. He nipped at her palm, wanting to play.

"What?"

"Why did you kiss me?"

Van chuckled. "You're a beautiful woman, and I lost my head."

Fox tucked her hair behind her ear, her gaze unwavering. "I would buy that if I thought it were true, but beauty had nothing to do with what I saw in your eyes. I was shocked."

He leaned his elbow on the table. "Shocked that I find you attractive? Why? You're a good-looking woman."

"Well, thank you, but no," she said, although a quick thrill dashed through her. "Ever since I met you, you've struck me as a sincere person who, although misguided in some areas, is honest."

"I'm always honest."

"Then tell me how you could kiss me if you don't trust me?"

He shrugged. "Well," he said, then shrugged again, clasped his hands together and shrugged again. "It's hard for me to trust anyone," he said quietly.

"And it's hard for me to kiss someone who doesn't trust me. I'm not out to hurt anyone or take advantage of Willow."

"I admit I misjudged you, but you're hurting yourself."

"How? I haven't smoked a cigarette since right before I had the heart attack, I haven't had any baby back ribs, and I haven't eaten one pat of butter. It hurts me to be so good."

"I mean the isolation. Don't you ever get tired of carrying the world on your shoulders?"

"If I don't take care of myself, there's nobody out there to do it for me."

"Stop! Just stop that bull 'I don't need anybody speech' you're about to start in on. You need Willow. You need to be here or you wouldn't have driven across the country in twenty minutes to get here. And you need me. As much as you don't want to admit it.''

''My situation isn't that simple,'' she said, uncomfortable with how the tables had turned. ''I'm all I've got, Van. My life was different from yours. I didn't have the large family to fall back on when I needed something. There has only been me.''

''And Willow.''

''Yes and Willow. She *is* the reason I'm here. And,'' she hedged, stroking Andrew's furry neck. ''I appreciate all you've done for me since I've been here.'' She drew in a deep breath. ''Thank you, Van.''

He burst out laughing.

''What are you laughing at?'' she asked, wishing she hadn't sat right under the light. The blush on her cheeks would light the road all the way to town.

''You're welcome. I had the feeling you were a woman that liked to smile and laugh. You should let her out more.''

She watched the slow, absent motion of his hands and wished he would hold her, touch her in gentle, easy caresses. Fox remembered how desire had burned in his eyes and wondered what it would take for him to act on his feelings. Her gaze traveled up his arms to his chest. How she wished to be held in his arms again.

''I think there's another reason why you don't trust me.''

''Are you a psychologist now?''

''No, but I know a little something about human nature. I think your lack of trust stems from your marriage. Everybody isn't like her.''

He smiled at that. ''I know, but our differences were enough to ultimately destroy us. Besides, I have to take care of Willow. People have been taking advantage of her for a long time and it's going to stop.''

''Did you ever think she might know what she's doing?''

''Fox, she's not like she used to be. I know Willow. She constantly talks about things from the past, like they're happening right now. And she's grown increasingly for-getful."

"Such as?"

"She thinks she has an account at the grocery store. Buford-Sam Sr., used to let customers run an account. The man's been dead for four years, yet Willow thinks she can walk out of there and not pay for her groceries."

"Have you talked to her and the grocer, or are you making an assumption?"

A guilty look flashed over his face. "She doesn't owe any money. I checked the day we went to the doctor. But that's not all, she's overdrawn at the bank. You heard the conversation. Four thousand dollars. I admit there is a strange situation going on, but we can't clear it up because she misplaced her checkbook. I'm worried about her."

She touched his arm recalling her conversation with Willow.

"I'm glad you told me, and my offer for the money still stands. I'll make sure to keep my eyes and ears open, but in the meantime talk to her. She probably has an explanation for everything that's happened."

Heat radiated up her arm and she pulled her hand away from his arm. Andrew raised his head, pleading for attention, and Fox gave it to him, caressing his soft coat.

"You've been here for a few weeks now. Do you miss New York yet?"

"I do," she said, nodding her head.

"New York is too complicated."

"No, it isn't." Fox felt herself smiling. "When was the last time you were there?"

"Thanksgiving, about four years ago."

"New York is a madhouse at Thanksgiving. That's one of the biggest tourist weeks of the year. You have to come in the spring or fall. It's beautiful then. When the first snow falls is always special and when they decorate the streets for the holidays is another of my favorite times of the year.

"Do you enjoy a season more than another?"

Van stretched his legs and hooked his thumbs in his belt loops. "Nothing is more beautiful that North Carolina in the fall. The changing leaves, the cool days before it gets cold. I always remember the last smoke-out before winter sets in."

"What's a smoke-out?"

"The last barbecue," he said as he traipsed down memory lane. "Mama, Daddy, aunts and uncles, cousins, and brothers and sisters come from miles around for the last, great smoke-out of the year."

"I bet the women do all the cooking."

He drew up, challenge lighting his eyes. "It's the men's job to barbecue the meat over the outdoor grill. Besides, we can beat the women any day with our homemade secret sauce."

"Come on," she said, disbelieving.

Van's dark eyes danced. "I've got the best secret sauce, this side of the Mason Dixon. It's been passed down ten generations."

He leaned forward to share a secret. "Willow doesn't even have it. Ray did, but not his wife."

"This is all made up. Willow is the best cook I've ever known." Fox laughed at the way he tried to inspire her confidence, but stopped before he dragged her into his charade.

"Maybe one year you'll come back and see for yourself. We have a great time."

"Maybe," she hedged. She could negotiate in Japanese with heads of companies, yet facing a horde of Van's relatives started her heart pumping. She breathed through her mouth, then inhaled deeply.

Sounds she'd grown accustomed to escalated, and Fox allowed them to soothe her anxiousness away.

"How did you come to be one of Willow's foster kids?"

Stroking Andrew's furry collar, she kept her eyes on her puppy. "There isn't a whole lot to tell. I was given up at a young age by parents who couldn't take care of me. Years ago I hired a private detective to find them and they are both dead.

"Apparently, my mother was a spunky woman who tried raising me after my father skipped out, but couldn't do it. I obviously inherited her spunk because I was never adopted. I was labeled a problem and stayed in the system for too long."

"Then how did you meet Willow?"

"She only took older children into her home. She came into my life when I was twelve. How she survived my puberty, I'll never know."

"A difficult time for lots of kids," he added softly.

"Willow did a lot for me. I would do anything for her. You should realize that by now."

Their gazes met, held.

"Yeah, I know now. Can I ask you something else?"

She gave him a sidelong glance. "Those types of questions are always loaded but go ahead."

"Where did your name come from?"

"It's the only thing my mother ever gave me. I am Fox Giovanni, daughter of Fiona Giovanni. She gave me a start, Willow gave me a middle." She shrugged. "I determine the end." Giving Andrew a final pat, she looked into Van's eyes. They were clear brown, like iced tea, and she wanted to float forever in his gaze. She felt herself drifting toward him, reaching out emotionally and knew she wanted him in her life. "I guess I'd better say good night."

Van pushed back from the table and when Fox stood, Andrew scrambled over. Van reached his big hand down and scratched the playful puppy behind the ears, making him bark happily.

He scooped Andrew up in one hand and brought the little brown dog to his chest.

"Hey, fella. You miss me?"

Andrew's excited barks made them both smile.

Fox watched the exchange, stunned at the tears that

stung her eyes. "You can take him, if you want," she said, hoping he'd decline.

"No, you go ahead. He'll settle down once you get him upstairs. Does he need to go out?"

"Oh, I forgot. He probably does. Come on, Andrew let's go."

Van put the puppy down and Andrew took that opportunity to scramble around the kitchen floor and hide under the table.

"Come on. Andrew!"

The puppy slid to a halt at Van's authoritative tone and thumped his tail against the floor, a smile on his chubby face. Van scooped him up by the scruff of his neck and, together, they walked him outside.

Stars dangled in the sky as miles away, someone shot off fireworks.

Fox gathered the silk jacket around her arms and waited while Andrew took care of his business, but her focus was on Van. He was more relaxed than he had been all day, and his easy mood transferred to her.

She loved watching him run in circles with the puppy and couldn't contain her laughter any longer. Giggles burst from her as she sank down on the bottom step and sucked a piece of apple candy.

Eventually Andrew came and huddled under her feet. Van sat beside her, a respectable distance between them.

Blue and red fireworks sizzled in the sky, then petered away.

"Pretty." She sighed. "Just like in my condo on the Fourth of July. Only the view from here is unhampered by buildings."

"You ever think of leaving New York?"

"No. Everything I need is there. Except for the Japanese, Chinese, or Russians, and I can travel for that."

"You sound like a workaholic."

She smiled, having come to that same conclusion about him. "I've been accused of doing too much before."

"Have you been all those places?"

"Last year alone. Later this year I've got a six-country tour, then I'll probably spend the rest of my time in New York."

"You sound as if you like it and miss it," he said as a shot of pink burst in the night sky.

She answered in Japanese. Van's quizzical stare made her laugh. "I said yes, I do."

He rose, his back to her as he looked up at the sky.

"I don't want to keep you from resting. You and Andrew should get inside."

Fox scooped up her sleeping puppy, walked through the door he'd opened for her. "Thank you, Van. Sleep well."

She caught a whiff of his cologne, memorizing it so it would follow her into her dreams. "Van?"

"Yes?"

"Next time you kiss me, mean it."

A grin spread slow and easy across his face and she was just a breath away from issuing an invitation, but stopped. He would come to her in his own time.

CHAPTER FOURTEEN

The cordless phone rested against her ear as Fox stirred cream into her coffee. "Doctor Rawlins, please. This is Fox Giovanni."

Sitting at the table, dressed and ready to go, Fox adjusted her already perfect collar.

"Dr. Rawlins is on another call," the professionally cheerful voice said. "Would you care to continue holding?"

"What?" Fox snapped, her patience tight as the shoe on her foot. "Sorry. Yes, I'll continue holding."

"Thank you." Music designed to induce calm wafted into her ear, and she took a deep breath of the spring breeze that fluttered the curtain by the sparkling window.

She'd tried every technique she'd learned to manage anxiety and had managed to keep an attack at bay, but didn't get any sleep. Some of her angst had surrounded fear that Rawlins wouldn't follow through on his thinly veiled promise of work.

But most of her anxiety centered around the idea of

pursuing a relationship with Van. Fox shook her head at how much she'd changed.

The heart attack had magnified the isolated person living a shallow existence that she'd become.

The old person wasn't who she wanted to be anymore, she realized when she'd pulled Andrew from the bathtub about three A.M. She didn't want to be alone anymore.

"Rawlins here."

"Doctor, this is Fox Giovanni. I don't know if you remember me, but I was in your office several weeks ago."

"Yes, Ms. Giovanni, I remember you. How have you been?"

"Very well. Thank you."

"And the nightmares? Have they continued?"

Crossing her legs, Fox couldn't keep a smile from parting her lips. Not since she knew Van had helped her through the toughest nights. "No. I get sensations from time to time, but for the most part they're gone."

"That's good news," he said cheerfully. "What can I do for you?"

"Well, I'm calling because we discussed my going to work and since I've been feeling better, I'd like to give it a try, and I'm expecting you to keep up your end of the deal."

Van walked into the kitchen, capturing Andrew's attention away from his chew toy, and he waddled over and yapped. Her heart fluttered when he winked at her and poured some coffee.

Andrew dashed in circles through Van's feet, catching his boot lace in his mouth.

"What kind of work are you intending to do? Resume your position in New York?"

"No," she shook her head, her attention drawn back to the conversation. "Nothing like that. Actually, Willow wants me to sit in on a town meeting. Just as an observer. Maybe offer suggestions to improve how the budget is handled."

"That hardly seems taxing, but I don't want to take any chances. Sit in on the meeting for an hour, then go home and rest. If you feel up to it, maybe next week we'll see how you do working up a budget. But I only want you to work in one-hour increments."

"One hour per day?" She clenched and unclenched her hand, caught Van watching and stopped.

"No. Per week."

"One hour per week! That's hardly worth my time. Doctor Rawlins, it takes me that long to get dressed in the morning."

"You're still on medical leave, Ms. Giovanni. You're supposed to be resting and I won't jeopardize your health."

"I'm too rested, trust me. All I do is sleep, eat, and sleep some more. Four hours a week," she bargained, pacing.

"Two and no more. Anything more I should know about? Are you exercising and taking your medication?"

"Yes," she nodded, aware even as Van sat down at the table with Andrew on his lap, he hadn't looked away from her. "I've been gardening, and cleaning, and I have a puppy to care for. He keeps me outside quite a bit."

"Good for you, but don't overdo it. I want to see you before the end of the week. Remember, one hour today, then home to rest."

Fox could hear him flipping pages. "At your leisure," Doctor Rawlins continued, "you may resume other normal activities."

Elated she'd won a battle, Fox stood and smoothed her short linen shirt, anxious to end the conversation.

"What other activities?"

Rawlins cleared his throat. "I was referring to driving and your intimate life."

"I see," she said, realizing her hand rested on her hip, as did Van's hooded gaze. Andrew had climbed onto the center of Van's chest and lay like a splatter of brown gravy. His tail thumped in quick tempo, keeping time with her heartbeat. "Thank you for telling me. Goodbye."

She lowered the phone into the cradle and leaned against the counter, crossed her feet at the ankles and folded her arms. "Good morning. I thought you were gone. I heard your truck early this morning."

Van continued stroking Andrew's head. "I came back a little while ago. We're all going to town together. Are you ready?"

"Almost. I still have to walk Andrew."

"What did the quack say?"

She tore her gaze away from his and picked up the comb from beside her matching purse. "He said I could work two hours a week. One today, then I have to come home and rest." She touched her hair, slid the comb in her purse, and gave herself a final check. Van's gaze met hers. "And he's not a quack."

"You and I will always disagree on that. Did he say anything else?"

"Aren't patient-doctor conversations confidential?" she teased, liking the flirtatious nature he brought out in her.

Van's brows shot up. "When does he want to see you back in his office?"

"Before the end of the week. Is there anything else, Mr. Compton? You seem inordinately preoccupied with my business today. I think you need to learn how to relax before *you* have a heart attack."

"Don't wish your bad luck on me," he said, his lips curving into a too sexy smile. He'd trimmed his mustache, she noticed, then dared herself to flirt.

"How do I look?" she asked.

"Turn around, slowly."

Playful moments were so rare, she hardly believed she was doing a pirouette for him. Fox propped her hand on her hip, her body burning under his casual examination. The cane-bottom of the rocking chair outside swayed, giving her country music to dance to.

Otherwise, nothing else existed. It had been so long

since she'd been receptive to a man's attention, Fox found herself hungry for it.

Slowly his gaze raised from the tips of her shoes, slid up her legs, past her hips and waist, crawled over her chest and neck, then met hers.

"I don't usually do this," she said, slightly breathless wondering if she'd gotten in over her head.

"You do it well," he finally said, his voice husky and warm. "You look gorgeous."

She burned with pleasure. "Thank you. I'm ready," she said after several quiet seconds, and opened the door. Andrew scrambled down from Van's lap and they both followed the puppy outside.

From the porch, Fox could see Willow's pink hat as she walked in the fields. "Is she feeding her animals?"

"Yeah, she'll be back in a few minutes. I guess we took too long. You want to get something to eat while we wait?" he said, having tied Andrew's leash to one of the pillars. He climbed the stairs, each step bringing his mouth closer and closer to hers.

She yielded to the attraction that lived within her and said, "No, I really want you."

His hands captured her around the waist, as a current of wanting connected them. Tilting her head back, she closed her eyes, afraid at what she might see if she looked at Van. She wanted to see the desire that had flowed like hot lava yesterday, but was afraid the brown depths would be clouded with suspicion and distrust.

As if a fairy had granted her wish, she opened her eyes and what lay within her heart was mirrored in his gaze.

His mouth approached slowly, her eyes sank closed, and their lips met. He took her tentative peck and transformed it to an open-mouthed, tongue-against-tongue mating ritual that had her rising to the tips of her high-heeled shoes in search of satisfaction.

Kissing Van crushed emotional shackles, and she heard

herself groan. Fox broke away from his mouth for a second, only for her lips to be recaptured.

Spirals of ecstasy curled through her when his arms completely encircled her and swept her off her expensive shoes. Fox groaned long and low again.

He whispered, "Do that again," and drew her body closer, his lips never leaving hers.

Obligingly, she gave in.

From across the field, Willow watched her nephew and Fox finally meet, not as adversaries, but as man and woman. "We did it, Ray," she said softly. Now the object was to keep them together.

Walking deeper into the woods, she found her favorite fallen tree and sat down. Maybe the couple wouldn't want to go to town after all. Unwilling to take any chances, Willow kneeled and prayed that they be bound together in love.

When she was done, she took the long way home.

"Your lipstick's all messed up."

When he was finally able to tear his lips away from Fox's, Van couldn't let her go. Her eyes were still closed. He longed to see them—wanted to hear her voice—had to be sure she wanted his touch.

"Lipstick?" she said from the curve in his arm. Her eyes slid open. "What's that?"

A low rumble bubbled in his chest. Oh, she was working on him. Pulling heartstrings his first marriage had stretched too taut to vibrate.

The other night while at Willow and Ray's old house he'd had an inkling he was in trouble, but now he was sure. The water had covered his head and he was drowning in love with Fox Giovanni.

It occurred to him they still stood on the porch. He

guided her backward and opened the screen door. The cool air from the kitchen soothed his physical heat, but he was nevertheless glad when she put the table between them.

"I'd like to watch television at your place tonight."

Her polished elegance had him hungering for her. He needed to hear she wanted him the way he wanted her.

"Tell me what you want."

In typical Fox style, she gazed directly at him. "I want you."

He closed the space between them. "We can go right now."

Andrew started to bark, drawing their attention.

Willow walked in. "Are you ready to go to town?"

Van wiped his mouth and came away with a hand full of red lipstick. He looked at Fox whose bruised, faintly pink mouth was curved into a small smile. She caught her lower lip between her teeth and looked innocent. Tonight wasn't going to be soon enough.

The phone rang and he grabbed it, wiping his hand on a handkerchief.

"Yeah?"

"Van, it's Denise." He glanced back at his aunt.

"Go on and get in the truck. I'll be right there." The door closed and he prepared himself, knowing the news wasn't good.

"Go ahead."

"The signatures are forgeries. I just wanted you to know the bank will be pursuing a criminal investigation."

"Thanks, Denise." Van lowered the phone and made a promise to find Bootsy and when he did, the man would be very sorry.

CHAPTER FIFTEEN

A problem had clearly developed among the elders on the town council of Slumber, North Carolina. They were all tired of each other. Bantering between rivals was the order of the day, and as hard as Willow fought to stick to her agenda, hell broke loose often.

A headache nagged and Fox tried to blink it away as she sat sequestered in back of the overly hot meeting hall. Her brain gyrated as Willow banged the gavel on the table. "Sit down, Lil' Jim and Sal, and stop that incessant shouting. Everybody's hearing aides are on."

The two men released each other with a final shove and resumed their seats.

She hadn't realized how tired she would be and planned to take a nice long nap once she got home.

"You need to step down, Willa," Lil' Jim said. "You still spendin' your dead husband's money! That's why you ain't worried about your fields getting plowed. But the rest of us didn't marry rich like you, and you're too selfish to marry a man like me and let me show you how to spend

Ray's money. I'm the treasurer of this council, and I think we should vote you out.''

Fox glanced over her shoulder when a hand whispered across her arm. She knew it was Van returning from his errands and just knowing he was there, charged the air even more. He sat across the room from her. Members of the council came to Willow's defense, but she didn't even dignify Jim's comment with a response. He was eventually pulled back into his seat by Sal.

Instead Willow focused her gaze on certain key members.

''We already agreed that the additional money should be spent on the children of this and surrounding counties that need to be immunized. However, a formal vote was never taken. We're going to take care of that today. Vote your conscience, gentlemen. I certainly will.''

The air hung thick from unwashed bodies and bad ventilation, but Fox ignored the physical discomfort and wondered how Willow could face such opposition and from people she'd known all her life. Admiration fell too short of how Fox felt for her mentor. She was humbled.

A refreshing stir of air filled the room when the door opened, followed by the delectable smell of home cooking. The young woman who'd given her a ride to Willow's walked in carrying large platters. She quietly lined a table against the wall with the aluminum pans, then hurried back to the door and guided a cart in with more food. A heavyset man followed her in, but made no move to help unload the cart. Van and he locked gazes and for a moment neither moved. The big man's hard gaze landed on Fox before he left the room. She immediately disliked him.

''All in favor of the immunization program signify by raising your hand,'' Willow said, recapturing Fox's attention.

Van helped the woman with the trays and she smiled at him shyly. Five hands flagged in the air and were counted.

"All those who want the money used to buy two tractors, signify by raising your hand."

Five different hands raised. Willow shook her head sadly. "A tie. As president of this council it's my job to break any and all ties. I vote for the immunization program." The gavel banged on the table, but not before a mighty roar split the room.

Van and the woman slid into the chair beside her and Van squeezed her hand before letting go.

Willow hammered the gavel until silence reigned.

"There is one more issue that needs to be addressed," she said, tiredly. "Last month we voted to have an independent consultant make recommendations on how to improve the way we handle business, how we spend the citizens' money, etc."

"You voted that in when most of us were all down with the flu. That ain't right," an elderly man in a wheelchair complained.

A nasty scar lined the old man's face and that of the younger man who'd entered behind Bert. Father and son. Trouble, she surmised.

"There was a majority to vote at the time, Cleophus," Willow said, looking suddenly tired. "I've found the person who is willing to look at our books and make recommendations on how to best manage the budget. She's doing it for free, so nobody can object to that. Gentlemen, meet Fox Giovanni."

A stone wall of disapproval greeted her as she stood and faced the angry glares. "Jim, please turn over the books so she can get started. This meeting is adjourned."

Wheelchair-bound Cleophus, Sr., rolled up to Willow, his face bloated with hate.

"You're going to regret this. I'll make sure of it."

"No, I'm not, Cleophus. But your whole family should regret all the wrong you've done to the people of this town. How are your crops?" she asked, her voice silky smooth.

His face turned ashen. "You don't scare me with your praying all the time, Willow."

"You should be. Yah!" Willow thrust her empty hand out at the man.

He drew back sharply, spun his chair, around and hurried from the room, muttering about witches.

Van, Fox, and Bert joined Willow, who quietly filled a plate with food.

"What was that all about?" Fox demanded.

"It suits Cleophus, Sr., to think I prayed for his crops to fail, but he knows better."

"What's wrong with his crops?" Noticing how quiet Bert was, Fox fixed a plate and handed it to Van, then prepared one for herself. He smiled his thanks.

"They won't grow," Van said. "Big Cle, Sr., thinks Willow prayed some spell on them."

"I don't have that kind of power, do I?" Willow's jovial personality burst and she began to chuckle.

"How's Walter, Betty, and Doreen, Bert?" Willow asked, her voice hoarse now.

"Everybody's fine, Miss Willow. I'm sorry Big Cle acted so ugly to you. You know how he's been since the accident."

Willow chewed slowly. "How old are you, Bert? Twenty, twenty-one?"

"I'll be twenty-three next year."

"You're not a child anymore, so I'm going to tell you something. Cleophus, Sr., has always been mean. Mean is how he got in that chair in the first place. Don't make excuses for him, and don't take any nonsense off that son of his."

"Excuse me, ladies. I've got to run. Will you be all right for another hour?"

"Take your time." Fox tried to keep the dreamy look off her face. Van kissed Willow's forehead, touched Bert's shoulder, and winked at Fox before leaving. He headed out the door and Fox was dragged back to the conversation at hand.

"I appreciate your advice, Miss Willow. I try to make everybody happy and it gets hard sometimes."

"That's because it can't be done."

"I worry about you sometimes, too," she said to Willow then turned to Fox. "I work with my fiancé and his family at their bar and I hear what men think about Miss willow running the council. Most are supportive—-some are not."

"They just have to get used to her."

"No," Willow said, rising. "They don't need to get used to anything. This is my last term."

Fox stopped chewing the tasty greens that filled her plate. "What are you talking about? You just asked me to help and you're leaving?"

"I'm not leaving right this second, but I can't do this forever, Fox." She came back to the table and took Bert's hand. "This town belongs to you young people. It's time for you all to take control and build a future for your families."

When Willow looked up, Fox felt a peculiar warming start in her feet and move to her chest as if Willow were speaking to her, too.

"What will we do without your leadership, Miss Willow? You're the smartest woman in this town."

"You'll find your way just like I did. Why don't you young ladies enjoy yourselves? I'm going next door to the center. Have Van bring the food over so it won't go to waste, and thanks for your generosity, Bertha. You're a fine young woman, just like my Fox."

Bert clasped Willow's hand and accepted her kiss on the cheek. "Thank you, Miss Willow. Tell the folks at the center I'll be by in a little bit. I think we can manage without Van's help."

"Peace and blessings, darlin's."

Shuffles, not footsteps, carried Willow from the room. The slack way her hair hung beside her cheeks and the definite droop to her shoulders had Fox out of her chair, but Bert stopped her.

"She's just going next door. I bet when I get over there, she'll be napping in Sis Miller's spare bed. Don't worry."

"I can't stand to see her hurt," Fox blurted. "I hated watching the council members mistreat her. She doesn't deserve that."

Bert surprised Fox by taking her by the shoulders and leading her back to the table. "You don't need to get yourself all excited about anything in this town. We're small-time compared to you. You're from New York City," Bert exclaimed. "You've got so much history at your back door and you can't forget those fine brothers from the Knicks."

"True." Fox laughed at Bert's dreamy enthusiasm. "But you all have space down here, a place to breathe and not run into someone. I've enjoyed it since I've been here."

"So," Bert said when Fox let the conversation lag again. "Are you feeling better? The first day you were wiped out."

"I feel fine."

"When you live in the country, you run into lots of older people who take medication for one reason or another. I carried your purse and your medication to your room and recognized it." Bert averted her shy gaze.

Although her limbs were long, she moved with graceful glides even as she ate.

"So you know I had a heart attack," Fox said, crossing her legs. Her silk stockings whispered as she rocked her leg.

Bert nodded and brushed a hand over her short, tightly curled hair. "How are you feeling?"

"Like a fool. I didn't want anyone to know. I'm already a spectacle of sorts."

"You can trust me."

"Why?" Although Bert was nice, Fox was still suspicious. She'd never allowed anyone to be her friend before for fear of the ultimate rejection.

"I'm trying to be your friend, that's why," Bert replied staring at her as if she were an alien.

A burst of laughter shot from Fox's throat. She caught herself smiling and tried to suppress it. "But you don't know me."

"Isn't that how you make friends by getting to know someone? Maybe even sharing a secret? I can't believe a sophisticated woman like you doesn't know that. *Loco,*" she murmured under her breath.

Fox shot back in Spanish, "Did you say I'm crazy?"

Bert answered back and they burst into a fit of giggles.

A floodgate opened and conversation came naturally about Bert's life in Slumber. The topic of conversation shifted to work and Fox gave a brief overview of her job at Fields. She didn't say much, far more interested in Bert's desire to return to college.

"Why did you leave?"

"Initially I couldn't go back because my parents couldn't afford to send me back, but that's not the problem now. It's personal now." Bert retied her long sneaker laces. Fox would never tell her, but she had the longest feet she'd ever seen on a woman. When she stretched her legs, Fox moved, giving her plenty of room.

"My fiancé wants me to stay here and helping to run his family business. He owns a bar/nightclub here in town and a restaurant."

Sadness dragged at her once-smiling face. To be so developed physically, she seemed young emotionally. Her insecurity reached into Fox, reminding her of her younger days.

Inspired by all the talks she and Willow used to have, Fox said, "What do you want to do?"

"I want to go back to school and finish my degree in Spanish and teach eventually, maybe even be a translator. Short term." Her eyes darted, excited. "Long term. I'd like to play professional basketball. I've been offered a basketball scholarship to a North Carolina school. Professional scouts are already wanting to talk to me."

"Congratulations," she said, but didn't feel Bert's excitement. "Why don't you go for it?"

"Cle doesn't want me to."

"Why? You could be set for life financially, and realize your dream."

"He wants me to stay here with him and raise a family." She folded her long fingers, letting them hang over her knees. "Don't get me wrong. I want that, too, but if I played pro ball, I could help my daddy and mom and my little sister Doreen have a better life than they have now." A faraway look entered her dark eyes.

"Yeah," she said trying to hide how upset she really was. Fox decided not to push. "I don't want to burden you with my small town problems."

Fox did something she had only done since her heart attack. She reached across the table and touched Bert's hand. "It's not a burden. I really hope we can be friends. If you want to talk about it, I don't mind."

Bert squeezed her hand supportively. "I had a good feeling about you when I saw you. I hope we can be friends, too. I guess I need to talk to my parents. They're a part of this decision, too."

"Have you discussed any of this with them?"

"Oh, yes. They're torn. They want me to go to college, but they'll miss me. I keep telling them the school is only six hours away. They can make a day trip on Saturday."

"So are you going to go for it?"

Her gaze dropped and she twirled the salt shaker between her hands. "I want to so bad. I told Cle."

Fox laid her sandwich down and pushed the plate to the edge of the table. "How did he take it?"

"He's furious. He says I don't want to be with him, and I'm only thinking of myself. He didn't used to act this way. But two years ago he was banned from professional wrestling and slowly he changed. Sometimes that man just isn't right in his mind."

"What are you going to do?"

"He gave me an ultimatum. Fox, I don't want to be alone."

Fox looked at her new friend. Long fingers spun the salt shaker and caught it. Spun it again, and caught it.

"Bert?" She looked up. "Decide if you can live with yourself if you don't follow your dreams. If you can, then you've made the right decision."

Nodding, Bert looked away. "Thanks. I'll think about what you said."

Rising, Bert gathered their plates, then began to drape the pans of food with foil.

Never having faced a problem like this, Fox was unsure what to say. She quietly worked alongside the woman until all the trays had been placed back on the cart.

"Oh. We got gravy on your skirt. Hold on, I know something that will get that out right away."

"Thanks," Fox said as the tall woman hurried away. Composed when she returned, a cloth draped Bert's hand and she used it to blot at the hem.

"I can do it," Fox said when she kneeled down for a better angle on the stain.

"Nah, I'm the expert. Hold on a sec."

"I feel silly with you kneeling down taking care of this old skirt. It really doesn't matter."

Bert blotted repeatedly for several seconds. "Got it," she said, displaying the hem.

Fox looked down at the damp spot her skirt, then up at her new friend. "So you did. *Gracias.*"

"*De Nada.*"

The door slammed behind them, and they turned.

"What the hell you doin'? Get up, Bert! You ain't got to wait on her."

"Cle, I'm not waiting on her. I was getting a stain out. Fox this is my fiancé, Cleophus Woods."

He looked Fox up and down and dismissed her. "It's time to go."

"I'm almost ready. Can you help take this food next door?"

He turned back waving his hand, brushing her off. "What do I look like? I don't have time to cater to people. You wanted to bring this food over there, now you deal with it. I need you back at the club at four." He glanced at Fox and said, "Don't be late." The door banged the wall after he barreled through it.

Fox didn't back down from his glare, having stood up to many men in her time. Cleophus was a big bully, and a dangerous one. "He must be a barrel of laughs."

"Cle's different," Bert said, as she pushed the cart out the door. They stood in the corridor of the town hall building. "I'm sorry he and Van got into it the other night at the bar. I was sure blood would be shed."

Fox blocked the cart. "What happened?"

"Van came looking for Cle's cousin, Bootsy. I'm glad Royce told me to come up from the kitchen or else things could have gotten ugly. Cle's taken to carrying a .45 on him."

A chill raced down Fox's spine. "Why is Van looking for Bootsy?"

Bert held open the door with her foot and didn't answer right away. "It has something to do with some missing money from Miss Willow. Everybody in town is talking about it. Especially since Bootsy had some money and nobody has seen him since early in the week."

"Van thinks he stole the money from Willow?" It was just money! Why couldn't Van have just taken the money she'd offered to him? Why was he so adamant to do things his way? The idea of him getting shot scared her to death.

Bert pulled the cart down the sidewalk until they stood outside the senior's center and rang the bell. "Yeah. Bootsy worked on Miss Willow's house several months ago. Next thing I knew Van was back at the house and Cle and Bootsy were pissed because Van accused them of cheating the building suppliers. Things haven't been right since. Cle's businesses are losing money everyday and Big Cle's crops have been plagued with bugs. They blame Willow and Van for everything that's happening."

"That's crazy."

"I know, but you can't tell them anything. Until things turn around, Van should watch his back."

The door to the center opened and several men poured out, greeted her and Bert and unloaded the cart. They disappeared back inside, happy.

Fox touched Bert's arm. "Would Van have hurt Bootsy had he found him?"

A faraway look glazed her eyes. "Long time ago, folks learned not to mess with those Compton's. When they were younger they were tough, and they solved problem with their fists. They were good boys though, and Miss Zenobia and Miss Willow worked hard to raise them right. They're all real fine people now and Van should be proud being the oldest. But a reputation can live a long life down here.

"Let's just say I'm glad Van didn't find him. I don't know what would have happened. Well, I've got to go home and talk to my parents."

Shifting from foot to foot, she shoved her hands in the pockets of the short billowy skirt she wore. "After all I said today, you might not want to be bothered, but maybe we could have lunch sometime."

A sense of elation filled Fox. She squeezed Bert's hand. "I'm glad you were honest with me. And yes, I would love to have lunch with you. How about early next week?"

"All right," Bert said, smiling. "There's a town council meeting next Tuesday. How about lunch, then shopping before the meeting."

"Sounds good," Fox said, Bert's grin contagious.

"Do you want me to wait with you?"

"No." She looked up and down the street and didn't see his truck, but spotted the bank. "He'll be along soon.

I need to take care of some business before he gets here anyway. Thanks for everything. Bye.''

Bert waved and jumped into the big Chevy with the sagging ceiling.

Fox watched her go, and took her time soaking up the warm sun as she walked to the bank. Once inside, she transferred eight thousand dollars into Willow's account, and felt immensely better.

Outside in the heat, she spotted an ice cream store and ladies boutique, stopped in both and made quick purchases. Under a shade tree outside the ice cream store, she had just settled on a bench when she spotted Van walking. He had this casual step that made her heart leap and her mouth dry. He slid beside her.

"Silk and cream? Not a great combination," he said, pointing to the drips of ice cream that dotted her shirt.

"The dry cleaner can get it out."

He'd been gone only an hour but she'd missed seeing him, hearing him, and most recently, tasting him.

How she needed him to want her, but as direct as she was at work, she couldn't tell Van how she really felt. Years without stating her feelings had stunted her growth, but she understood the feelings she carried deep inside.

She licked ice cream that ran down her hand. "This might not have been a good idea." She covered the melting cone with her mouth and sucked. It shimmied down her throat and she swallowed repeatedly, taking it all down.

"Watching you eat ice cream is like watching a sin being committed," he said gruffly. Sliding close, he took her hand and caressed the cream from her palm with his handkerchief. His gaze never left hers as he dabbed the sticky substance from between her fingers and off her wrist.

"We're in public," she whispered.

"What am I doing?" he asked, just as low, as if he weren't making love to her hand. "I'm ready to go back to Willow's." Filled with invitation and promises, his husky voice made tingles travel up her legs and throb in her center.

"What about Willow?"

The street surrounding them hummed with pedestrian traffic as Fox tried to reacquaint herself with reality. Mothers pushed strollers into the ice cream store for a bit of relief from the heat.

Fox licked her lips, her body burning.

"Is she still at the center?" He glanced around the street, but she liked the sensual feeling she got when his gaze landed back on her. Her nipples pressed painfully against her silky brassiere.

"Yes."

"I might have to come back for her if she's not ready. You need to get home so you can rest."

"Van, I feel fine."

"Doctor's orders. Besides, I thought we had plans for tonight?"

"I didn't forget," she said breathless.

"Just checking."

They walked back to the center in a silence filled with sneaky glances and brushes of his arm against hers. It didn't matter if it was his gaze that touched her, or his hand guiding her across the street. Being close to Van made her feel whole. Fanning herself, she swept her hair off her neck.

"Doesn't it ever rain down here?"

He chuckled. "City folk are always complaining about the weather. It's too hot or too cold. Aren't ya'll ever happy?"

"Of course, we're happy but we're not used to such heat. I need a cold shower," she murmured.

"We can remedy that tonight."

She tried not to look into his eyes, lest he see it wasn't just heat that had gotten her overworked.

His black truck was parked in front of the center waiting to deliver her home. Home, she thought. *Has a nice ring.*

"Van!" They both turned to see Royce heading toward them, a limp in his fast step.

"What's the problem Royce?"

Fox tried to hear what the two men were whispering, but was held back by Van's strong arm.

"What is it?" she demanded.

Royce got one look at her before his eyes darted around and he limped away.

Van held her shoulders, gripping her tight. "I need to go check on something and I'll be home later. Can you drive back to the farm with Willow?"

"Yes," she grasped his hand. "Check on what?"

"Men's business. Now let me go." He shook her, but she didn't release him. "I've got to go get Willow."

"I'm not letting you go until you tell me the truth. Bert told me the entire story. Are you going after Bootsy?"

"No."

"Don't lie to me," she pleaded.

"Woman!" Van yanked her close and dropped his mouth on hers. His lips bruised hers then gentled, setting off sparklers inside her head and chest. Her legs melted and she felt her body sag against his. He'd backed her up against the truck and clasped her face between his hands. Their foreheads touched.

"I'm not lying to you. I'm going to talk to somebody who might know where he is. No fighting, I promise." His smoldering gaze met hers. "Take Willow home and I'll see you later."

"How will you get home?"

"Don't worry about me. You get some rest."

"I want to go with you," she pressed, trying not to sound bossy, but feeling bossy nonetheless.

"Where I'm going is no place for a lady."

"You're saying that just to get rid of me." He chuckled at her bravado, looking down at her silk and lace. "And don't let the clothes fool you," she snapped. "It's just window dressing."

"It's who you are, sweetheart. Please go home and rest. I thought we had plans for tonight?"

"I don't appreciate this code of the South where men get to have all the fun and women get to rest. Let me come with you, Van. Don't pacify me."

"I'm not," he said, suddenly serious. "I need to take care of some business and you can't come."

He smoothed his fingers down her cheek, but she moved away from his touch and leaned against the truck.

Bert's prediction of trouble between Van and Cleophus's cousin filled her with dread. She wished she could wield power like she did at work and make Van listen to her. But Van wasn't an employee who had to follow her orders. He followed orders she couldn't control, rules she didn't make.

"Bert told me Cleophus carries a gun. Don't mess with him, Van."

His eyes clouded as he lifted her hand. His palm engulfed hers, making it appear small and powerless.

"If anybody messes with my family, they have to deal with me." He squeezed her hand gently. "Bootsy needs to be taught a lesson and if he comes after me, he'll be dealt with."

The way he talked scared her. "You can't fight a bullet."

"No, but I can beat the man. It's about honor and family, Fox. Bootsy and Cleophus know they messed with the wrong people when they stole from my aunt. Eventually they'll pay. That's the way it is." He dropped her hand. "Do you want to come with me to get Willow?"

"No, I'll wait here."

Turning, he headed into the center.

Worry ate at her until her breathing escalated. Fox propped her hands against the truck, fighting for calm. Squeezing her eyes shut, she examined her life. For years she'd protected herself from real risks and real emotions.

She'd worked for the same company since graduating college, and kept herself isolated from issues that didn't concern the bottom line in business.

Only that reality no longer existed. She no longer cared

about the fiscal new year, or whether she'd make president before she was thirty-five.

Now she cared about people who would die for each other. Their unfathomable commitment to each other made tears sting her eyes. She was a businesswoman who had been relied on to identify and solve a multitude of problems.

How come she couldn't make one man see that his life was more valuable than honor or family?

Van and Willow emerged from the building and Fox quickly wiped away her tears of worry.

"Sure you can drive this thing?" he asked softly.

"We'll manage. Come on, Willow. Let's go home."

"It's hotter that a Baboon's behind," Willow exclaimed, fanning herself, inadvertently breaking the tension.

Van swept his aunt into the high seat and came back around to the driver's door.

Fox lifted her skirt and allowed him to help her into the truck. He tugged at the seat belt and she snapped it into place.

"Be careful."

"I can take care of us," she said, looking down at him. "You go take care of your men stuff."

"Come on. Chil', I need some air. Van, I trust you'll come home in one piece."

He stared into Fox's eyes. "Yes, ma'am."

Fox pressed her lips together and didn't say a word. She hated starting his truck and driving off without him, but she did.

CHAPTER SIXTEEN

The rain finally came. Driving sheets of water slashed the earth until the packed dirt surrendered and allowed the liquid access. Van stepped lightly, his foot sinking ankle deep in mud, but he didn't care. He was almost home.

Tomorrow everything would be beautiful and green, and then the real heat would come.

Though it was late, he was glad he'd had Royce drop him at the top of the lane instead of driving him to the front door. Every once in awhile, he liked making the one-mile trek and watching the magnificent house grow up from the ground until its grandeur overwhelmed him.

Willow's place was his past and his future, and no matter where he was in the world, the farm would always be home.

Slinging water from his eyes, he let guilt crawl over him for not making it easier on Fox when she first arrived, but now he couldn't imagine the house without her.

Yet she didn't fit the profile of the woman he'd imagined her to be.

Fox wasn't from the country. She couldn't cook worth a damn, and she didn't know squat about tending animals, but she worked hard to please Willow and him, too, he realized. And she loved that silly little dog.

The house loomed ahead, the kitchen light burning a muted yellow. Fox's room was dark and uninviting, but that wouldn't deter him. Only she could tell him no.

He entered the cabin, stripped at the door and headed to the shower. After the shower, he stepped into some shorts when he heard the front door close and the television flip on.

Ignoring the buttons on the shirt he'd barely pulled on, he wandered into the living room where Fox stood in the center of the floor, holding the remote control.

"You're in one piece." She lined the controller up with the corner of the table and took slow steps toward him. He waited until they faced each other. Her bare toes touched his, and he looked down at the bright red polish that decorated the nails. A thread of his control snapped, and she drew his hand up and stroked her cheek with it.

"I wouldn't have it any other way."

Her seductress eyes closed, then she opened them, smiling.

"Me either." She raised on her toes.

He'd dreamed of taking her in his arms so many nights and fulfilling his fantasy of making love to her, but had kept pushing the thoughts away. The time hadn't been right.

Tonight the time was never better.

Her parted lips slid along his and opened to his probing tongue. Their tongues met, danced in slow rhythmic circles before she pressed forward and he claimed her mouth. Her hands burned his cool skin as they climbed his bare chest and captured his face.

He grabbed her waist, bent her backward deepening the kiss, and she answered with equal passion, yielding as his mouth ravished hers. The simple shirt she wore was too much, and he drew it up and off her beautiful brown skin, bringing her body back to meet his.

With her fingers, she pushed his shirt until it fell from his shoulders, and he plucked the center clasp of her bra and watched it pop. Freed from the confines of the black bra, her breasts swung free and he lifted her in his arms and propped her up on the high couch back. He claimed her nipple between his lips, devouring her flesh, inhaling her until he thought he'd explode if he didn't claim her.

Ragged breathing filled his ears as he moved from one breast to the other, but he didn't stop sliding his tongue and mouth over the sensitive tips until she cried out his name on a quiver of orgasmic ecstasy.

The gold ring she wore on her thumb caught in the hair on his chest and he growled from the pleasure-pain, but he almost lost control of his legs when she dipped her head and soothed his nipple with tickling licks.

Kisses rained on his chest and neck and he glanced once at her hooded eyes and caught his breath when she cupped him between his legs and stroked.

Van pulled her down from the couch and lifted her skirt, her panties no match for his seeking hands. She worked to free him from the confines of his jeans and briefs, but he got there first and sighed into her mouth when she folded her palm around him.

Bracing her against the sofa, he plunged and heard her long inhale and then, *"Yes."*

Permission granted, he drove deeper and deeper into the tight canyon, his manhood and his mind engulfed within Fox. Her legs circled his back and with each thrust her nipples drew twin lines of desire up and down his chest. Her nails dug into his shoulders, as all of her tightened around him in silky grasps and breathless gasps.

The spiral of orgasm started at the bottom of his feet, weakening his calves and he grabbed her butt tight, knowing he was going to lose control. Wrapping his arms around her, he pushed faster and let the sensation shatter him.

Recovery came slowly for Van. He still gripped Fox in his arms, but in the midst of their powerful climax, had wedged her against the back of the sofa.

Hair covered her face, and her small hands still grasped his shoulders.

Van shifted her weight, holding her more firmly against him and away from the back of the rough sofa. Regret filled him at how earnestly he'd pushed into her.

"Fox, talk to me, are you all right?"

When she didn't answer, he knew that was a definite bad sign.

"Do you feel okay, sweetheart?" he asked, but she kept herself turned away from him. Finally her shoulders slid up slowly.

"Woman, if you're playing games, I'll . . . I'll . . ."

"I need to lie down," she whispered against his neck.

Van slipped from her. "It's your heart, isn't it? Do you need your medicine? I wasn't thinking." Stumbling around the living room, his pants still bunched around his ankles, he headed in aimless circles. "I didn't even think about your heart. Oh hell. Oh hell. Do you need an ambulance?"

"I want to lie down, Van," she repeated, folding her arms around his neck. "In your bed."

"You do." He stopped abruptly. "Your heart is fine, isn't it?"

"My heart feels great. How's yours?"

"Like it wants to jump out of my chest. You scared me. Look at me," he coaxed.

She slid up and brushed her hair back. The tousled mass of jet strands framed her radiant face and for the first time since she arrived, he smiled. "You feel good?"

"I feel fabulous."

"Let's go lie down."

"I'm glad you thought of it," she said on a breathy sigh. He carried her to his room and lay her on his bed before stripping the remainder of his clothes.

"Van," she exhaled raggedly when he turned her on her stomach, unzipped her skirt, tugged the khaki material off and tossed it to the floor.

"What is it, sweetheart?"

His hands slowly moved up the center of her bottom to her back. He softened the spot where her back and butt met, and pressed his lips into her shoulder blade.

"Do you have any ice cream?"

Slowly he moved down her back, his hands claiming her perfectly round behind again. He hardened just from listening to her voice and feeling her warm skin.

"Are you hungry?"

Her muscles quivered at his touch. "I just had a taste for it, among other things," she whispered.

"Tell me what you want and I'll get it for you."

She pushed back on her knees, while tugging his hands until he collapsed on top of her. Instinctively, he found her secret garden and was welcomed.

The soft gasps from her lips, and the tiny convulsions that lured him into her downiness nearly broke his control, but he pushed until involuntary quivers made her cry out. Then he let go and poured himself into her.

Van studied Fox as she polished off a bowl of chocolate ice cream. She'd made his ratty blue robe look sexy as she curled her feet beneath her and licked her lips. He lay at the end of his bed, tired and pleased.

"Where did you go this afternoon?" she asked, examining her hair through the reflection on the shiny silver spoon. It rattled against the bowl when she set both on the bedside table.

He weighed telling her the truth, knowing her reaction would be strongly opposing. Tears had shimmered in her eyes when he'd come out of the center with Willow, but he never intended to make her cry. She had looked so sophisticated in her soft peach silk, almost too perfect to touch, but she'd welcomed him with open arms. He wouldn't hide the truth from her. He could count that as the first wrong move he'd made in his marriage.

"I heard Bootsy was in an illegal gambling joint two counties over, but when I got there he'd already left."

She shook her head, strands of her hair sticking to her lips. She pulled them away. "It's foolish to fight over money. What would Willow do if her beloved nephew got killed in her honor?"

He yanked on her toes wanting to shake her somber mood. They'd just made fantastic love. Why was she ruining it with talk of death?

"Willow would throw me a party, darlin'." When she didn't laugh he said, "Come here, Fox. Sit beside me." He covered his naked lower half and sat up. She stood, as he knew she would, pulled the robe together and sat primly beside him.

Her fingers flitted at the gold cross and necklace circling her throat, then dropped to her lap. "What is it?" she asked, her eyes on her tightly fisted hands.

"I don't want you to be upset with me, but you've got to understand how things are done down here."

Crossing her legs, the velour slipped from her thigh. Her foot patted the floor and he wished he could turn back the hands of time and make her smile again. She breathed deeply and exhaled.

"How things are done doesn't make it right, Van." Folding her fingers around her knee, she spoke softly. "When I was about eight I had a friend, and we were inseparable. We shared a bedroom, walked to school every day, sat beside each other in class, and were together so much, people actually thought we were sisters. Then one day she didn't walk home."

Her shivers broke his heart, and he gathered the blanket

around her shoulders and drew her to him. "What happened to your friend, sweetheart?"

"The foster parents we lived with were very tight lipped, so I didn't find out until a couple days later that she'd been adopted. Nobody bothered to care that I might miss her or that she might miss me. That's just how things were done."

Fox held herself stiffly, but Van didn't break his gentle hold of her. She wasn't alone anymore, he wanted to tell her, but held back. Pain radiated from her in waves as her voice, void of emotion petered off. Since she'd arrived, he'd been curious about her life, her upbringing. But this pain he hadn't anticipated. She struck him as a lone tree on an island and he couldn't imagine anything so sad.

The week she'd spent in her room was the most tortuous time of his life. He'd wanted to talk to her, tell her someone cared for her, but fear kept the feelings trapped inside.

"What was your friend's name?" he asked, sliding her hair behind her ear.

"It was Shelly." She laughed short and harsh. "I was that unimportant."

Her brows wrinkled, and a tear streaked down past her nose, wetting her lips.

"That was so long ago."

"I remember it like it was yesterday," she said, her voice dry and tight. "I went to live with Willow several years after that. By then I'd decided being angry suited me. People left me alone."

"I bet Willow wasn't having any of that. She could coax a smile from a dead man."

She was controlled, too much so. "Willow just let me be. If I wanted to talk she listened. If I was quiet for days, she never said a word. She was my best friend."

Leaning against the foot board, he drew her close to his chest. The robe plumped her up, but beneath she was frail and small. "Why are you telling me this, Fox?"

She leaned up and slowly raised her head until their

gazes met. "Because I don't know how many more special people I can afford to lose. Cleophus and his father are dangerous men."

"You're talking like something bad is going to happen and it's not."

Her fists pressed against his chest. "Why do you act as if you're invincible? You're just a man. You can't fight the battles of the world."

"You don't understand, Fox."

"Because I never had a real family?"

"That's not what I'm saying," he said, holding her when she tried to escape. "I'm saying families stick together. Good, bad, or indifferent. They protect one another from people who try to break them down. A feud has been brewing between the Compton's and the Woods's for a long time. It's high time it was put to rest."

"What you're saying is so ridiculous. Van, you're a grown man. You're too old for a street brawl."

"I'm not old," he said, raising her chin with his finger and tasting her lips. "And you're right, but it's not up to me. If Bootsy and Cleophus do what's right, nothing will change."

"Just don't go back to his bar. Promise," she stressed, her face inches from his.

"Fox," he said unable to resist her serious gaze. She was reaching out to him and he felt himself respond. "Woman, quit being so bossy."

"It's what I do best," she said. "Promise."

"I'll take it under advisement." At her resistance, he said, "Serious advisement." Snagging her bottom lip between his, he sucked until her warm mouth became pliant and soft in a luxurious kiss. "You do this much better." Working the knot in the robe belt loose, he pulled her on top of him.

"What?"

He kissed her deeply and shook in his urgency for her. "Make me want you," he said, when she grabbed hold of the footboard and leaned closer to his mouth. A low, sexy chuckle crawled up her chest. Van dipped his head intent on pleasing her. He swept the robe from her back and filled his mouth with her soft breast.

He claimed her slowly, loving the texture of her skin as it slid beneath his tongue and how sexy her sigh sounded in his ear.

She pleased him by being easy to please and, he worked harder, wanting her to have all the pleasure he could give.

When she finally slept, she didn't crowd the corner of the mattress, but wrapped herself in a ball in the center of the bed and snored in satiated huffs.

He couldn't help but smile, then pulled her into his arms and allowed sleep to claim him.

CHAPTER
SEVENTEEN

The rooftop outside Van's window faced away from the main house and allowed Fox the solitude she desired without being inside.

How long had it been since she'd been so thoroughly satisfied? Too long, she thought, lifting her face to the dawn morning and accepting the breeze that stirred her skin. Too long.

Van was a fantastic lover, but he was so much more than someone to roll in the bed with. Thoughts of a future with him assailed her, and she allowed the fantasy to grow and include children, and a nice house somewhere on a wide open tract of land.

Visions of him in a white shirt and tie made her frown. Van wasn't a corporate man. He worked outside, preferably in a paint-splattered T-shirt, jeans, and work boots. He worked in the heat, had calluses on his hands, and didn't ever stop to wipe at sweat unless it dripped into his eyes. Just one of the hazards of the job, he'd told her once.

She'd had the most difficult time staying away from her

window when he'd pull off his shirt to work, his chest bare
to the unrelenting sun.

Fox closed her eyes and inhaled the fresh morning air
as a wave of old insecurities drifted through her.

What if Van didn't share her loving feelings?

Reaching into the robe pocket, she rooted around for
a cigarette and didn't find any. A smile parted her lips.
She'd quit smoking, she recalled, nearly a lifetime ago.

A lifetime she had to return to in just twenty-one days.

How could she leave behind her new friend, Bert, her
first and only pet, the woman who'd been like a mother
to her, and most of all, the man she loved?

Behind her, she could hear him stir in bed and Fox
turned, watching him through the open window as he
slept. Her heartbeat sped up, galloping at the decisions
she had to make and the uncertainty of her future.

Taking one last look at the pale brown dirt that stretched
as far as the eye could see, she wondered if she could
leave such serenity for the fast pace of New York and an
occasional twig that passed as a tree?

Crawling through the window, she curled next to Van
and decided tomorrow would bring answers to her questions.

Pounding rain against the roof awoke Van who was surprised and confused to find himself in his own room
instead of sitting in the rocking chair beside Fox's bed
with Andrew on his lap. He looked down at the woman
that had cuddled next to him.

Fox did everything gracefully, including sleep.

Her long legs draped his and her hand lingered possessively on his thigh. Her shoulder-length hair had grown
since she'd arrived and was splayed on his pillow, and her
sometimes troubled eyes were closed in peaceful sleep.

He couldn't resist touching her arm, drawing his finger
down her rib cage and watching her nipple blossom. His

body stirred at the unspoken invitation. Knowing if he didn't get up, he'd take her again, Van extricated himself from her body and walked naked to the bathroom.

A shower restored him and he headed to the kitchen, started a pot of coffee and waited impatiently for it to finish brewing. He carried a steaming cup to the living room and sat.

Fox was going to leave in a few weeks.

There, he thought, he had faced what had been nagging at the back of his mind for a week. She was going to go home to New York.

Hot liquid slipped down his throat, but the taste wasn't stronger than his feelings. How had he allowed himself to fall in love with a woman who he'd known all along was going to leave him?

Shaking his head at the impending hurt he'd have to face, Van turned around instinctively.

Dressed, Fox walked toward him and picked up the shoes she'd left at the door last night.

"I thought you were gone," she said.

"Can't do much today on Willow's roof until the rain passes. Coffee?"

"Uh, no," she said, taking a few steps toward the door. "I'd better get back and walk Andrew. No telling what he's done to my room."

"I'll come with you," he said, rising.

"I don't need you to come with me."

"Then what do you need, Fox?"

She dropped her shoes, wringing her hands. "I don't want to go walk Andrew in the rain, and I don't want to leave here right now. I don't want to feel insecure and squishy about being with you, and I don't want to think about tomorrow until it gets here."

"Squishy?" Van gathered her in his arms, putting his own anxieties aside, and tugged on her ear lobe with his lips. She never had to leave as far as he was concerned.

"A sophisticated woman, fluent in four languages, and you say squishy?"

"Six," she said, resting her head against his chest and hugging him to her. "Squishy is how I feel." Her voice took on a soft quality he'd never heard. "Van, I don't want you to let me walk out that door so I can spend the rest of the day in my room hiding, thinking you think what happened wasn't supposed to."

His mouth moved down her neck as he drove her shirt up with his hands. It landed with a soft plop on the floor, followed quickly by her skirt. "Don't ever think that. And you can't avoid me. I'll find you wherever you go."

He urged her leg up over his thigh as their tongues tangled. Her breasts puckered against his and he ran his hands over her smooth skin, before sweeping her into his arms.

"Today is a good day to sleep in," she sighed, when he carried her up the stairs and laid her on the bed.

Van covered her body with his. "It certainly is."

Staring at the budget she'd prepared for the town council and the separate list of recommendations for investments made her eyes blurry. Fox closed them tight and rested her head in her hands, berating herself for working so hard. When had one hour of work turned into two days?

A computer would have made the proposal easier to complete, but the lack of automation was indicative of a bigger problem. The people might not be receptive to her recommendations.

Opening her eyes, she laid the handwritten forms on the table and stretched. Andrew snored lightly as he slept in his box, despite the hammering and sawing that shook the air.

She snapped her fingers and was rewarded with a cheerful smile as he woke up and waddled over. She scooped him up, then settled on the floor against the bed.

"Hey, boy. How are you today?" His fur was soft and warm and welcoming.

Andrew barked, and Fox cuddled him close, closing her eyes. Below her she could hear Van's voice issuing orders to the men he'd hired to paint in four of the remaining rooms on the lower level.

Willow had gone to the prison for the day and had stated at breakfast she would stay in town with Sis Miller tonight.

The last few days with Van had been heavenly and being alone with him tonight would signal the culmination of a great week.

Around Willow they conducted themselves like responsible adults, but at night they became shameless lovers. Fox liked to hear Van talk, and loved even more to hear him laugh.

Through him she learned simple things, like which way was north from looking at the sky, and how to tell poison ivy from poison oak.

He'd walked her all over the farm, teaching her about plants she'd never remember and animals he couldn't convince her to touch.

Smiling, she listened as a car headed toward the house, but didn't move. It wasn't for her anyway.

Fox continued to scratch Andrew's chest when a knock sounded on her door.

"Yes?"

"You decent?"

"Come in," she said, and drew her legs beneath her.

Van came into her room, looked down at her position on the floor and gave her a quizzical stare. But he didn't ask if she was okay, and Fox was glad.

"Hello," she said from her comfortable position. "How's it going downstairs?"

"Busy." He sat down beside her and accepted Andrew, who leaped into his lap. Van's five o'clock shadow had begun to darken and she couldn't stop thinking how sexy it would be to give him a shave. "The stairs are done and tomorrow I have to put finish on them. You might want to use the back stairs for a couple of days.''

She nodded. ''Why are you up here? You never come up here if someone is in the house.''

''The Whites are here,'' he said, not looking at her. ''They're back from vacation and came to pick up the dog.''

Her breath whooshed out, and Fox looked at Andrew and then at Van. Her throat closed up and she blinked, pulling her lips in. ''I see. I guess they want him right now.''

''Yeah.''

She slowly got to her feet and picked up the chew toy and roll of socks he liked to play with. ''I'd better get his things together.''

Van rose, Andrew still in his arms. ''Look, are you sure you want to do this?''

''It's not my choice. Andrew was never mine.'' She gathered his other things and walked to the door, avoiding looking at her puppy or Van. ''Let's not keep them waiting.''

Taking the back stairs where the air was thick and hot made her head light, but Fox ignored her discomfort and stepped into the kitchen.

An older couple stood on the porch their backs to her. The man wore blue overalls and the woman a flower print dress. Neither seemed to have much life in them, but Fox kept putting one foot in front of the other until she had reached the screened door.

''Hello,'' she said to attract their attention. The couple turned and gave her the once over.

''Hey,'' they replied in greeting. ''That the dog?''

Van stepped out on the porch, holding a squirming Andrew in his arms.

''His name is Andrew,'' Fox said.

The woman looked at her. ''What kind of name is that for a dog? We plan to call him Dan.'' She took Andrew from Van's arms and began to walk down the stairs, while the man took the box and other items from Fox's limp hands.

"Thanks, Compton. Bye, Miss." He tipped his hat and stomped down the stairs. He put Andrew in the bed of the pickup along with the box and drove away.

She squinted, watching the raggedy sky blue truck disappear. Fox turned and walked right into Van's chest. She backed away from him.

"Sweetheart, are you going to be all right?"

"At least I got to say goodbye."

She suddenly couldn't stop the fountain of tears that gushed beneath the surface. She managed to get through the screen door and to the back stairs when Van caught up with her. He tipped her face up and looked into her eyes.

Fox tried to smile, but two tears slid down her cheeks.

"I was brave this time," she whispered.

"Oh, sweetheart," he said, and gathered her to him. Fox cried until the lump in her throat was small enough to swallow.

"They better take good care of my dog." She wiped at her tears, her chest still tight with loss.

"Or what?" Van thumbed tears from her cheeks and planted small kisses along her face.

Fox hiccuped, controlling herself. "I'll call somebody at the IRS and have them audited." He laughed, and she had to laugh, it eased the pain some. "He'll be fine." They climbed the stairs slowly. Fox walked into her room and sat on the side of her bed.

"Who's going to play with me now?"

"You want to play?" Van went for his belt and when her eyes widened, he winked. "Is that an offer?"

"There are people painting in the room below us," she hissed, smiling despite herself, crawling back on the bed.

"I know. They won't mind if the chandelier starts swinging." He tugged at her hands, pulling her to her feet and cupping her breasts. "Come on," he urged seductively.

"Van. They'll hear," she said, breathless from his touch. He could get her hot just looking at her.

Fox wrapped her arms around his neck and kissed him. "You're doing a good job of distracting me, but I don't want to distract you from your work."

He ran his callused hands beneath her top and over her satin bra and she shuddered.

"You think making love to you isn't work? Hah," he said, sucking on her neck.

"I'm not work, I'm fun," she said, giving in, letting herself feel the salty pain of loss and sugary sweetness of pleasure.

Fox closed her eyes and reached for the pleasure Van's hands gave her. He stripped the belt, denim shorts, and panties from her legs and through her silk blouse cupped her breast with his mouth.

"Ah," she whispered, arching when his hands sought out her heat. "They'll know, and I'll be so embarrassed."

"Then don't make a lot of noise like you usually do," he said, sliding his mouth between her legs.

"Van!" she cried into the pillow, keeping it there until she exploded into sweet completeness.

"That was terrible and unfair." When the web of desire cleared, Fox tried to regain her composure.

"I'd better keep practicing," he said, and grabbed her to him. "Let's do it again."

She swatted at him. Gathering her clothes, she held her blouse in front of herself with both hands. "You are turning me into a tramp."

"Never," he said. He rose slowly, evidence of his unspent desire pressing at the front of his jeans.

"Where are you going like that?"

"Back to work. I'll work faster so I can get back to you tonight."

The endearment pressed at the back of her throat and

she wanted to say it, but stopped herself. She had never told another living soul she loved them.

He walked to the door and she wished he'd go through. She *needed* to be alone. "I was thinking you might want to go to town later."

Fox drew on her robe and cinched the waist. "Tonight?"

"Yeah. Interested?"

"Are you going to the place ladies can't go?"

"A woman like you is too good for places like that. Besides, I don't go there anymore. Do you want to go or not?"

"Yes, I want to go."

"I'll get you back in time to get a good night's rest."

"You're so thoughtful." She'd used the same sweet voice more and more with him.

"Bye, sweetheart."

She waved until the door closed. Walking barefoot across the room, she dropped onto her chair and snapped her fingers, then remembered with a jolt Andrew wasn't there.

The room grew too big and she rose and straightened the line of shoes Andrew always managed to scatter, and picked up the ball she'd bought for him when she was in town.

A premonition hit her, pulling her mouth down into a somber line. Andrew's leaving was a clear sign her life was about to unravel, yet again.

Fox laid the ball on the table, gathered her towel and fragrant soap, and headed for the tub. Her days were numbered in this town. She knew it as well as she knew her name.

CHAPTER EIGHTEEN

Black pants hugged Fox's thighs and legs like a second skin, and the gray top she wore screamed money. She looked hotter than he'd ever seen her, and Van wished they were alone so he could show her how much he loved her.

Another man walked into the hall, gave a low whistle at the view, saw him and cut if off. Fox was looking good to just about everybody.

Van circled the pool table again, blocking her from curious onlookers who had gathered to watch the game.

She stretched across the table, braced the stick and sank a ball neatly in the center pocket. "I'm about to beat you," she said, as she chalked her cue.

"You scratched."

"You're a poor sport." A smile teased her lips as she glanced at him with serious, yet bright eyes. Her competitive spirit vibrated around them and he instinctively knew she would be a tough opponent at work. Soft and meek were not words he'd use to describe Fox. He'd seen her tough, then silky, hot as coals, and cool as a diamond. She pleased him, immensely, and that scared him.

She didn't acknowledge the men who had gathered around their table to gape at her, but locked her gaze on the pool ball. Patting the pocket with her stick, she neatly sank the eight ball.

"Pay up, you owe me a diet soda."

"You scratched," Van said, already digging for his money. Arial, the waitress, came and took his money with a smile. She lowered Fox's already prepared soda to the round table behind them and scooted away.

"You're a poor loser." Fox took a sip of her drink and glanced around the room over the top of her glass. He caught a grimace on her face, and followed her gaze. Two men he barely recognized were arguing over a basketball game, growing louder with each basket scored.

He could see where the verbal disagreement was heading. He hated second guessing himself, but Van wondered again how Fox had talked him into billiards instead of dinner and a movie.

A pang of discomfort settled around him. Barney's pool hall was in a renovated warehouse in an older part of town. It wasn't meant for shiny gray blouses and skintight black pants. It was a place for men to hang out, drink, and tell lies about false conquests. He suddenly lost his taste for beer and loud music and set down the bottle.

"You want to shoot again?" she asked.

"No, let's go."

"Van, are you being a sore loser?"

"He's a loser, all right." Cleophus walked down the stairs and stood by their table, blocking the game.

Men gathered in clusters already wagering on the outcome of the inevitable fight. Van wished Fox wasn't so close to Cleophus. The man had an angry glint in his eye only hours of steady drinking could cause.

"What do you want, Cleophus?" Van asked.

"I came to tell your girlfriend to mind her business.

She's been running her damn mouth to Bert, and I'm here to tell her to shut the hell up."

"Watch your mouth—" Van started toward Cleophus, but was edged out by Fox.

"Why are you scared of a woman like me? You wouldn't have anything to worry about if you got your act together."

Hoots filled the room. Cleophus's eyes reddened, his gaze never leaving Fox's face. "Compton, your girlfriend has a big mouth."

"Fox, let me handle this," Van said, feeling deadly and dangerous. She shook off his hand.

"You're a bully, Cleophus," she said coolly, a disgusted look marring her face. "Why don't you go home and learn how to be a real man? A man Bert isn't afraid to talk to?"

A glass broke in the back, but nobody moved. "You don't know nothin' about me. You come in here with your city ways and think you run the world. I run this town."

"I'm impressed," she said, a sardonic twist to her mouth. "This town is suffering from lack of vision. The people here deserve better if you're all they have to count on."

Van pulled Fox behind him and noticed out of the corner of his eye when the club owner scurried away, probably to call the deputy. Damn.

"You need to be taught a lesson," he slurred, pointing at her.

"Back off Cle—"

Fox shoved Van's hand aside still staring at Cleophus. "I've got news for you. You're not worthy to be on the bottom of Bert's size-eleven shoe. I hope she drops you like a bad habit."

"Bert is my bid'ness. Got that, you citified bitch?" He lunged for Fox and Van hit the big man solidly in the nose.

His fist stung as he drew back ready to deliver another blow, when he was converged on by other patrons. Cleophus had fallen between a small table and the wall. He was out cold. Aided, Van was sure, by the amount of liquor that reeked from his sweating pores.

Van grabbed Fox's hand and pulled. "Come on." Dropping three fives on the bar, he hustled her outside the hall and to the truck.

"What's wrong with you?" she demanded once safely in the cab.

"You couldn't just let me handle things, could you?"

"Handle what? He was looking for me."

"He was looking for trouble."

"You got your wish. You've been dying to punch him."

"Letting our women run wild isn't how things are done down here, Fox."

She turned in the seat, staring at him. "I'm not running wild. I spoke my mind. I can't follow predetermined lines for communication, Van. I speak when I have something to say, not when a man tells me to."

She recognized the rural route that intersected the road to Willow's, and knew their evening had come to an end.

Van drove with a focused determination that told her the depth of his anger. His hands gripped the steering wheel, and his foot mashed the gas pedal. The headlights provided the only light as she stared into enduring blackness.

Two fast approaching yellow dots scampered to the side of the road, and Fox breathed a sigh of relief that the creature had made it safely across.

She wasn't safe from Van's anger, though. It knotted her insides, causing her heart to beat at a thunderous pace.

They turned suddenly, and Fox held on as familiar trees on Willow's lane zoomed by.

The truck came to a rocking halt, and before he cut off the engine, she dropped to the driveway and started toward the house. He called her name.

Thunder rumbled in the distance and she stopped. "What's this really about, Van?"

He walked slowly as if the weight of the world controlled

each step. "You and me. Fox and Van. We're different. Down here the men are men and the women are women."

"I'm not allowed to have an opinion?"

"Of course. But you have to be careful not to step on each other's toes. You have to let me fight the battles. That's how it is."

She shook her head, helplessness and fear racing through her. "I can't be controlled by rules I don't know or understand. I would never let someone speak for me."

"Would you ever let anyone love you?"

"Yes," she whispered. "Yes. But this is different. I've always stood up for myself. There's never been anyone else."

"Part of loving someone is trusting, compromising, understanding. I didn't understand that the first time around. I think I know it well now."

His words tightened around her, leaving her gasping for air. He loved her, he was saying. She understood that in one part of her brain, but would he feel the same if she wasn't exactly what he wanted? Insecurities of so many years ago surfaced from each time she'd failed to make adoption.

Slouch a little, they want a short child . . . Smile, they want a happy child . . . Quit being that way . . . reverberated in her head and she shut the thought off, gritting her teeth.

Nobody was going to change her, because she didn't want to be another way. She dragged her gaze back to Van who watched her through hooded eyes.

"I need time to think this through," she said.

"If you love me, too, then what's the problem?"

Her head and heart pounded intensely. She reached for the most handy excuse. "Van, I have a life a thousand miles from here, and I can't give it up. It's all I've ever had. And I don't think you want to give up the life you're comfortable with. I wouldn't want you to grow bitter and angry because I couldn't make you happy."

"Slumber isn't such a bad place," he said softly.

"Neither is Manhattan."

Lightning brightened the sky and the hurt that weighed on her took its toll. With nothing more to say, she opened the screened door and walked to her room.

Her body felt heavy, as if she was swimming upstream, and her head throbbed from unshed tears.

Lying down fully clothed, she turned her face into her fluffy pillow. One hot tear slid, followed by another until they came too fast to count. She embraced the thick pillow, sobs wracking her body until the wind howled louder than her cries.

Van lay awake and alone. The cabin groaned in protest at the assault of wind and rain, but held strong. Daylight would brighten the sky in a few hours and he was glad he hadn't started on Willow's roof.

He continued the silent argument that had raged within him all night long. If he loved Fox, why couldn't he accept her for who she was? For a moment, he'd been proud to see her stand up for herself, but his ego had kicked in. How were the men viewing him? He couldn't let her fight and stand idly by and watch.

She'd made another point. He lived here, not in New York, and he had no plans to repeat the final reason for his divorce.

A crack and snap of a tree branch sent him to his feet. This wasn't an ordinary storm. The wind cranked louder, beating down the door and walls like an unwelcome relative. He dragged on his jeans and boots and grabbed a shirt on his way out.

The door to the cabin was snatched from his grip, alarming him.

Propelled into the wall of the cabin, he fought against the forceful swirls and called Fox's name, but his voice was grabbed by the wind and swallowed.

He battled against it, making the short walk to the house

in triple the time it normally would have taken and managed to get inside.

"Fox!" Whistles echoed off the walls in the large empty rooms, bouncing back as the wind roared. "Fox," he called, wanting her to answer, afraid she would not.

The main staircase leading to the second level had been sanded and the first coat of the sharp smelling finish applied, but neither mattered as he charged up the stairs.

Halfway up, something crashed and he retraced his steps. The door off the back stairs was closed and he pulled.

Fox was huddled on the floor, the comforter from her bed covering her, and portable radio from the kitchen clutched in her hands.

He sat behind her and gathered her in his arms. She leaned into his chest, touched his cheek. "A tornado is coming."

"Shh, I know." He took the radio, turned it off and placed it beside them. It only played snow from a bad reception, and if this were the end, he didn't want a stranger's voice to be the last thing he heard.

The mighty winds wreaked havoc with Willow's land. Groans and snaps pounded the house, while glass popped and objects scraped against wood.

Fox's heartbeat thrummed against his chest, and he embraced her tighter, closing his eyes when something heavy hit the side of the house.

"I love you," she whispered. "If I never say it again, I don't want to die not having told you how I feel." Her hands clutched his face, her breath mingling with his. He looked up and couldn't see her, but knew she was there.

"I love you, too."

Loud tearing made them jump, but she didn't panic and Van was proud. He just held her a little tighter.

Rain pounded like the hooves of a thousand horses and Fox kept quiet, praying a lot, sleeping little until her eyes finally refused to obey the command to stay open.

Van had created a cocoon with his body and the blanket,

and had stretched them out long ago on the floor. She'd gladly embraced him, and wondered if lying in each other's arms, anticipating death was how they'd spend their last night together. Van's limitless love made her whole, and Fox knew if they survived the storm, she would never be the same.

Silence woke her.

Sitting up abruptly, she scrambled to her feet. "Van!" she whispered. Panic raced up her legs, clutching her throat that he wasn't at her side.

She breathed in, unable to control the anxiety attack, her first in weeks. Gasping, she pushed at the door, but couldn't get it to budge. Ordering herself to calm down, she managed to regain some semblance of control and threw her weight against the door.

It wouldn't move. Fox crawled up the stairs, through fallen debris from the cracked ceiling and managed to get the upper door open. She searched the top level of the house for Van, more concerned with each passing moment for his safety.

Maybe he'd gotten hurt or was needed, but when had he left? She could have sworn he'd held her until just moments before she'd awakened. Her thoughts flitted to Willow and she wondered as to the older woman's safety in town, and prayed she was okay.

Fox hurried through the kitchen, opened the door and barely caught herself from falling. Part of the porch was gone.

She pushed the hair from her eyes and wondered if she were in a nightmare come true. The devastation was enormous.

Van's cabin was gone and so was the chicken coop, and some of the trees on the lane. She closed the door to the horror and clung to the strict control that had governed her life.

She had to get out of the house and find Van and Willow, now.

Hurrying up the stairs, she gathered extra towels, blankets and bandages and stuffed them into a garbage bag.

From the kitchen she gathered three jugs of bottled water, liquor and packages of nonperishable staples. A twist tie fell from a drawer and she used it to bind her hair, before opening the door and facing the horror again.

Mean looking daggers of wood jutted up from the porch, so she decided to take an alternate route and kicked out an already broken window.

She was outside at her car, which had sustained body damage, when she saw a black truck tearing across the pasture.

She honked, waving. Relief hit her full in the chest and she closed her eyes savoring the sight of Van's truck.

He pulled in beside her, searched her with his eyes, then nodded. "We're needed in town."

"I'll follow you," she said, shifted into gear and headed to Slumber.

CHAPTER NINETEEN

By late afternoon, all of the townsfolk had been accounted for. The destruction was widespread, but had claimed no lives.

The injured had been taken to the hospital, while all others had been asked to stay in the gym until water and power lines were functioning again.

To Fox's amazement most of the people were calm, having experienced this type of emergency before. She worked alongside Sis Miller, calming other older folks who were confused and scared by the day's happenings.

Van had left her at the gym and had gone off with some official looking men to assess damage, but she'd spotted Willow who seemed tireless and reassuring to the people who loved her.

Finally their paths crossed and she hugged Willow tight before pulling back to look at her. She brushed long gray braids that had escaped from Willow's bun. "How are you, Willow?"

"I'm blessed. How are you darling? You look sad."

"I'm fine."

How could she complain about her affairs of the heart, when everyone in the gym had been a victim of such mass destruction? Her problems seemed minuscule compared to theirs. She released Willow, and they moved aside as another load of blankets was delivered from the rescue mission.

A swell of people surrounded and separated them, but she could feel the intensity of Willow's gaze. It beckoned her and when they came back together Willow held Fox's hands between hers.

"Willow, I'll be leaving soon."

"Why, Fox? Have you not found all you've ever desired right here?"

The words lanced her pain, allowing it to bleed into her chest. She wished she could explain the fear that had haunted her for weeks and the new doubts that crowded the loving feelings she'd developed over the past weeks. She needed time to sort out her feelings. It was time to return to New York.

"You've been great to me," she said, around the lump in her throat. "I'll never forget your hospitality. But, I'm better. You know I didn't come here to stay forever, and I need to get back to work."

Willow drew up to her five-foot, four height, and leaned back to look Fox in the eye. "I hope I was much more than hospitable to you, Fox. I wanted you to find your home here. Many of us don't have a perfect life. Look around you. But we don't walk away from those we love."

"It has to be this way for now. You probably know Van and I, we . . ." She rubbed her cheeks, then folded her hands. "We fell in love. But we need time. We're so different. Our styles don't mesh."

"Does Van know you're leaving?"

"I told him last night. I wanted to give you my recommendations for the council. I'll stay the week to help you get the house back in order. The cabin is gone and the house sustained some damage."

Willow nodded, her eyes sad. "Darlin', if I thought I could convince you to stay because of that, I would. But you've got to stay for the right reasons." She squeezed Fox's hands. "There are plenty of young people in town who'll need a job to help them make some extra money." She pressed her lips to Fox's brow, then pulled back slowly.

"We're going to have the town meeting tonight while everybody is already assembled. Where's Van?" They moved among the children who played board games and cards on the floor.

Fox spotted Dr. Rawlins checking on some of the elderly people who clustered in a group by the locker rooms, and planned to talk to him.

"The last time I saw Van, he was leaving with the men to assess the damage. I can't leave before helping clean up the house."

"No, darlin. You go. That house is going to be fine."

Willow lowered herself into a chair next to an old woman who breathed with the aid of an oxygen tank. The woman reached over and Willow patted her veined hand. "That old house has survived many a storm and lived on. Van told me about the porch and cabin." She shrugged and continued to pat.

"Things. That's all they are. It's family, good friends, and love that counts. I'm going to rest my old bones now. You see to those youngins over there."

Fox started away and was called back.

"Turn around, chil'," Willow said, rising, "you've got something . . . Here it is."

The twist tie fell into Fox's palm. "Oh, I'd forgotten I'd put that there. Thank you."

Willow closed her palm, their hands—so similar—gray and cracked from the endless amount of work they'd endured. "We've all got our lifestyle. I think yours and mine's is a lot alike." With a pat, she headed back to her seat and began to talk to the woman with the oxygen.

* * *

The gymnasium was filled to capacity as if two teams had announced the rivalry ending game. Fox sat to the side as the elders of the town each gave his report on storm damage. The hardest hit areas were being seen to first by the investigators, but the governor had not called in the National Guard.

Men trickled in and out to eat and rest after patching roofs and rounding up stray animals. Fox noticed Bert hard at work and headed in her direction. Her face was pulled into tight lines, and her cheeks seemed hollow.

"What's the matter, besides the obvious?" Fox asked.

Bert hugged her tight, then dished out another plate. "I'm sorry." Shame and guilt weighed down the words.

Fox whispered to the woman who served food beside to Bert and guided the statuesque woman away from the table. They walked into the hallway. The door closed shutting in the noise.

"What's the matter?"

"I heard about your run-in with Cleophus. I'm so sorry." Unable to meet Fox's eye, she studied the lockers. "I shouldn't have said anything to him about us talking, but he put his own spin on things and decided you influenced my decision."

"Bert, I know it wasn't your fault. I shouldn't have provoked him. I didn't mean for things to get so out of hand."

Bert shook her head, her long fingers clasped.

"It wasn't your fault. He and I were on the rocks anyway, and when I made the decision to go on to college, he didn't take it well. Besides, his anger was so misplaced, if he could come after you, he could come after me anytime he wanted. I don't want to live my life that way, so I ended it."

"I'm glad you're going to do what makes you happy. When do you leave?"

"In August. I'm going to go to a sports camp for the remainder of the summer and sharpen my skills. Don't be surprised if you see me on TV one day playing for a professional team."

"I won't." Fox smiled at her friend. "I want you to call me in New York the minute you sign your contract."

Bert rolled her eyes. They shimmered with unshed tears. "You're leaving? What did Van do?"

Fox laughed, despite the ache in her chest whenever she thought of him. "He didn't do anything. We just need to take some time."

"Do you love him?" Bert asked.

She propped her cheek on her hand and fought the tears that threatened. She finally nodded. Bert draped her long arm over Fox's shoulder and gave her a tight squeeze.

"Then it'll be a hard decision to make, but you'll make the right one. Somebody gave me that advice once."

The two women hugged, each caught in her own pain.

"Is there a Fox Giovanni out here?" A man asked from the open gym door.

Fox pulled back. "That's me."

"You're up next."

Smiling up at Bert, she gave her hand a squeeze. "I've never had a best friend before. Let's keep in touch."

"Definitely."

Fox hurried to the microphone and delivered her report on the budget, followed by the recommendations for the town. The general response was mixed, but when she stepped away, she knew she'd done what had been asked of her. Dissension came high and bitterly from several council members, but Bert and Dr. Rawlins came to her defense, swaying the tide of anger and focusing on the needs of the people. Fox smiled her appreciation, but headed for the door. It was time to go.

She didn't wait for Willow to close the meeting and walked outside. Drips of rain salted her gray blouse, and she remembered she hadn't changed since last night. People milled around the door so she stepped into the street, got into her car, and drove back to the house.

CHAPTER TWENTY

Van knew the moment Fox pulled off from the house on her way back to New York. He was at Ray and Willow's first house staring at the debris that had been struck by lightning, when the radio crackled and Wayne delivered the news.

Cursing to himself, he acknowledged, then kept pumping water onto the smoking wood to make sure the fire was completely doused. He hoped the wood wasn't indicative of his life, but he wondered if he could have saved this relationship from crashing and burning.

Late that night, he pulled up to Willow's and walked through the rarely used front door. He stared at the shiny foyer, glistening in its opulence and the majestic staircase that winked against the moonlight.

The house had held up well. He followed the sound of voices to the kitchen and stopped short when he saw Bootsy sitting at the table with Willow.

"What are you doing here?" he demanded.

The man shot to his feet and grabbed his hat. "I came to return Miss Willow's money."

"You give her back every dime?"

"Yes, sir." He swallowed, saying, "plus interest. To repay her for taking supplies, I'll fix her stairs and porch at my cost."

"We were just negotiating that, Van. I don't want this hard-working young man to be out his money to fix my stairs. But I do reckon he can come around and help get the job done."

Van moved into the room, fixing Bootsy with a gaze so hard, he almost fell off his chair. "Why should we trust you? You're a thief and a liar. Why shouldn't I call the deputy and have you arrested, or better yet, just take you outside and whip your behind? Excuse me, Willow."

She nodded.

"Van, I know I did wrong. I stole Miss Willow's checks and cashed them. But I've got my head on straight and I want a chance to prove I'm an honest man. I was wrong," his voice quivered.

Dropping his bag beside the counter, Van said, "I don't know."

Willow looked at him. "Darlin', we believe in forgiveness. Now I reckon we've got two choices. We can let him have a chance at redemption, and if that doesn't work out, then you can take him out back and whip the devil out of him. Excuse me, Van."

He nodded. "Be here Monday morning at seven. No excuses. Don't make me come looking for you," he said to Bootsy.

Van touched his aunt's shoulder while giving the man a hard stare. "Willow, I want to talk to Bootsy. Man to man, outside."

His aunt's gaze rested on him and he gave her a reassuring pat. She clasped her hands together and slowly rose to her feet, then shuffled on down the hall to her room.

Outside, stars winked in the sky and the cool air hung thick with rain. The roof definitely needed to be patched, but he wasn't going to worry about that now. Bootsy stood a short distance away from him and Van was taken back to their days of youth. Bootsy had always been a follower and usually with the wrong crowd. He remembered him as being weak, even as a teen, but his sympathy had died for the man long before he took advantage of Willow.

People like Bootsy didn't care about anyone but themselves.

"Where did you get four thousand dollars?"

"What does it matter to you? I gave it back."

False bravado, Van noted.

"You're a user, Bootsy. Always have been," he said quietly. "Probably always will be. And as bad as you deserve a butt whooping for ripping off my aunt, I don't want anybody else to get hurt because of you. Where did you get the money? Did Ma Shelia give it to you?"

"You know my mother don't have that kind of money."

Van advanced toward the man and grabbed him by the collar.

"Last time," he said, shaking him like a rag doll.

"I borrowed it from my sister in South Carolina!" Bootsy gasped. "That's where I was. I was working, man. A job. First job I've had in a while. After I took Miss Willow's money nothing went my way. I couldn't sleep, eat, work, nothing. Everybody turned against me." His dark eyes were scared.

"I figured either the devil had finally got ahold to me, or . . ."

Van released the trembling man and smiled. "Or what?"

"Or Miss Willow got ahold of me." Bootsy shook his head, wonder and respect shimmering in his eyes. "I don't know, Van. But I decided to change my life while I still had some to live. I'm real sorry for what I did to Miss Willow. I know I have to face the bank, too, but I really want to get my life together. My sister is giving me a chance, but I want to make right what I did to your aunt."

It had been eleven years since he and Bootsy had had a fist fight. A long time since they'd rolled in the dirt and pummeled each other for no reason. Van didn't see a reason to do it now.

"It takes a big man to admit his mistakes." After a moment of silence, Bootsy extended his hand. Van looked from the extended palm to his face and reached for it.

"I'll be back Monday," Bootsy said before walking slowly down the lane and heading toward town without a backward glance. The man disappeared into the darkness before Van climbed the stairs and walked into the house. He immediately started replacing panes of glass from the kitchen window.

"That can wait until tomorrow," Willow said from behind him as she placed a tin of cookies and glass of lemonade within his reach.

"I'd rather do it now."

"When are you going home, Van?"

His head snapped up. "What?"

"Surely you want to go to your house and check on things."

He shrugged and kept working. "I hadn't even thought about it. I'll send one of my brothers over there tomorrow."

"You go. You haven't been home in weeks for taking care of me. Spying on me." His eyes widened when he looked up at her. "I appreciate how much you care for your old aunt, but it's time you got a life."

"I wasn't spying. I care about you and felt maybe something was wrong. So I decided to do some work on the house and make sure you were all right."

"You've been taking very good care of me," she said with a satisfied lift to her voice. "I didn't realize how much until I found out you deposited twelve thousand dollars in my account at the bank. I would say I'm doing mighty all right having you as a nephew."

The pane of glass nearly slipped through his hands.

"Twelve thousand? I didn't deposit twelve thousand dollars in your account. I put four thousand in there."

"Well, I wonder who my other benefactor was?"

"Fox," they both exhaled at once.

"That woman," he sighed.

"She's a priceless gem." Willow laughed. "I wonder why you let her get away?"

"She wouldn't have been happy here."

"She looked quite content until somebody tried to put her in a place she didn't belong. Nephew, it's time for you to show your hand. I'm getting old and don't have too many more lessons in me you don't already know. If you love her, go get her."

Willow finished her lemonade and washed her glass in the sink. Four thousand dollars from Bootsy lay in a neat stack on the table.

"Since you been minding my business, I trust you'll make sure that gets into your account tomorrow."

Van pushed the stack of bills around with his finger. All the worries of the last few weeks slipped away. Willow was fine.

The house was a mess and he was alone.

Things looked the same, but on the inside he'd changed. "I love you, Willow," he finally said. "I would never do anything to hurt you. I'd already decided if you were losing your faculties, you would live with me."

"I knew I raised you right." Her eyes gleamed with pride and love. She grasped his shoulders. "Now go get my daughter, and bring her home. She belongs here, too. Course if you need a reason, tell her I said I don't trust the regular mail with her money."

Van embraced his aunt.

He released her. "I guess I'll have to go to my house. All my clothes were swept away."

Willow patted his shoulder and ushered him to the door. "You know the last time I was in New York they had lots and lots of big tall buildings with plenty of stores filled with clothes that are probably your size." She kissed his cheek. "Call me when you get back. Peace and blessings."

Van stood on the porch of the house he'd called home for the past two months and knew he'd be back. But when he came back, he planned to have someone special with him.

CHAPTER TWENTY

Fox sat in her new chair in her new office and tried to concentrate on the staff members who sat before her catching her up on six weeks of work. She sighed and placed her elbow on the table.

"Excuse me, Ms. Giovanni?"

"Yes?" she said, her attention dragged back to the group of managers.

"You said something."

"No, please go on."

"Would you like to take a break? I can reschedule for another time if you're not feeling well."

"No. I'm fine. Please continue." Fox forced herself to concentrate on what they were saying, issued her directives, and dismissed them.

They all seemed to be immensely pleased to be out of her company and she was relieved also. Work had become a grind.

The soft jewel tones for the office had been selected by her new secretary, and Fox decided she liked them. She wouldn't have chosen anything so bold, but the colors brightened her low mood.

Two days back in the office, and she still hadn't gotten back into the groove of things. Everything seemed so foreign—from the constant ringing phone to the formal use of her last name every time somebody wanted something. She'd forgotten so much.

But her thoughts kept straying to a simple time and a simple place where she'd found and left a part of herself.

Walking from her office, she headed to the cafeteria, a place she'd never visited before and grabbed a diet drink. Curious stares followed her progression, and she smiled just to shake them up a bit.

Back in her seat, she stripped off her jacket and laid the bangle bracelet on her desk, wishing she could strip off her hose and go barefoot.

"Ms. Giovanni," the secretary interrupted through the intercom. "There's a package out here for you from Willow, no last name. Shall I bring it in?"

Fox's Cross pen slipped from her fingers and her head raised slowly. "Yes. Please bring it in."

Rising, she waited as the door slowly opened, then gasped.

"Andrew!"

The puppy bounded over to her, jumping into her arms. She scooped him up, burying her face in his fresh-smelling fur and let him give her kisses on the cheek. "How did you get here?"

His bark was stronger than when she'd last seen him and he was heavier, but he was still her Andrew.

The door closed and her heartbeat tripled against her ribs.

"Your dog insisted on seeing you today."

She laid eyes on Van and drank him in. He was a sight for her sore eyes. She gave Andrew a final hug and let him down.

He scampered over to Van's shoe and tugged on a tassel.

Fox let her gaze stretch from his shined black shoes to the sharp gray suit he wore. The power tie nearly buckled her knees and she smiled.

"You look good."

"I didn't want to embarrass you."

"Never. Come in, sit down."

He sat across from her on the white sofa that had been placed in a corner of her office. Surrounded by a small table and chair, it mirrored the sitting area in her room at Willow's. "You came all this way just to bring Andrew?"

"It seems he was very unhappy at the White's. I knew he wouldn't be able to get past security. We all thought it best he be with his real Master." His eyes softened. "I also brought you this." Her gaze followed his hand as he reached inside his jacket pocket and pulled out a long white envelope.

Fox hurried to her desk and returned with the pearl-handled letter opener. She slit the envelope.

"Nice nails," he said.

"Thanks." She withdrew a cashier's check made out in her name for eight thousand dollars.

Catching her bottom lip between her teeth, she tried not to smile, but it blossomed anyway. Her day was suddenly looking brighter.

"You knew?"

"Willow found out. Why did you do it?"

She reached for his hand, so glad he was there. "I didn't want you to worry about Willow. I love her enough to cover for any mistake she might have made at the bank." Tentatively, she asked, "Have you made any decisions?"

As he looked at her, a smile crept up his lip. A thrill filled her and she knew she couldn't let the man who made her so happy leave her alone again.

"Willow might be forgetful, and check the stove ten times a day, but she's got it all together. In fact, I think she'll be taking care of me when I get old."

"I'm glad to hear you say that." Fox surged to her feet. "Are you hungry? I know this great place to have lunch. Come on," she said, grabbing her long, winter-white coat. "I want to take you there."

"All right," Van said with a slightly confused look on his face. "What about Andrew?"

Fox made a phone call, and they delivered Andrew to the security office.

Because of the inclement weather, they cabbed over to her favorite Italian eatery.

Fox pulled Van down the stairs at Café Ormond and greeted Antonio, whose eyes widened. "Ms. Giovanni! How good to see you feeling better. And who have we here?"

"This is Van Compton. Van, Antonio."

"Ah." He smiled, shaking Van's hand. "You are the reason for the smile."

"Yes," she said, unable to mask the love she never knew could burst from her heart. "I'd like to see Andrew, please."

Antonio nodded. "Of course. Andrew!"

The young boy appeared from around the spindled divider and hurried toward her. A smile brightened his face, and he took her hand.

"Hello, Andrew," Fox said softly.

"Hello, Ms. Giovanni. I'm glad to see you."

"I'm glad to see you, too. Andrew, I wanted to say thank you. You saved my life."

"You're welcome. I knew you were going to make it. I could feel it in here." He touched his chest over his heart.

Fox took hold of Van's hand and couldn't stop tears from filling her eyes. "Andrew, since you were my guardian angel, I owe you. If you ever need anything, call, and it's yours. It's like a wish. If you ask, it will be granted."

"Wow, anything?" His eyes sparkled with excitement.

"Anything."

"Thank you!"

Fox hugged him tight, then let him go. She watched the boy who'd changed her life by giving her something to believe in.

Antonio shook her hand, then Van's. "Your offer is kind. Andrew is a very special child and we've all been blessed to know him."

"Yes, we are."

"Come this way, we have a nice private table in the back for you."

Van held Fox's chair until she was seated. How had she almost let him get away?

"You look beautiful," she said.

"You do, too." Wine was delivered and poured. He lifted his glass, and she hers, they touched rims and sipped.

His gaze never left her and she looked up into eyes that admired and loved her. "I'm wondering how I could have ever let you almost get away?"

He leaned close to her and whispered. "Stop flirting, you're going to make me blush."

A giggle escaped her, and before he could sit back, she captured his face and ran her hands along the jaw she loved for its strength. "I only flirt with very special people."

His brows lifted. "You thought Andrew was special."

"I've only flirted with the person I fell in love with."

"He sounds like one lucky man."

Fox hated crying, but she could feel the tears backing up in her throat. She kept them at bay, her voice cracking. "I'm the lucky one."

He caught her hands and kissed them. "How lucky?"

"Lucky that you'd come after me. I thought if I returned to New York, I could regain the life I once lived. I did all the things I used to do, but they weren't satisfying anymore."

"What would satisfy you now?"

Her eyes couldn't contain her tears and they slid down her cheeks. "Van, I love you."

He kissed her with such tenderness, she hiccuped a sob. Tipping her chin, he waited until she looked at him. "I love you, too."

She accepted the clean handkerchief from him, blotting tears from her eyes. The cloth reminded her of home and she knew this one was hers forever. "I'm so glad you're here."

"Actually"—his soft voice caressed her—"I was wondering if more permanent arrangements wouldn't be more suitable for us. There's got to be a demand for renovators and remodeling in this big city. I made the mistake once of letting someone go, I won't do it again."

Fox giggled, as her heart did a little leap.

"I can't imagine you living up here. It's too cold. There's no place big enough to park your truck, and there's not enough room for my dog to run and play. No," she snuggled up to him. "New York isn't suitable for you."

"What did you have in mind?"

"I wonder how you would feel about having a wife, with a dog, and a slightly battered car, who doesn't have a job, but has her own money, and is very independent, and prone to getting herself in trouble because she doesn't know when to keep her mouth shut?"

He sucked air through his teeth. "She sounds like a handful."

"She is," she said tearfully.

"Well," he began, and pressed her hands to his lips. "I wonder how she would feel about having a husband that never drives her car, has a job, but hates to wear a shirt to work. He has his own money, and a house, too, but doesn't want to stop his beautifully outspoken wife from speaking up on behalf of her stubborn husband when he gets himself into a roar about her being outspoken."

"I think she can live with that." Fox glanced around the room, her life coming full circle.

"This is the commitment I've always wanted," she whispered. "How shall we seal this deal?"

Van took the glass from her hands. "With a kiss," he said, and touched his lips to hers.

Dear Readers:

Thank you so much for your encouragement on my previous novels, *Now or Never, Whisper To Me—Silver Bells* anthology, *Silken Love,* and *Keeping Secrets.*

It has been an honor to write love stories that touch people's hearts, relate to an occasion in their lives, or simply give them a few hours of joy. My stories have reached the far corners of the world, and it's because of you the readers. Thank you, I am eternally grateful.

Please continue to keep me in your prayers and write and let me know what you'd like to see in the future.

My address is P.O. Box 956455, Duluth, GA 30095-9508. Enclose a phone number and SASE for quick response.

Peace and blessings,
Carmen

ABOUT THE AUTHOR

Carmen Green was born in Buffalo, New York. She received a bachelor of arts degree in English from Fredonia State University College in Fredonia, New York.

She currently resides in Georgia with her husband and children.

THESE ARABESQUE ROMANCES
ARE NOW MOVIES FROM BET!

Own More Movie Tie-In Editions From *ARABESQUE*

Own the Entire ANGELA WINTERS
Arabesque Collection Today